# FANFARE

## Renee Ahdieh

Fanfare

Revolution books may be ordered through booksellers or by contacting:

Revolution Publishing Inc.
http://revolutionpublish.com
marketing@revolutionpublish.com

FANFARE

Front cover artwork by Laura Kreitzer

Library of Congress Control Number: 2011929213

ISBN: 9780983353706

Printed in the United States of America

To Victor for always believing in me.
Mere words are not enough.

To Ela for everything that is beautiful
about Cris . . . and so much more.

# FANFARE

*The way of love is not
a subtle argument.*

*The door there
is devastation.*

*Birds make great sky-circles
of their freedom.
How do they learn it?*

*They fall, and falling,
they're given wings.*

Mawlana Jalaluddin Rumi

# ONE

It's anti-capitalistic to love someone. I mean really and truly love someone. My theory on why the divorce rate is so high stems solely from this concept. Think about it: We go through life programmed to believe that success comes when you strive to be the best at something, whatever it is and no matter the cost. What is good for the individual will ultimately be good for the whole as "success" trickles downward.

This selfish need for domination is the driving force behind any triumph of the free market. The profit margin is king, and the little man or woman is a means to an end.

In our work, and in our daily lives, it becomes nearly impossible to free one's mind from this winner-takes-all mentality. Then you come home, and you're supposed to switch off this self-destructive mindset and love your family, your friends, your pets ... whatever allegedly makes you happy. It's impossible.

Real love is selfless. Instead of putting your own needs first, you put yourself at the bottom of the list. You are no longer in control. See? It's anti-capitalistic to love someone. I wonder if this is why love fails so often. Two dueling personalities in one individual: one trying to be a success in the world and another trying to be a success in the heart. Selfishness and selflessness ... the ultimate death match.

As Hawthorne wrote: "No man for any considerable period can wear one face to himself and another to the multitude, without finally getting bewildered as to which may be the true."

And ... (drum roll please) ... you're now divorced. Or in my case, dumped.

These were the thoughts I mused to myself as I stood in the mall surrounded by a hoard of teenyboppers accompanied by their enablers. This was hell, and real love had gotten me into this mess.

In an attempt to be a selfless vessel for anti-capitalistic love, I had (idiotically) volunteered to take my young cousins, Stephanie and Maria, to a celebrity autograph signing. Who the hell would have thought it would take this long? Five hours later, we were still waiting in a line the likes of which I hadn't seen since opening night of the last Batman flick. That was a good movie. I should probably watch it again.

The day before, when I told Hana I was taking Steph and Maria to this promotional thing at the mall, she spoke incessantly about the ridiculous movie starring this celebrity. Hana was such a know-it-all, and (of course) she had read everything about this actor and the background behind the film. She had even inhaled the two books these movies were based on in less than four days over our trip to Cairo this past winter. Given the haze my life had existed in for the last six months, it was no surprise I had no idea what she was talking about. All I knew was that Steph and Maria were obsessed with these books about a ghost who fell in love with a teenage girl. We were in line to meet the sad excuse for an actor portraying the aforementioned ghost. He had inadvertently become the fantasy of every screaming tween around me. Thomas something-or-other.

"Cris!" I heard behind me.

Dammit. Now was not the time to have to deal with this.

"Hey Becky! Hey Mariam! What's up?" I said with a falsely bright smile.

"What are you doing here? Are you in line meeting that guy from that ghost movie? God, he's so cute! I wonder what Ryan has to say about that!" Becky teased.

The sounds of hell amplified. "Hah-hah. Actually, Ryan wouldn't have a whole heck-of-a-lot to say about it. We…broke up." I grimaced reflexively. It would take a while before my face stopped reacting to the truth of my words so involuntarily.

"Really? I thought you two were engaged!" Mariam gasped.

Thanks a heap. I totally needed to hear that again.

"We were. Now we're not." And don't ask anything else. I plastered the biggest smile I could muster on my face to prevent the inevitable chorus of "Oh, you poor thing" from escaping their lips. I had dealt with enough pity, just to the point where I could stand it. *No más, por favor.*

I hated the uncomfortable looks on their faces almost more than I despised their pity. There was never a better conversation killer amongst women than having to admit that you were *this* close to the dream and it was taken away from you. Hey, at least I wasn't jilted at the altar. Then Ryan would probably be a dead man instead of just a selfish jackass.

"Well, you seem to be taking it pretty well. I mean, you look great!" Becky said nervously.

"Seriously, Cris. I had no idea. Don't worry though. I know you're probably tired of hearing this, but you'll have no problem finding someone. I mean, you're terrific," Mariam said with a kind smile.

Since Becky was engaged and Mariam had been dating the same guy for the past two years, I knew that the safest course of action was to pretend to believe her lie so she wouldn't feel guilty or smug about being happily in love.

"Definitely. Thanks so much!" I said and clutched onto my smile until I was sure they believed it.

I had to love the awesome power of my big-ass smile. Even when I summoned it from a place of extreme anguish, the flash of teeth that dominated my small face could convince anyone of its veracity.

"Well, see you around!" Mariam said as they began to walk away.

"Let me know if you want to get some coffee sometime." Becky smiled kindly at me.

"Sure! Take care!" Thank God; they were leaving.

Steph and Maria gabbed in excitement to the girls next to us, so they weren't paying attention to the growing flush of red on my face from the newest encounter with my ugly reality—a reality that tore a fresh, albeit small, hole in my battered excuse for a heart. I yanked my iPod out of my purse and pulled out my *In Style* magazine. I wouldn't talk to anyone else while I stood in hell. The blaring sounds of the band Rage Against the Machine echoed in my ears and successfully drowned out the ancillary din of the mall. We inched forward.

My phone buzzed in my purse. I cursed under my breath while I fished around for it in the Black Hole. Have you ever noticed how your phone can turn into a friggin' bar of wet soap whenever you needed to find it in your bag? Finally yanking it out successfully, I had two missed calls and a new text message. Only one person I knew was that annoyingly persistent: Hana.

Sure enough, the text message read:

Hana (3:37 pm): did u see him yet? he's cute in a scruffy english kinda way.

I typed out a response while music blared in my ears. The frenzied screams grew louder in front of me. Two more steps forward.

Me (3:39 pm): No. Can't see anything. Left my glasses in the car.

3

Hana (3:41 pm): u idiot! u look like crap when u squint.
Me (3:41 pm): And I should care b/c...?
Hana (3:42 pm): b/c u should always care. sight's important u moron.
Me (3:43 pm): Whatever. Call u later.
Hana (3:45 pm): yeah. naz will kill me when he sees the txt msg bill. ttyl.

I highly doubted Naz would say anything more than "Can you stop texting Cris?" to Hana whenever he saw the bill, much less kill her. Nazir Fateri was the most patient man I had ever met. As luck would have it, he had married my best friend. Even with my shitty string of bad luck, it was impossible to feel unhappy around Hana and Naz. They were meant to be together, and it showed in every aspect of their lives.

I had met Hana when we were freshman at the University of North Carolina almost seven years ago. Initially, I thought she was one of the most pretentious girls I had ever met. Hana had been trained by her Korean mother to be a hyper-achieving little machine. As we began to spend more time together, I saw past her carefully constructed façade and found a girl with a wicked sense of humor and one of the biggest hearts I had ever encountered. Hana was also fiercely loyal. If people tried to mess with anyone she loved, she would chase them down like a rabid dog until they bled, cried, or did both...preferably both.

I remembered the morning after that terrible night—the night my heart ceased to be anything more than a mechanism for pumping blood. I hadn't slept at all, and my voice was cracked and dry. There were no tears left to shed. I picked up the phone to call her at an absurdly early hour.

*"Hana?" I cleared my throat.*
*"Cris?" she whispered hoarsely, still half asleep. "What's wrong?"*

After our phone conversation, she called Gita, and both of them drove three hours to help me move my things out of Ryan's house; a house he had bought for us to live in together; a house I had decorated with the carefree heart of a person unable to fathom anything but champagne and sunshine in her immediate future. Love had made me into a disgusting, cautionary tale.

Life sucks, and then you die. If my father could see me now, he would chuckle. I laughed blackly to myself.

I focused back on my magazine and turned the music up even louder. Out of the corner of my eye, I watched Steph and Maria. They were so excited as they clutched onto copies of their books, posters, and some random pictures of this guy. I couldn't understand for the life of me what was so wonderful about meeting some actor who didn't care one bit about them. He had probably met thousands of little girls just like Steph and Maria, and they all most likely annoyed the crap out of him. In my mind, I pictured a self-absorbed, perfectly coiffed douchebag with a chip on his shoulder the size of Texas and an entourage Diddy (or whatever) would be proud of. I couldn't really think of anyone I would wait hours in line to see for just a few impersonal moments. Okay, so I lied. I'd probably wait in line to see Brad Pitt. Honestly, I had never even heard of this actor dude until yesterday.

Steph began to jump up and down, so I glanced up. We were almost to the table. I tried not to squint while I attempted to see this guy through the throng of squealing tweens as they pressed and shoved to get a better position. If anyone pushed me, I'd bring out the Puerto Rican inside with a vengeance. I may be short, but I sure knew how to yell and throw a good punch; it came with my heritage.

One girl leaned over the table and started to scream as he reached over to hug her. There go his eardrums for the day. I had a glimpse of a shaggy mop of hair that appeared like it desperately needed to be washed. Man, maybe I should have brought my glasses. Squinting did make my small eyes look unusually beady. Damn Hana for being right *again*.

"Cristina, can you do me a favor?" Steph asked quietly. She was barely able to contain her anticipation as we stepped ever closer to Junior High Heaven.

"What's up?" I said with a smile.

"Can you ask Thomas to hug me too? I don't want to ask him. It's too embarrassing."

No, no, no! Why did I choose this particular occasion to be anti-capitalistic? "Stephie, it's okay! He won't mind. He just hugged that other girl. Have some balls! Ask him yourself!"

"No, I can't! Please?" begged Stephanie. She gave me an unforgivably pleading expression.

"Me too, me too!" Maria whined.

I gritted my teeth in extreme irritation. I desperately wanted to be selfish and refuse to help my little cousins. After all, I had already volunteered to spend my Sunday in a mall waiting in line with them to meet a silly actor from an even sillier movie. Wasn't that enough?

I closed my eyes and sighed. My love for my family and for my friends was all I had left.

"Fine!" I hissed through my teeth. The jumping up and down like little rabbits began anew with even more vigor.

Finally, we were next in line. My cousins were seriously unable to contain themselves. Now that we stood less than five feet away from him, I took a closer look. He was pale with stubble shading his face, and his hair did, in fact, look like he had forgotten to wash it for the past…week? It was long and hung in a pile of disarray on his head. His eyes were light grey with a hint of green, framed by unkempt eyebrows and a well-defined jaw. Altogether attractive, but I wasn't entirely sure what all the fuss was about.

"Thomas! We love you!" gushed Steph disgustingly.

"You're so cute!" chanted little Maria.

"Thank you so much," he said good-naturedly.

If anything, he seemed extremely uncomfortable and a bit tired. I was surprised to discover he was not the pretty boy of my earlier musings. He looked like a guy who had just woken up a few minutes ago and was forced into a designer suit, when all he really wanted was a cup of coffee, the newspaper, and a moment of silence. Instead, he was thrown into a room full of screaming, pre-pubescent girls, and ordered to "dance monkey, dance!" or else. Visions of the Roman Coliseum in its heyday came to mind, and I couldn't stop myself from laughing softly as I contemplated a den of hungry lions wearing Hannah Montana T-shirts.

He patiently signed all of the ridiculous paraphernalia my cousins handed to him and glanced up when he heard my laughter.

"Are you listening to something funny?" he asked quietly with a melodic British accent.

"No," I said calmly.

"What are you listening to?" He smiled crookedly at me. I honestly felt bad for him. Poor guy needed a nice shot of whiskey and some earplugs. Hell, so did I.

"Rage Against the Machine," I responded.

"Well! That's decidedly unfunny and a bit surprising," he said as he studied me with a look of quizzical amusement.

Irritation flared at his snap assessment. Years of being judged solely based on my ethnicity did not work in his favor. I didn't struggle to make people expect more from me all my life to be stereotyped by a studio puppet.

"Yeah, I guess it would make more sense to you if I said I was listening to Daddy Yankee." Man, I sounded like a bitter shrew.

His eyes widened, and he put his hands up in a gesture of mock surrender. "I didn't mean anything by it! I was just surprised, that's all! I don't have many occasions where I'm surprised whilst on these junkets. I'm sorry." There was no mistaking his honesty.

Damn. I felt like a huge bitch. "I'm sorry, too. I've had an interesting day." I tried to smile without showing my embarrassment, and he graciously smiled back.

"When are you starting your next movie?" Maria asked in an attempt to regain his attention. I could tell that both Maria and Stephanie were irritated that Thomas was talking to me instead of them.

"I'm not sure yet," he said warmly. "But I really hope you go to see it."

"We will!" they replied in unison.

Both of my cousins looked up at me with expressions of expectation. Crap, now that they were mad about the distraction, I definitely couldn't get away with conveniently "forgetting" their earlier request.

"Um, Thomas?" I asked, wishing the floor would just swallow me and take me on an express train to the farthest reaches of hell.

"Tom," he said automatically.

"Yeah, uh, Tom. Would you mind giving my cousins a hug?" I was going to give it to them in the car for making me do this.

"Sure." He paused expectantly with raised eyebrows. I guess he wanted to know my name.

"Cris," I replied ruefully.

I placed my iPod down on the table so I could collect their newly autographed treasures and knelt to put all of it back in their backpacks. They squealed and blushed. He actually kissed each of them on their cheeks. The screams of the girls behind us nearly deafened me.

I looked up and smiled earnestly at Tom. He was definitely not a douchebag.

"Thanks," I said softly.

"Anytime," he replied.

My face was beginning to burn again with unexpected embarrassment. I grabbed my cousins and made a beeline for the nearest exit.

7

"Did you see that, Cris? Did you? He *kissed* me!" Steph was beginning to freak out.

"Yeah, yeah, yeah. It was fabulous," I said as I tried to control my frustration. My heart beat unusually fast, so I took a deep breath to calm my nerves.

We were just about to make it outside of the mall when Maria chirped, "Cris? I'm hungry. Can we get something to eat?"

I inhaled again slowly and closed my eyes. I shouldn't be this irritated with my poor little cousins. It wasn't fair. Smiling at them as patiently as I could, I said, "Sure! What do you want to eat?"

A snack turned into shopping around for a new pair of tennis shoes for Steph and earrings for Maria. Before I knew it, another two hours had gone by, and my Sunday was shot. The only redeeming factors were the huge smiles on their faces from an excellent day filled with memories they would probably cherish until the next It-Boy came into their lives.

I almost wished I could go back in time to when I was their age. I had been obsessed with Ricky Martin (haha!). I guess if I had spent the morning waiting in line to see Ricky and was then treated to junk food, tennis shoes, and earrings, I would say my weekend was pretty much made. One day, both Steph and Maria would realize how much more it took to make them happy than it used to, and a day like today would seem like a blissful epoch from their past.

We piled into my little black Civic, and I reached into my purse for my iPod so I could plug it into the adapter.

"Dammit!" I said angrily.

"What's wrong?" Steph asked.

"I think I left my iPod in the mall. We have to go back in." I groaned.

"Do you think someone stole it?" Maria guessed.

"I don't know! Maybe I left it on that table from earlier. We'll check at lost and found." This was what I got for trying to be good.

We marched back into the mall and to the information counter. Of course, the meet-and-greet had ended an hour ago, so the table that was swamped earlier that day was no longer there. Information directed us to lost and found.

"Hi," I said with chagrin as I walked over to speak with the individual who monitored the small room where my iPod hopefully waited for me.

"My name is Cris, and I think I lost my iPod earlier at that autograph signing in the center of the mall."

"Yes, a number was left for you."

What? Why wasn't my iPod left for me?

"A number? Um, okay," I said with frustration.

He wordlessly handed me a small piece of paper with a telephone number on it. Nothing else was written on the paper.

"Uh, did they say anything else?" I asked.

"They just asked that you call later on this evening."

*Man, I swear.* If some stupid teenagers took my iPod and expected some sort of reward, I would hunt them down and tell their parents. I was seriously pissed, and once I got my hands on the junior racketeers, they were going to wish they hadn't tried to make a quick buck.

What a perfect end to an excellent day. We walked back to the car in silence.

"I'm really sorry, Cris," Maria said quietly as we took our seats.

"Don't worry about it, chica. I'll get my iPod back."

I sure would. In fact, I would get it back today. Screw waiting until tonight to call this little hustler. I grabbed my cell phone and ruthlessly punched in the numbers written on the small piece of paper. It rang several times before it cycled to voicemail. I cleared my throat, intent on leaving a stern message. The final ring chirped before the recorded greeting.

"Hi, this is Tom's cell. If you managed to wrangle this number, you're either a close friend or family member or have otherwise managed to impress my agent greatly. In either case, I should respond shortly. Thanks."

It beeped and waited for me while I sat there in shock. "Uh, um," I stammered. I couldn't just hang up! Caller ID had ruined that escape.

"Uh, this is Cris. Um, I think you might have my iPod. Could I, um, have it back, please? This is my cell. Uh, can you please call me back?"

I hurriedly pushed the End button to complete the worst voicemail message in the history of voicemail messages. I had asked a movie star to give me my iPod like a kid on the playground who wanted her ball back. Why the hell had he taken it anyway?

"Cris? Are you okay?" Steph asked me when she saw the look of utter disbelief on my face.

"Yeah, sweetie. I'll be fine." My mind swirled with thoughts, and most of them centered on my extreme curiosity. I could not fathom why he would take something he could simply leave with lost and found. If he gave the mall a number, why didn't he just give them my iPod? Maybe he had forgotten about it and only remembered too late to leave it at the mall? Sure. That had to be it. But then why would he give me his cell number and not send some minion to take care of it? I was certain he had many people at his beck and call. The questions burned in my mind as I drove to Steph and Maria's home to drop them off.

After stopping inside to say hello to my Aunt and Uncle, I began the half hour drive home to my mother. I had managed to conceal my heavily distracted mind from my Aunt by sticking to banalities, but I knew I would not get away with that at home. Mami missed nothing, and now that it was just the two of us, her eyes were even more watchful. What I wouldn't give for a semblance of privacy. As much as I wanted to move out and live on my own, I knew I wasn't ready to leave her. Too much had happened this year, and it was too soon for her to lose her daughter right after she watched her husband succumb to cancer.

It was time for another reality check. Lately, I had given myself lots of those. It was a major reason why I managed to maintain an air of sanity. Each time I wasted precious moments of my life dwelling on things I had no control over, I forced myself to review the facts.

Fact: This guy is a movie star.

Fact: You are nobody.

Fact: You don't want anything to do with him.

Fact: Men make absolutely no sense.

Fact: Men lie.

That was it. I was done. There was no reason to continue obsessing about being given Thomas's personal cell phone number. It didn't matter. I would get my iPod soon, and then this would just be another funny story to file away for a rainy day.

Renewed by my reality check, I hummed quietly along with some tuneless song on the radio and let the music take over my thoughts. I've always had a love affair with music, and nearly all of my most consequential memories had rippling harmonies in the background. I associated almost everything important in my life with some form of music.

My Cuban-born father was a classical cellist. As a little girl, I would sit on the floor while he played. I would place my tiny hands on the base of the gleaming wood instrument and revel in the vibrations singing through my fingers with each resonating note he drew across the strings. He would smile down at me. *Tu eres la luz de mi vida.* I was the light of his life. He was the rock in mine—the only man I could ever trust. My mother was born and raised in Puerto Rico and walked to the silent beat of drums. When she was younger, when her knees didn't give her trouble, she would dance in the kitchen while cooking us dinner, even when no music could be heard.

I couldn't live without music. Now that my father's quiet laugh and sparkling eyes were no longer in my life, the connection we shared through music was the closest thing I had to being with him.

I walked in the door of the little house I shared with my mother. "Mami?" I called out.

She sat in front of her TV, watching her soap operas on Univision. God help whatever schmuck owned Univision if anyone messed with Mami's *telenovelas*.

I plopped down onto the sofa to dutifully tell her about my day. We spoke solely in Spanish at home and, even though I no longer considered it to be the language I conversed most adeptly in, there was always a sense of innate comfort to the Spanish words that rolled off of my tongue I didn't necessarily feel when I spoke English.

I fixed dinner while she sat on the sofa and told me how much her knees had pained her that day. Mami was the quintessential martyr, and I didn't know what she would do with her day, or talk about, if she were actually absent a slew of debilitating ailments. I listened patiently. She knew that my threshold was about twenty minutes, and she milked every moment of it. After we ate, I went through the mail and made sure there were no unpaid bills before I went upstairs to check my email and take a shower.

My phone began to ring as I made my way up the stairs. It was Gita.

"Hey babe! How was your Sunday?" she asked.

"Man, it was boring as hell." I groaned. I proceeded to tell her about waiting in line forever to meet some tween idol.

"C, you're such a good cousin. I don't think I'd do that crap for my own sister!"

"You're lying, Gita. I know you would, and then you'd call me at night to complain about it just like I'm doing right now." I laughed.

"Well, at least let me try to make you feel good about sacrificing your entire Sunday for them. I spent mine at the library studying accounting crap. Seriously, remind me why I'm going to school while working full-time. Spout the lies about opportunity cost and whatnot so I can feel like I'm not killing myself for nothing," replied Gita.

"You know that—" *Beep.* "Hey Gita? I have a call on the other line, give me a sec."

"Hello? This is Cristina."

"Hi. This is Tom." I nearly dropped the phone when I heard his softly accented voice.

"Uh, hi?" I squeaked.

"Am I calling at a bad time?" He actually sounded a little nervous.

"Um, can you give me a second? I have a call on the other line."

"Truly, I don't want to be a bother. I can call later."

"No, no. Just give me a sec." My hand shook a little as I pressed the button to switch back over to the conversation I was having with Gita. *Calm down, Cristina! You're acting like an idiot.*

"Gita? I have to go, but I'll call you back."

"Right, it's actually still Tom." Great. Dumbass.

"Sorry. Let's try this again." I fumbled around with my phone a second time. I really should have read that damned manual at least once instead of pompously discarding the packaging and placing ill-gotten faith in my own technological aptitude.

"Gita? I'll call you back," I said in a rush.

"Okay, sure! Bye!" she replied.

"Tom? Sorry about that," I said while attempting to slow my speech.

Jeez! I really wasn't enamored at all, but I think the whole famous thing was getting to me. I pursed my lips and steadied my shaking voice. I'd rather eat shit than have him think he could make me freak out just because some idiots in Hollywood thought he was easy on the eyes.

"Don't apologize. It's not a big deal." Again, I felt like I detected a faint level of anxiety in his voice that caught me off guard. Wasn't being obnoxiously self-assured a staple characteristic of the cinema elite?

"Are you nervous?" I blurted without thought. Strike two, Cris.. . or maybe three. I'd lost count.

"Uh." He exhaled in surprise at my bluntness. "Actually, I am. I don't normally call girls I just met in passing. It's not exactly at the top of my list of fun things to do."

Right. Sure. Pretending to be the awkward guy was apparently his current trick for tricks. "I guess you don't normally take their iPods either," I said with a sarcastic laugh.

He chuckled softly. "No, I don't typically do that. I actually rescued your iPod. You should probably thank me. Some girl thought she'd struck gold."

"Unless 'gold' is code for a lime green iPod with a giant scratch across the screen, I don't know why she would want it. There's probably not much on there that would interest her. I'm not into the Jonas Brothers."

"So I noticed. What exactly draws you to angry music with a politically-charged message?"

I thought for a moment. "Irreverence and rebellion." If he asked, I would give it to him straight. I had enough experience with word games to fill a book that would make *The Brothers Karamazov* look like a walk in the park.

He laughed comfortably this time. "I can see both of those things in you."

"How?" I asked carefully.

"I actually noticed you before you made it up to the signing table. You were squinting oddly at me."

"Yeah, I couldn't see anything. I left my glasses in the car."

"That was probably unwise. Sight's important."

"So I've heard." Freaking Hana.

"I thought you hated every moment of standing in line. Whenever your friends came over to talk to you, you couldn't wait for them to leave. Most girls like having the distraction and the attention of their peers, especially in public. I dunno, I think it makes them feel desirable."

Man, he had noticed a lot. "How did you manage to sign all those autographs and notice enough around you to make social commentary?"

"Are you kidding? Do you know how many times I've had to sign my name in my life? Honestly, I'll bet if someone handed me a pen in my sleep, I'd wake up with my name tattooed over half my body and all across the sheets."

"So, you're subconsciously a narcissist? Interesting—a narcissistic movie star. There's a new one."

"And here comes the irreverence. Aren't you supposed to be charming? Usually, girls I meet go out of their way to be charming to me. You actually went out of your way to suggest that I'm a racist wanker."

I grimaced. "Yeah, I'm sorry about that. Do you want to know the funny thing? I actually like Daddy Yankee."

He laughed loudly. "A Latin girl who likes reggaeton. It's downright shocking."

I was surprised at how easy he was to talk to. "I can be charming 13 when I want to be. It just wasn't my day."

"I honestly prefer the irreverence. It helps to ground me."

"If you're telling me that you dislike hearing a bunch of girls say how gorgeous you are, I'm going to scoff in disbelief." Shit, I'd used the word "scoff."

"Scoff away. I actually hate it."

"Please." I snorted.

"I really do."

"Explain."

Awkward boy was back with a vengeance. "I hate feeling like I have to live up to some figment of perfection they have in their imagination."

"So, you can't handle the pressure of being scrutinized. My next question is painfully obvious. Why would you go into the film industry if you hate having people treat you like eye candy?"

"Truly, I have no idea how to answer that question. It was just an opportunity that fell into my lap, and it seemed foolish to throw it away."

"Yeah, I hear the money's good, too." I smiled in spite of myself.

"It definitely helps. In truth, I'm quite a miser. If you saw the way I lived at home, you'd be really surprised."

"You know, I believe you. Enough about this conversation has surprised me into believing that I shouldn't make snap judgments. Movie stars are people too."

He laughed again, then sighed regretfully.

"Is something wrong?" I asked.

"I actually have to go; I have a plane to catch."

I could swear he almost sounded like he wanted to keep talking to me, and I couldn't stop a surprising feeling of loss from creeping into my stomach. Man, I was pathetic. I must really miss late-night phone conversations with a cute guy.

"Well, how am I supposed to get my iPod?"

"I really am sorry about that. I'm going to New York tonight, but I can have it sent to you sometime in the next few days."

"That's fine. If you lose it, I'll sue the hell out of you. Then I can quit my job and sip Mai-Tais along the Caribbean."

"You really are refreshingly irreverent," he said with a chuckle.

"And you really are incredibly surprising," I admitted.

"That's a start. Goodnight Cris."

"Goodnight Tom."

*A start?*

# TWO

You need to understand that we are finished."
The frigid words cut at my soul with biting stabs. Eight
sharpened daggers hell-bent on merciless destruction. The end of
dreams, and the beginning of nightmares.

"What are you talking about, Ryan?" My voice was steady and
calm. I had already mastered the ability to talk my way out of uncomfortable situations. This false sense of control belied the screams
building in my throat.

"How much clearer can I be? Do you want me to say it, Cristina?"

"I want you to tell me why." Even in my nightmare, I looked
refreshingly unruffled while witnessing the heart-stopping destruction of my carefully designed future.

Frosty blue eyes glared at me. There was no warmth to be seen
in their bleak wasteland.

"There's someone else."

Finally, my face showed some signs of understanding. It began
at my eyes and rippled through my features with slow deliberation.
Pain. More pain than I thought existed—pain outside the realm of
physical reality. I would rather have felt thousands of small needles
pricking my skin protractedly, one at a time. There was no music in
this memory—only the silence of a death. When a soul screams its
last, can anyone hear it?

"Why?" My voice broke. Something suffocated my lungs slowly,
as though I were drowning from inside out. I clasped my hands
behind my back in an attempt to maintain my posture. I would not
give him the satisfaction of seeing me crumble like a beaten dog.

"Why do I need a reason?"

"When you destroy a dream, you have to have a reason," I whispered.

"You're not the person I fell in love with. I will never be the person you want me to be."

*I can change!* I wanted to scream. *I can be whatever you want me to be!*
The screams were held back unconsciously by my pride—a blessing
I clung to months after the fact. *Just don't leave.* My mouth refused to

form the words that my heart ached to say.

I wouldn't beg. I wouldn't be pathetic.

"But I love you," I said simply.

"It's not enough."

He looked at me with the blue eyes that had shared four years of laughter and tears… four years of successes and failures. Four years of love. Now they were the eyes of a stranger.

"I'm not staying here tonight. When I come back on Sunday, you won't be here. Take whatever you think is yours."

His eyes narrowed as he watched my world unravel with the gaze of a detached observer. "Don't worry. You'll find someone else. You're very easy to like." This was the moment in my recurring nightmare where I really wished I had held a sharp object in my hands.

He turned around quickly and walked down the shadowy hallway towards the front door. I forced my feet to stay glued to the carpet. Dramatic visions of me sprinting after him into the darkness and collapsing on my knees in the wet grass flew to mind.

*Please, Ryan! Don't do this to me! Don't destroy us!*

No. Never. He could not take my pride from me too.

The room grew colder, as though he had taken all the warmth away with him. Alone in my anguish, I fell to the floor and dug my nails into the carpet to prevent them from clawing at my skin. Cold. Dark. Suffocating. The vision blurred….

I woke in the darkness the same way I always did: with a gasp. The tightness in my throat and pain in my cheeks were now predictable. I tried in vain to stop the vicious cycle from completing yet another circuit as the hot, stinging tears coursed soundlessly down my face. I couldn't prevent them. If I did, the pain would remain and grow until it consumed me. I lay still in my bed and breathed deeply to silence the rapid thud of my pounding heart. Sometimes I wondered if my subconscious recreated this scene to remind me that my heart still worked. If it did, my subconscious was seriously fucked up.

I silently moved aside the sheets and padded through the darkness to my bathroom. The cold water was soothing on my cheeks and neck. I turned on the light and stared at my reflection. I had a small face with dark brown eyes rimmed in thick lashes that stood in contrast to the lighter bronze tone of my skin. My mahogany-colored hair hung past my shoulders. I was pretty—nothing to write home about, but definitely not a troll. This was one of the trite things I said to myself from time to time in an attempt to move past the pain of reliving my own personal anguish… a mini-therapy session with me, myself, and I.

I bit my lower lip as I continued to peruse my swollen face and red eyes. This was going to be one of those nights. Maybe this recent bout of subconscious self-flagellation was brought on by my conversation with Tom. I was unusually happy those few moments on the phone with him; it reminded me of the good times in my relationship with Ryan when we would stay on the phone until sanity left us, and we laughed together at nothing.

Taking a deep breath, I walked over to my desk and pulled out my cat-o'-nine-tails. The innocuous box shook in my hands as I lifted the lid. My pain returned, renewed. The engagement ring glittered in the shadows as the light from the bathroom caught its faceted prisms. I was unable to toss it, just like I kept the letters he had written to me when he was deployed in Afghanistan. The pictures and other mementos had been burned or thrown away not long after it happened. I had agreed to do that mostly for Hana. She needed that therapy since I refused to let her even speak to Ryan for fear I would lose my best friend to a prison ward.

I lifted the sparkling lie from the box and put it on. It still burned my skin, but it wasn't self-flagellation if you didn't feel pain. Gita would probably beat me if she knew what I was doing. Hana would just go to the bathroom and cry. I stood there and tried to summon a semblance of the happiness I had felt when the lie rested on my finger in earnest. A time when not even the birds could touch me as I flew through the air on a high of self-content: the best drug in the world.

It had become harder and harder to retrieve those sentiments. This was what everyone meant when they said "Time heals all things." I had personally amended that statement in my mind. Now it went: "Time kills all things." I was probably one of a few select people who would actually laugh at that joke given my situation.

I curled back into bed and pulled the sheets over my head. I had no reason to feel lonely. I had my loving mother, wonderful friends, my health, and a good head on my shoulders.

I had no reason to feel lonely....

# THREE

The buzzing sound of my phone's message indicator yanked me from my sleep. 6:18 am? Who the hell would text me that early?

> Blocked ID (6:18 am): r u awake?

What? Irritation poked a hole of lucidity through my cloudy mind. If this turned out to be a wrong number, I'd be pissed.

> Me (6:20 am): who is this?
> Blocked ID (6:21 am): tom, i know it's early, srry

*Huh?* Why in God's name was this guy text messaging me? Maybe he had the numbers mixed up. He probably thought he was texting someone else he was supposed to meet or something.

> Me (6:22 am): This is Cristina in North Carolina
> Blocked ID (6:23 am): i know

He knew? So he honestly meant to text message me this early in the morning? I could have used that extra forty minutes of sleep, but my curiosity was killing me and my mind was whirling again.

> Me: (6:25 am): Do u know what time it is?
> Blocked ID (6:25 am): yes, r u mad?
> Blocked ID (6:27 am): hello?
> Me (6:27 am): I'm thinking.
>  Prolly not.
> Blocked ID (6:28 am): that's a load off, what r u doing?
> Me (6:28 am): I was sleeping. Now I need to go to work.

```
Blocked ID (6:30 am): what do u do?
Me (6:31 am): I'm a social worker.
```

Man, I couldn't believe I just told a movie star what I did for a living. I almost wanted to make something up, like tell him I'm a porn star or teach skydiving classes. A social worker? Yuck. How terminally uncool was I?

```
Blocked ID (6:32 am): i bet ur good
at it
Me (6:32 am): Riiight. What r u doing?
Blocked ID (6:33 am): hair and makeup
Me (6:34 am): LOL
```

I really couldn't help it. I just pictured him sitting forlornly in a chair while someone torturously applied some cakey mess to his face and dumped product after product onto his hair to achieve the same look he managed by simply failing to bathe regularly.

```
Me (6:35 am): Did u actually wash ur
hair this morning?
Blocked ID (6:36 am): what do u mean?
Me (6:36 am): Oh come on. Ur hair is
jacked, and u know it.
Blocked ID (6:37 am): my hair is sup-
posed to be my trademark
Me (6:38 am): Bum chic is ur trade-
mark? I can find a bum with ur hair in
5 mins.
Blocked ID (6:38 am): ouch, that hurt
Me (6:39 am): I'd apologize, but u
did wake me up at 6:15
Blocked ID (6:39 am): i'm a selfish
ass, srry
Me (6:40 am): It's ok. Why r u in
hair and makeup?
Blocked ID (6:40 am): vanity fair
shoot in central park
```

God. Why the hell was he talking to me, again?

Blocked ID (6:43 am): r u still there? should i not have said that?
Me (6:44 am): No. Sometimes I forget what u are.
Blocked ID (6:44 am): i like that about u
Me (6:44 am): It's just disconcerting.
Blocked ID (6:44 am): how so?
Me (6:45 am): Do u honestly want to know?
Blocked ID (6:45 am): of course
Me (6:45 am): I don't know why ur talking to me.
Blocked ID (6:46 am): i don't have anyone else to talk to

Seriously? He was probably surrounded by tons of people fetching him Evian and a whole-wheat bagel while measuring him for his wardrobe and figuring out what poses would work best. *He had no one to talk to?*

Me (6:47 am): Srsly? Aren't there tons of ppl around?
Blocked ID (6:47 am): yes, but they don't want to talk
Me (6:48 am): Were u mean to them? Did u kick their dog?
Blocked ID (6:48 am): lol, most ppl don't really want to talk to me
Blocked ID (6:48 am): it's kind of like window-shopping
Me (6:48 am): Why not? U seem ok... not too crazy J
Blocked ID (6:49 am): just ok?
Me (6:49 am): I mean, aren't all actors a little screwed up in the head?
Blocked ID (6:49 am): only the good ones J
Me (6:49 am): R u a good actor?
Blocked ID (6:50 am): not yet, but

i'm trying
Me (6:50 am): Well then I don't get
it.
Blocked ID (6:50 am): think a/b it
Blocked ID (6:50 am): these ppl care
most that i look sharp in their mag
Blocked ID (6:51 am): not a/b if i'm
happy, c what time they woke me up?

I could almost picture him laughing to himself at his own joke.

Me (6:51 am): Yeah, the nerve of
those bitches. . . .
Blocked ID (6:51 am): lol
Blocked ID (6:53 am): am i keeping u
from something?

I waited a moment more while I stared at the tiny screen of my cell phone. It unnerved me how easy it was to forget my misanthropy whenever I talked to him. I almost felt happy right now. It was the first time I felt happy in the morning in ages. This was not good. It wasn't going to go anyplace that was healthy for me, and I needed to stop this. Soon.

Me (6:55 am): Actually, I need to go
to work.
Blocked ID (6:55 am): oh i'm srry
Me (6:56 am): Plus, I pay per text.
Blocked ID (6:56 am): shit
Blocked ID (6:56 am): at the risk of
sounding redundant, srry again
Me (6:57 am): Don't worry a/b it.
Take care.
Blocked ID (6:57 am): what's ur
email?

Ugh. Part of me had already began to type my address in response to the involuntary thrill coursing through me. The more cautious side of my psyche, the side I should have listened to whenever things went downhill with Ryan, told me to stop and think about it instead of just doing what felt right.

I had deduced a few things about Tom in the short set of conversations we had shared so far. He seemed intelligent and witty. As I recalled how he handled my fawning cousins, I also knew that he could be kind even when it was unnecessary. The thing that gave me the greatest pause was the overwhelmingly obvious inference I had made from his words and actions: he was lonely. It shocked me a great deal when I truly realized this. A lonely movie star?

It wasn't a big deal to give him my email address. Hey, it wasn't like I had anything exciting going on in my life that would captivate him for any extended length of time. Plus, he had been so sweet to Steph and Maria yesterday. I couldn't lie to myself either... I really enjoyed talking to him. This was something I could manage. If things got out of hand, I knew I would be able to tell him to find some other mundane distraction from his fantastically glamorous existence. Anyway, I was sure his fascination was akin to a runway model observing the common hausfrau grocery shopping for her family.

I had no romantic interest in yet another man with screaming red flags surrounding every aspect of his life. "Those who cannot remember the past are condemned to repeat it," were the philosopher George Santayana's words. I reflected on that quote whenever the desire to give someone a chance would pop into my head. I knew better. I could handle this.

**Me (7:00 am): 7crisp@gmail.com**
**Blocked ID (7:00 am): thnx**

A curious flutter in my heart immediately put to question my rational musings of only a moment ago. I furrowed my brow and gritted my teeth with renewed certainty. Movie Star Tom was a temporary diversion in my unbelievably boring existence—completely meaningless, entirely disposable. Absolutely not a big deal.

During lunch I decided to call Hana to see what she thought of the situation. Since I was pretty sure some semblance of discretion was in order, I made my way back to my car to talk to her. She answered the phone, but I could barely hear her. The music in her car was absolutely deafening with its thumping bass and unintelligible vocals. If classical music stirred the memory of my father, and my mother walked to the beat of Latin drums, then Hana Fateri cruised to life with the most ghetto gangsta rap as a soundtrack. Honestly, it was one of these things I loved to tell people just to shock them.

Picture this: A half-Korean girl who dressed in designer everything, loved to cook and spend time with her family—essentially a homebody whose favorite pastimes included going to the beach and watching movies with her husband. Charlotte York speeding around in a black BMW to the booming sounds of Three 6 Mafia. Oh, and by the way, she knew every single word of whatever song currently polluted the air and could rap word-perfect along with the tune—lots of colorful stuff about bitches and hos. As a result of her musical predilection, Hana also had one of the more colorful vocabularies I had encountered. To me, all of this just added to her charm. Any form of love is blind.

"Hello?" I said even louder.

"Cris? One sec." She shuffled the phone and turned down the music.

"Dude, how do you even hear the phone ringing with the music that freaking loud?" I asked.

"Save it. What's up?"

"Are you busy?"

"Nope. I have to show houses around three o'clock, but right now I'm just taking things to the post office."

"Well, I wanted to talk to you about something, but I don't want you to overreact or read too deeply into it," I warned.

"What happened?" Her curiosity piqued.

"So, the other day when I took Steph and Maria to that meet-and-greet thing at the mall, I accidentally left my iPod on the signing table. I went back to the lost and found to get it, and it turned out someone had picked it up and left a cell number for me."

"Are you wasting my time with a Gita story?" she asked with a hint of irritation in her voice.

I laughed. Gita was notorious for talking up a situation prior to relating its events in such a manner that made the actual story incredibly anticlimactic. Essentially, she was a shiteous storyteller.

"Just give me a second. So I called the number and left a voicemail, and the dude called me back last night. We had a nice conversation, and he text messaged me this morning."

"Whoa! You have a crazy stalker? Awesome. Are you going to mess with him?" she asked in amusement.

I paused for effect. "See, none of that is what makes the story interesting. What makes it interesting is…the dude who took my iPod is that Thomas guy from the movie."

Dead silence.

"What?" she whispered. Rendering Hana speechless already 23

earned me a pat on the back.

"Thomas, the actor slash ghost, took my iPod. We talked on the phone last night and texted each other this morning."

"Are you fucking kidding me?" she shrieked. Her voice had risen with each subsequent word so that, by the time she finished, all I could hear were shrill reverberations in the phone.

"Dude. You don't need to yell."

"Tell me *everything*. Don't spare a single detail," she demanded.

Hana and I were wont to psychoanalyze everything about men in the obsessive fashion of women everywhere. Gita gave us much-needed balance because she thought wasting time pondering the words and actions of men was basically the equivalent of learning how to make poop edible. At the end of the day, it didn't change the fact that it was still poop. Gita was honestly more like a guy than most guys I knew. If I told Gita this story, she would probably say, "That's nice, C. Now, get back to work."

I related the events in superfluous detail. She gasped and echoed my statements at all the appropriate intervals.

"I think he likes you," she stated with certainty.

"Well, it doesn't really matter now, does it?" I responded testily. I had already known she was going to say that, but for some reason it made me even more uncomfortable to hear the words in actuality.

"Why the hell not?" she insisted.

"In case you've forgotten, he's a movie star. I'm not Cinderella, nor am I Julia Roberts from *Pretty Woman*. I never wanted to be. Plus, he doesn't strike me as the type of guy who wants a project," I stated with complete honesty.

"Cristina, don't be too judgmental."

"That's funny coming from you. If I told you he was a recovering heroin addict, you'd be urging me to call 911 so the police could be dispatched for the dual purpose of retrieving my iPod and making sure he wasn't using again."

"Now, that's not fair. Honestly, if he works in Hollywood, he could be a recovering heroin addict, too. Thomas, the actor slash ghost slash possible heroin addict," she deadpanned.

We both laughed.

"So, what are you going to do?" she asked.

"I don't know. I was thinking… is it outrageous for me to think we could be friends?" As I said the words, I realized how much I wanted them to be plausible. I had no desire to tell the actor slash possible heroin addict that I never wanted to talk to him again. The truth was I definitely wanted to continue our conversation. I hoped that didn't mean anything ominous.

"I don't know, Cris. Hollywood-types may not be good friends for us groundlings," she said unabashedly. "Why don't you Google him? I know a little bit about him from the random gossip blogs I read everyday, and he doesn't seem like he would be too big of a toolbag. I can't remember anything terribly deleterious. Actually, I always thought he seemed kind of awkward...like I wanted to take him home, fix him a bowl of soup, and demand that he tell me what's wrong."

"Then why does everyone think he's so amazing?" I asked.

"Well, he's freaking adorable, first of all. Secondly, he's a decent actor. He's also got this tortured artist vibe to him that intrigues the minds of angst-ridden teenage girls."

"Yuck. I'm done with tortured anything. All he has to do is tell me he reads Nietzsche, and he's earned an express ticket to Who-the-Hell-Cares."

My ex had loved to read morbid philosophy about existentialism, Marxism, nihilism, and any other bleak-ism out there. I pseudo-blamed his penchant for reading this sort of "life has no meaning" crap for why he decided it was okay to ruin mine.

"Google him. See what you find out there and use your best judgment. If he likes talking to you, he can't be all that bad. I just hope he's not one of those twisted fucks who likes to study the insects in their natural environment. Maybe he's in info-gathering mode. Like a Strasberg method-acting weirdo...maybe his next role is a Puerto Rican tranny." She laughed uproariously at her own joke. Hana didn't care at all if you failed to find her funny...she oftentimes found herself funny enough for several people. Luckily, her dark humor was usually right in sync with mine.

I chuckled with her. "I need to go, but I'll call you after work. If you talk to Gita, tell her what's going on so I don't have to tell the story again. I never called her back last night...damn, maybe I'll send her an email."

"Okay. Love you. If you get invited to the Oscars, lose the bastard and take me."

"Haha. Dream on. Love you, too," I said with a smile.

I went back into the office, sat down in my cubicle, and took a deep breath. I opened up a browser window and typed in www.google.com. *I can't believe I'm doing this crap.* I always mocked Hana endlessly whenever she told me she wasted hours Googling random people on the net. She spent a great deal of time amassing large quantities of useless information, and the "Google Technique," as she called it, was Phase One of any sleuthing enterprise. I never thought I would stoop to her level.

I typed in his name and hit Search. Approximately 10,400,000 results. Suddenly I felt like I was the size of the parasite that causes amoebic dysentery. I didn't even want to know how many results would come up if I typed in "Cristina Aleida Pereira." Maybe ten? At the top of the endless list of hyperlinks were several articles insinuating that Tom was unhappy in Hollywood. I glossed over those. I'd lost my faith in responsible journalism back in the election cycle of 2004.

I spent a few nanoseconds on a couple of fansites and quickly decided that estrogen-fueled shrines were not the best place for me to figure out whether or not someone had a normal personality. I did see a couple of pictures of him in a tux that made me smile. He cleaned up nicely. Finally, I clicked on a few links that sent me to www.youtube.com to watch some of Tom's interviews with various media outlets. Jackpot.

I spent the next hour at work obsessively watching clip after clip of him promoting movies and oftentimes being asked the same series of predictable questions. Hana was right. He did seem awkward . . . not necessarily like he lacked confidence, but more like he wanted to be somewhere else. I desperately wanted to know where else he wanted to be. This was bad. *Stop it, Cris. That's enough.* Damn Hana for suggesting answers and promoting chaos at the same time. I X-ed out of all the browser windows with frustration. If anything, my sleuthing had only exacerbated my curiosity. Shit.

I opened up my work email and mechanically responded to several of the more pressing issues. Fielding phone calls and organizing the projects on my desk took up the rest of the day.

When I got home, my mother wasn't back from work yet. Feeling the need for some comfort food, I scrounged around the kitchen for the ingredients to make *arroz con gandules* and some chicken with *tostones.* After doing all of the preparatory work, I made my way upstairs and turned on my laptop to send an email to Gita.

There were several unread messages in my inbox. Gita had sent me a link for one of those "Send this to ten people to brighten their day, *or else*" forwarding chain emails. Why were your friends allowed to spam you? Those bullshit chain emails in particular always triggered an irrational mini-conniption in me. Kind of like an email-induced form of roadrage. I forgave her because I loved her, but that didn't stop me from clicking on Delete and damning ten unnamed friends to a day of darkness.

When I looked below her message, I saw something that made me catch my breath: It was an unread message from the sender "Tom A." with a subject line that read "question(s)." I tried to ignore the signs of my heart coming back to life with curious acceleration as I clicked on the message.

> From: Tom A. <bobdylan85@yahoo.co.uk>
> To: Cris Pereira <7crisp@gmail.com>
> Date: Mon, January 12, 2009 at 4:32 PM
> Subject: question(s)
>
> ---
>
> it occurred to me as i went about my day that i might be coming off a bit dodgy. i hope you believe me when i say that it's never been my intention to make you uncomfortable. maybe this next move will just be the final nail in my coffin, but i did want to reassure you that i'm not some creep with a fixation. all evidence to the contrary. honestly, i liked the fact that you were completely unimpressed by me. i'm unimpressed by myself on a daily basis, and it's nice to find someone else who shares the sentiment—it helps me feel like i do exist in the real world, even if only for a moment. sometimes it's not enough that my sister calls me a git every chance she has, and that my mum constantly reminds me that i'm an idiot. you also answer my questions with your own thoughts instead of trying to figure out what you think i want to hear—it makes me smile that you don't seem to give a rat's ass. the long and the short of it is: i like talking to you. it makes me feel normal. i hope you don't mind that. if you do, just tell me. i don't want to be a bloody nuisance—like that guy who just won't leave you the hell alone. anyway, i have two questions for you. if you don't want to hear from me again, don't bother responding. i'll take the hint and bugger off.

27

```
what's your favorite place in the world and
why?
why is algerian raï music on the same ipod as
k-pop?

tom

p.s.-your email address made me laugh. crisp?
```

When I finished reading the email, I was surprised and taken aback by the fact my facial muscles felt sore. As I absorbed each sentence, the smile that began with a delighted smirk had grown centimeter by centimeter until it stretched the skin of my face with the good pain of something unexpectedly funny.

Hot on the heels of my warm amusement came cold frustration. Tom the Movie Star didn't make it easy for me to "remember the past" and act accordingly. I wanted desperately to click the Delete button and forget about the email, forget about the momentary absence of pain, and forget about him.

So, he was listening to my iPod? *Hmmm.*

I looked over his charming message again. The same silly smile began to manifest itself on my face.

I sighed in surrender as I hit Reply.

 # FOUR

From: Cris Pereira <7crisp@gmail.com>
To: Tom A. <bobdylan85@yahoo.co.uk>
Date: Mon, January 12, 2009 at 7:57 PM
Subject: Re: question(s)

So . . . I have to admit I sat here staring at a blank email for awhile trying to figure out what the heck I was going to write about.

I guess that I should just begin by answering your two (more like three) questions. We'll see where it goes from there.

1.) My favorite place in the world is probably Paris. I know, I know . . . how cheesy, right? A girl who loves Paris, blah blah blah. Honestly, it doesn't even have anything to do with the whole "City of Love" thing. When I was in college, I did a year abroad in France, and it just kind of stuck with me. One of my favorite places to just "be" in Paris is the Musée d'Orsay. I have a weak spot for Impressionist paintings . . . something about the mundane mixed in with the slightly psychotic . . . haha, hope that doesn't scare you too much. I'm not a big fan of perfection in art. I prefer flaws . . . I think it's easier to imitate something perfectly, but it's not so easy to copy an unintentional imperfection.

I also travel to eat, so Paris is a no-brainer. I'm serious when I say that. Whenever I travel, I plan my day around where I'll be eating. One day this shit is going to catch up with me and I'll be as big as a house. Maybe then I'll rethink priorities when going abroad. Until then, c'est la vie.

2.) This question made me laugh. When I was

living in France, I became friends with one of the most wonderful people I've ever met in my life. His name is Samir, and he was like a big brother to me. His entire family had moved to France from Algeria about ten years before, and I had a great time learning about their culture by hanging out with him. His family worshipped this Algerian Raï singer named Khaled, and it definitely grew on me.

About the K-pop . . . yeah. My best friend is half-Korean. It's impossible to avoid having Korean pop music on my iPod. I'll confess that occasionally I find myself dancing around to some of the more obnoxious, bubblegum shit when no one is around. You asked.

Well damn. That's a pretty long email. Watch, now you'll think twice about asking me multiple questions! You may be the guy who won't leave me the hell alone, but I'm definitely the girl who won't shut the hell up.

Here's a question for you . . . What do you want to be when you grow up? :-P

Cris
P.S.–What's wrong with my email address? Looks like someone has a crush on Bob Dylan.

From: Tom A. <bobdylan85@yahoo.co.uk>
To: Cris Pereira <7crisp@gmail.com>
Date: Tues, January 13, 2009 at 2:13 PM
Subject: Re: Re: question(s)

last night i was invited to a party at a hotel in nyc. i've been there before, but this was the first time i went where i received a fair amount of acknowledgment as i made my way around. i'm sure you won't be surprised when i tell you i pre-ferred it more the last time. my ego appreciates the attention for a while, but then i just really wish i could carry on alone without any sort of outside expectations. i'm not sharp enough to come up with witty rot for extended periods of time. i'm sure if people actually sat down to talk to me, i would bore the piss out of them in under five minutes. i probably shouldn't be telling you this as i'm counting on you wanting to talk to me for longer than that. as to what i want to be when i grow up—i'm not daft enough to think that i can hang onto this fluke for very long. it's near impossible to achieve anything in this industry, and to continue achieving is probably a complicated mix of elements beyond my control. it would be fucking unbelievable if i could be successful enough to call my own shots in life. i've always thought that i'd like to do something with music. i wonder if anyone would buy music i made? i dunno, maybe i could help with one of those programs that encourage kids in school to learn how to play an instrument. greater good, jolie/pitt stuff. that would truly be amazing. i realize i haven't really answered your question . . . i guess the best response i can come up with is this: i have an idea of the type of person i want to be when i grow up. if i'm doing something with myself that helps me be that type of person, i'll be happy. in conclusion, i have no idea what i want to be when i grow up.

what was the best day of your life so far and why?

tom

p.s.—a 'crisp' is what you yanks call a 'chip' in the uk. this is a really old email address. i used to be obsessed with bob dylan as a kid.

From: Cris Pereira <7crisp@gmail.com>
To: Tom A. <bobdylan85@yahoo.co.uk>
Date: Wed, January 14, 2009 at 9:03 PM
Subject: Re: Re: Re: question(s)

Zimmerman:                                          31

You know, it's really funny because my best friend Hana (the one responsible for the K-pop) told me that whenever she sees you in an interview or on TV (don't ask, she's the biggest stalker I know, and she doesn't care), she wants to take you home, cook you dinner, and force you to tell her what's bothering you. After I read your email, I totally get it. Stop picking on yourself so much! Trust me, you'll never get a girl's attention if you keep telling chicks how boring and stupid you are, even if it's the truth–haha. I think you're overcompensating because you think people assume you're a narcissistic bastard–being a "movie star" and all. Just stop it! It's okay if you think nice thoughts about yourself once in a while. I won't tell . . . probably.

You know, this was a pretty loaded question. If you had asked me this six months ago, I would have had a totally different response. I think the best day of my life was probably your choice of many the year I was eighteen. The reason why I can't pick just one is because it's all become a blur as time passes. It was my first year in college, and I had more fun than should be allowed. Trust me, I paid for all that fun the rest of the time I was in school. They should give you a disclaimer on your first day–it's really easy to wreck your GPA, but it's amazingly difficult to fix it. I stupidly wanted to be a doctor! Ha! They don't want people in medical school who fail freshman calculus (twice). Anyway, it was just such a great time for me. I made some of the best friends I have, and we would all stay awake just wasting time and talking until the sun rose–trying to remind us that we had a purpose other than socializing in college. Not that it mattered. I laughed and carried on more that year than I can remember, and anytime I need to cheer myself up, all I have to do is think of some silly memory
from that time. I know I'm being cryptic, but

it's difficult to explain. I just felt at peace with myself and with my life. Everything was new and anything seemed possible. I miss that feeling.

What's one thing you feel like you must do before you die? (And don't feed me some crap about climbing Mt. Everest. Reality would be a good place to start.)

Cris
P.S. I'm still obsessed with Bob Dylan.

From: Tom A. <bobdylan85@yahoo.co.uk>
To: Cris Pereira <7crisp@gmail.com>
Date: Wed, January 14, 2009 at 11:58 PM
Subject: Re: Re: Re: Re: question(s)

chip,

shit, and i really did want to climb Everest . . . seeing as how you managed to turn a question about one day into an answer about one whole year, i think i'm allowed a certain amount of liberty in my responses as well. i used to say to people that i liked traveling, but it's become more of a hassle than a pleasure as of late, so i stopped saying that. honestly, i think that if i could travel freely again, it would be something i'd like to do before i die. i've been to so many amazing places, but i've never really had the chance to do the things you're supposed to do whilst there. my time is really not mine, not that i'm complaining or anything (god forbid i get another one of those lectures on being positive). for example, it's a load of rubbish that i went to rome and never got to see the colosseum—if you know what i mean. i bet you're wondering why i didn't just say 'i'd like to see the colosseum before i go' to the people in charge of my schedule, but whining doesn't sit well with me (all evidence to the contrary). so that's my 33

'answer' to compliment your non-answer. i'd like to travel freely before i die. maybe i could make a list of places i'd like to go. what do you think?
    can i call you tomorrow at lunchtime?

    zimmerman
    p.s.-don't think i missed your bit about a 'different answer six months ago.' i'm just being temporarily polite.

It was nearly two o'clock in the morning. The crazy rantings of my mind were making it impossible to sleep. Screw it. I decided to call Gita. I needed some unemotional, ruthlessly detached advice.

Throughout the last week, I had become worried when I realized that the emails I shared with Tom were quickly becoming a highlight of my day. I had no idea where he wanted this to go, but I knew that all I needed right now was a friend, nothing more. It seemed premature to say this to him…plus, I might be incredibly presumptuous in assuming he had anything more than a friendly interest in me. I mean, seriously. I knew I wasn't even trying to be modest when I thought this way. I was fairly certain that famous people usually rubbed elbows (and other parts of the body) almost exclusively with other famous people. How else do you explain how all of these gossip blogs Hana obsessed over and magazines I glanced at in the checkout aisle at the grocery store managed to stay in business? Hot movie star with nameless nobody just doesn't sell. It's almost like a convoluted American version of the caste system…anyone not possessing several pairs of oversized Oliver Peoples' sunglasses need not apply. I just couldn't let this get out of my control.

If I told him that I just wanted to be friends, I was worried I might look like a fool.

I pressed four on my speed dial. It rang several times.

"Hello?" a groggy, highly irritated voice answered.

"G? It's Cris."

"Holy shit dude, what time is it?" She sounded like her throat hadn't seen water in three days.

"I think it's around two," I said dismissively.

"Is something wrong?" she groaned.

"Not really."

"Then why are you calling this late, babe?"

"I really need to talk to you," I said in as urgent a tone as I could muster.

"Well then, call Crazy . . . she's probably still awake." I could already hear her starting to hang up the phone. Gita needed sleep like no one I'd ever met in my life.

"I don't need to talk to Hana. I need a voice of detached reason," I blurted quickly.

"Is this about that actor guy?" she asked pointedly.

"Yeah. Please don't hang up!"

"Ugh, make it quick. You know how much I love sacrificing sleep to talk about boneheaded men. Most guys are the biggest waste of time in the world. Do you know how much more productive women would be if we didn't have to worry about freakin' men?"

Gita was extremely analytical when it came to meeting and dating men. Her objectiveness often bordered on cynicism, and she had a strict one, two, three rule—if she found more than three things glaringly wrong with a guy, he was out. She had dated several times, and most of her relationships were long-term, but Gita was definitely more focused on her career than anything else. Her Indian parents were not happy about that, but Gita didn't care one bit. She cruised through life to the beat of her own bhangra music.

"Yeah, yeah. What happened to making this quick?" I said.

"Talk."

"So . . . we've been emailing back and forth . . . it's been really nice. Tonight he asked me if he could call me at work tomorrow, well actually, today."

"So?" she yawned.

"I don't know, G. I'm not ready for a relationship, and emailing is one thing. It's kind of impersonal and I can control how the conversation goes."

"Cristina, are you serious?" she sighed.

"What?"

"Did he ask you to move to LA and have lots of babies with him?"

"No." I already knew where this was going.

"Then why the hell are you wasting time pondering his reasons for wanting to call you?" Her voice was firm, no nonsense.

"I just don't want to lead him on or give him any expectations. I mean, I don't even know if he likes me! I want to handle it right from the beginning. I can't clean up another mess retroactively."

"Cris, you need to stop trying to control everything like life is a 35 scripted saga. It's not. Right now, you're just talking about a phone call. Next time, call me if he asks you to have his lovechild. That's something worth worrying over."

"Are you sure there's nothing I should be concerned about?" I murmured. I felt like a neurotic child suffering from hypochondria. *There are no monsters in the closet.*

"Of course I'm not sure. All I know is it's just a phone call. Chill out. Go to sleep. And for God's sake, don't call Hana. All this situation needs is another obsessive mind pondering every nuance as if it were Shakespearean theater."

"Okay. Thanks G. Believe it or not, you've helped me a lot."

"I believe it. Love you, chica." I heard her yawn in the background. Gita Talukdar... the frontrunner in the Cut the Shit Campaign.

"Me too. Talk to you tomorrow."

From: Cris Pereira <7crisp@gmail.com>
To: Tom A. <bobdylan85@yahoo.co.uk>
Date: Thurs, January 15, 2009 at 2:27 AM
Subject: Phone Call

Zimmerman:

Sure. I usually take my lunch break between 12:30 and 1:30.

Chip

---

I stared at the email from my Sent inbox for a few more minutes, then I forced myself to shut down the computer.

God only knew what tomorrow would bring.

# FIVE

All morning at work, I knew it looked like I had done a long line of cocaine when I first woke up. I was annoyingly cheerful and almost hyperactive in my interactions with my colleagues... kind of like a squirrel with a nervous disorder. I knew that they noticed, and it bothered me to no end.

Usually, I was a fairly bubbly person and purposefully exuded an inordinate amount of energy in nearly everything I did. It helped me a great deal to be this way, especially whenever life took a turn for the worst. People with the propensity to pity me usually forgot about their concern whenever they saw my smile and heard my laughter— even if both were secretly forced. Regardless of my typical modus operandi, I was probably taking it too far today.

I tried hard not to let my nerves get the better of me... damn him for making me wait to find out what he couldn't say via email. It was a lot easier to feign detachment and disinterest when I didn't have such a large chunk of time to obsess about the burning question mark in my inbox. Ugh.

As soon as 12:30 hit at the top corner of my computer screen, I pulled out my phone and began making the walk outside to the car. Again, I didn't want anyone to know that my rather mundane existence of the past few months had just taken a small shock to the nervous system.

I sat down in the car and put on some Stravinsky. The last two movements from his *Firebird Suite* were usually like a soothing balm to my scorched psyche. It would do me no good at all to make him realize how much my mind turned to thoughts of him recently. I didn't even want to admit it to myself: I was really beginning to like Movie Star Tom, and it was destined to cause me problems sometime very soon.

The vibrations of the phone in my hand startled me just as a swell in the music elicited a drawn-out breath of relaxation from my tensed frame. The crescendo of violins retreated softly into the background as I lowered the volume and cleared my throat.

"Hello?" I said as nonchalantly as possible.

"Hi." I imagined him smiling as he said the word. Shit, why did I let my imagination take control of me?

"How's your day been so far?" Again, I thought I did a fairly good job of straddling the fence between mild interest and common courtesy. Right?

"I've actually been a bit nervous." He laughed warmly.

"Why?"

"Well, I keep thinking that I'm doing a decent job of seeming normal to you, and now I proceed to muck it up by asking you to do something I'd venture to be a bit of a stretch for you...and now I'm rambling nonsensically. Two very good reasons to be nervous."

My responding laugh was edgy and high-pitched...reminiscent of an idiotic schoolgirl. Excellent.

"See? It's now contagious." I saw him smiling again as he said the words and couldn't help my heartbeat from accelerating ever so slightly.

"How about we make a deal...I'll stop laughing like an idiot and you stop rambling nonsensically." My voice sounded more normal.

"Deal."

"Shit, I just had to stop myself from laughing like an idiot," I said with a grin.

"I'd forgotten how much I liked the sound of your voice," he said in a lower register.

No, no, no! My heart skipped a beat. This would not happen.

"See, now that better not be the only reason why you wanted to call me." I pretended to sound irritated in an attempt to change the direction of the conversation.

"It's not. Regardless, you have the cutest accent."

"What? I know the guy who says words like 'manky' and 'bollocks' is not telling me I have an accent." I attempted to say the strange colloquialisms with the same inflection a British person might use...at least I thought so.

"God, that was the worst fucking impression of a British accent I've heard yet. Swear to me you won't do that again."

"I worked hard as a kid so that I wouldn't sound like a foreigner, thank you very much. I'll only swear not to do a British accent again if you swear to pretend that I succeeded in my attempt. I'd rather not worry that I sound like Rosie Perez for another day in my life."

He laughed loudly. "It's not a marked accent. It's very slight. Like I said...I think it's quite cute."

"Humph. Watch out, England! Cristina is loose and bastardizing

38

the public's perception of your charming accent. Shakespeare and Jane Austen are turning in their graves!" My horrendous imitation even grated against my own eardrums. Blech. I sure wasn't Gwyneth Paltrow.

He laughed again. "To hell with it...I'm just going to ask. I have way too much fun talking to you."

"Ask me what?"

I heard him take a deep breath. Suddenly the cheeky attitude I had developed within the last few seconds of our conversation vanished and was subsequently replaced by its predecessor (aptly named "panic").

"So...I had a rather...brilliant idea last night. Well, I think it's brilliant, but you may think it's a bit...mental."

He was being extremely careful in his choice of words—a fact that doesn't usually bode well for the other person involved in the dialogue. It reminded me a bit of my father. Whenever he had something unpleasant to say, he would usually take his time, as though he were an elocutionist teaching a slow-minded person how to speak.

"Just spit it out, Zimmerman," I joked in an attempt to force both of us to relax and stop taking this conversation seriously. It was easier to pretend something didn't matter that much when you could control the timbre of the exchange in your lighthearted favor.

"Hah. Fine. I'm going to be in Atlanta from tomorrow through Sunday. Initially, I was planning on having your long-absent iPod mailed to Raleigh, but...I'd rather you come and get it yourself."

"Excuse me?" They were the only words I could manage to squeak out.

"If I were to, for instance, have a ticket waiting for you at the airport tomorrow to come to Atlanta for the weekend, would you come?"

I couldn't even think straight. Was he serious? He wanted me to come to Atlanta? *Why?*

"Cris?"

"Give me a second." My brain worked overtime hashing out rationalizations both for and against this insanity.

"I don't want to make you uncomfortable. I hope I'm not coming off as a complete tosser. Like I've said before, I really like talking to you." He sounded completely forthright, but he was an *actor*, after all.

"But why the hell would you want me to come to Atlanta?" I blurted out thoughtlessly.

"For the same reason I want you to respond to my emails. I think I'm quickly becoming fascinated by you...in a very non-stalker-like way."

"Non-stalkers don't offer to buy girls they hardly know plane tickets to visit them," I bit out.

"Very true. Do you see now why I was nervous?"

"Not nearly nervous enough," I murmured.

"Did I offend you? I'm truly sorry if I did. I feel like I'm doing a terrible job of properly expressing how much I would like to hang out with you this weekend. I know it's too soon to ask, but I wish you would trust me when I say that I just want to relax and spend time getting to know you."

"What do you mean by that?"

"Exactly what I said. I want to get to know you better and, unfortunately, I don't have enough time to park myself in Raleigh to do so."

"I don't know," I said honestly.

"Look, I don't want to pressure you. My closest friends live and work in London, and if I could get them to come and visit for a weekend that would be fantastic. I've resigned myself to the fact they won't be able to come...at least not with any frequency. That basically means I need to make some friends in the states or exist like a tortured hermit for the duration of the time I live here."

Friends? He wanted friends? If that was all he wanted, I could be okay with that.

"Tom, I don't want to fly to Atlanta to visit you."

A brief moment of silence. "I totally understand," he said softly.

"But...I will drive down to Atlanta to pick up my iPod on Saturday."

"Isn't that a bit of a drive? Why don't you just fly?" His voice had instantly become more animated, and my heart matched its intensity alarmingly. Really bad, Cris. You had better watch yourself.

"I don't feel comfortable taking a plane ticket from you."

"Why not?" he asked with surprise.

"I don't know. I need to feel like I can come and go on my own schedule. Plus, I don't like to feel beholden to others. If I wanted to fly, I could buy my own plane ticket."

"I've said it before . . . you really are quite surprising," he said thoughtfully.

"Yeah, I still don't know why you think that."

"And that's exactly what makes you so fascinating. Can I at least get you a hotel room so that you don't have to drive so much in one day? I can ask my agent to reserve one in your name."

I thought for a moment. "It sounds like a fair compromise."

"Excellent. Would you mind calling me when you've left?"

For a moment, I felt my heart jerk to a sudden stop. Whenever things were good, Ryan had always wanted me to call on my way to visit him and when I returned home. It hurt to hear another man's voice asking me such a secretly intimate thing.

"I'll call you when I'm an hour away," I said firmly.

"Another fair compromise."

"I can't believe you're making *me* come and get the iPod that you essentially stole!" I joked.

"I have to say it was one of the better filches of my life," he stated with mock pride.

"You realize that this basically makes you an asshole."

He laughed. "I'll take it as long as you're coming this weekend."

"You'd better. I'll see you soon."

This time, I definitely heard him smile. "See you on Saturday, Cris. Thanks—from your friendly non-stalker."

"You're welcome, Tom."

Oh, Holy Mother of God... this was not good.

 # SIX

As far as my mother knew, I was going away for the weekend to Charlotte to hang out with Hana and Gita. If I told her the truth, she probably wouldn't believe me anyway.

My friends were the only ones who knew the truth—I was driving to Atlanta to spend time with a movie star. The sheer lunacy of the situation would have driven me to crazed bouts of laughter had I taken a moment to detach myself from the startling reality. A movie star thought I was fascinating. God only knew why. Unfortunately, I was beginning to find the movie star irresistibly charming as well. Complete idiocy. There was nothing like rebounding with every girl's fantasy. It was sure to make my ability to select a proper lifelong match that much easier with such an excellent basis for comparison. In actuality, it was every girl's fantasy but mine. All I wanted was to rewind time and still have Ryan. The boring truth to my sad dream was beginning to eke out a hole in my brain that I needed to fill with something more constructive. A fun weekend out of town just might be the answer.

I decided about halfway through the drive to Atlanta that I would use this opportunity to cement in both our minds that we were destined to be passing friends. Of course, I was still pretty sure he didn't want anything more than that anyway, so that conversation was probably not going to be too difficult. Surprisingly fascinating or not, I was newly damaged...definitely more of a project than anyone should willingly take on for the moment. I hoped I didn't have to tell him what had happened to me. I'd avoid it at all cost if I could help it, as it was excruciatingly embarrassing to tell anyone that I'd been cast aside for some bimbo my fiancé had known for all of two minutes. Four years of solidarity thrown away for two minutes of spontaneity. Men were such a pain in the ass to understand.

I called when I was sixty miles away from Atlanta.

"Cris?"

"Hey. I'm about an hour away. Where should I go?"

"Do you know how to get to Peachtree Street? I'm staying at the Ritz-Carlton," he said quietly. I assumed he was in a room with other people who might be listening to his conversation. I heard the slight din of voices in the background.

"Swanky."

"Hah. Just check-in under your name and then call my cell once you're settled. I'll send my agent Melissa to get you."

"Okay. Um, is there something you want to do?"

"Well, I'm actually getting ready to leave a press conference. I'm free for the rest of the evening."

"I guess we can figure it out whenever I get there," I said with a slight sound of unease. I still had no idea why he wanted to hang out with me.

"Sure. See you soon."

"Bye." After I hung up the phone, I spent the rest of the car ride trying to quell the confusion and focused on being myself. I was sure to have a better time if I didn't feel so completely bewildered and uncertain by this situation. Cris Pereira was not a girl who suffered from a lack of confidence... I just suffered from an apparent inability to maintain control of my life.

The life that I had sought to create for myself with a careful precision akin to delicately constructing a house of cards had been decimated by an errant blonde breeze named Amber ... seriously, her freaking name was Amber. Wasn't that the quintessential stripper name? Now, anytime I heard the name "Amber," I became irrationally angry, as though it were my trigger word. For a moment I thought of that scene in the movie *Zoolander* where Ben Stiller's character was brainwashed into killing a Prime Minister by the song *Relax*. Hah! If only....

I pulled into a space in the parking deck of the Ritz and checked in. Whoever had made the reservation spelled my name correctly. Pretty shocking. I walked into my room and took the requisite look around before calling Tom's cell phone. He told me that Melissa would be downstairs in ten minutes to bring me to his suite, so I took the time to brush my teeth and run a comb through my hair.

I had decided not to spend an inordinate amount of time obsessing over what to wear. This wasn't a date, and I wasn't interested in having him walk away with any impression about my appearance other than boring normalcy. If it looked like I tried too hard, it wouldn't serve me well on that account. I opted to wear some of my comfortable jeans and a long-sleeved, fitted black top. It was my favorite shirt because a multi-colored, Warhol-esque depiction of Che Guevara was emblazoned on the front. It was a screaming shout-out to my heritage, and my father had loved to see me in it. I wore simple black flats even though heels would have better served to hide the fact that I was a vertically challenged five-foot-two. My people were not celebrated for their height. Instead of growing upwards, God blessed us with the burgeoning backsides that gave rise to Jennifer Lopez's infamous insurance policy. No matter how much I worked out, I could never hide that part of my genetic inheritance. My hair was slightly wavy in spite of all the torturous attempts to flatten it, and I wore a bit of powder and mascara. Clean and neat... nothing that appeared to have taken any extra effort.

A knock at the door startled me from the studious glance of my appearance in the bathroom mirror. I walked to the door and slowly pulled it open. The woman in front of me appeared to be around forty, and her dark blonde hair was pulled back into a severe ponytail that looked like it might be giving her a tension headache. She was pale, and her visage appeared to be utterly no-nonsense. Her clothes were perfectly pressed and tailored to her extremely thin frame.

In ten words or less: this lady did not take shit from anybody.

"My name is Melissa Nash. I'm Thomas's agent. He asked me to bring you upstairs to the suite."

She didn't blink or look me in the eyes once. In fact, it appeared as though she had chosen to introduce herself to a spot on the wall behind me. If I had to venture a guess, she was not a member of my fan club.

"Hi Melissa. I'm Cris," I said as cheerfully as possible. I threw her a sunny smile in an attempt to defrost her icy demeanor. I failed.

She raised her eyebrows at me as she stared at my face for the first time. She probably thought the same thing I did: Why does *he* want to spend time with *her*?

"Follow me." She turned. I had to quickly grab my purse and jacket from the bed in order to keep up with her.

Following her down the hall reminded me of being in grammar school in Puerto Rico. I had always been an innately curious child and easily distracted by things around me. As a result, I usually fought to catch up with the person in front of me. We walked down the hall in linear formation because I could barely keep up with Melissa Nash. I felt utterly ridiculous running behind her to match her long strides— the preying mantis and the tiny ant.

When we stepped into the elevator, she turned to look at me again with her frosty grey eyes. "Thomas wouldn't want me to say this to you, but I feel that it's incumbent upon me to state that discretion is key when socializing with him. If you attempt to abuse this situation in any way, it will not work out to your advantage in the end."

"Damn, and I thought I was blunt," I responded caustically. If she was going to a bitch, she had better be able to take what she could dish.

The eyebrows arched again. "It's my job to sift through the bullshit and get to the point."

"And I'm sure you do your job very well. I have no intention of abusing anything. I know you don't have to trust me, but I also don't have to like you." Awesome, Cris... off to a rip-roaring good start in the world of Hollywood.

"Fair enough. Don't do anything stupid and we'll get along passably." She looked away from me again with dismissive arrogance.

I pursed my lips in irritation. This evil preying mantis thought I was a gold-digging skank out to capture as many moments as I could sell to the highest bidding paparazzo. I wasn't even going to go through the trouble of trying to prove her wrong. I was certain that she believed unfailingly in her ability to accurately judge others. She was not going to let a tiny Puerto Rican girl prove her wrong. After years of fighting to make everyone like me, I'd realized that sometimes it was just impossible. You can't fight a war with a psycho and expect to win anything but battle scars. Win the battle, lose the war kind of stuff.

As the elevator doors opened onto the highest floor, I gazed about, and the nervousness returned with a vengeance. Two burly-looking security guards dressed in black stood on either side of large double-doors directly in front of me. I felt like a kid in my Che shirt and jeans. They nodded to Melissa and opened one of the doors. I shot the security guard on my right a look that must have made him feel bad for me because he winked and smiled kindly. I returned the gesture. At least now he might hesitate before dragging me out of the suite at the first mistake I made and tossing me unceremoniously onto Peachtree Street.

Thomas was deep in amused conversation with another man whose appearance almost made me laugh out loud. He looked like an absurd cartoon character who wore tight, black pants and a grey turtleneck sweater that hugged his small body. He had dark brown facial hair on his pointed chin that was cut in zigzag patterns up his jaw line. He wore many rings on his fingers and a large watch that sparkled even from halfway across the room. Zorro meets Liberace. Excellent.

Tom turned when he heard the tapping of Melissa's heels on the 45 marble in front of me.

"Cris!" There was no way to ignore the broad smile on his face when he saw me. I grinned back at him in an effort to hide my awkwardness and discomfort.

"Che?" Zorro asked with puzzlement as he stared at my shirt. "¿De donde sos?"

"Puerto Rico. My father's originally from Cuba." It was a lame explanation for why I wore a shirt with an Argentinean Marxist's face emblazoned on it, but he asked.

"Well, I certainly didn't think you were from my homeland, not with that ass…it's good to know I can still tell the difference," Zorro said with the flamboyant air I had come to expect from an incredibly secure gay man. I'd bet money on it. His accent was cultivated in a manner that was especially meant to impress exoticism on anyone foolish enough to believe in its full authenticity. He most likely spoke English better than many people born and raised in the States. In spite of all his affectations, I was going to like this guy who smiled at me while scrutinizing every last detail of my appearance.

"Cris, this is Esteban Alvarez. He's in charge of making me look decent," Thomas said with a comfortable grin in Zorro's direction.

"And it's incredibly fucking hard. He's impossible to work with. Such a man. Jeans and T-shirt type…no taste at all. Well, at least you're not a disaster. He wasn't lying about that. We *are* going to need to work on your wardrobe, though." Esteban drawled and gesticulated the entire time he spoke. I could not help the smile that grew on my face.

"Thanks?" I said pseudo-sarcastically as I arched my eyebrows with amusement.

"Oh, you are cute. You're welcome." He smirked back at me with a look of begrudging acceptance. Esteban and I would get along well. Thank God. After dealing with the Preying Mantis, it was nice to know I had one kindred spirit amongst Tom's entourage.

"So," Tom said as he put his hands together in a staid gesture while looking at me expectantly. "What should we do?"

"Well, that depends on what you'd like to do. I've only been to Atlanta a few times, and I'm most familiar with a rather unconventional part of it." I smiled in memory as I said the words.

"And what part would that be?" he queried.

"Koreatown."

"Ah, K-pop took you there," he said with a grin.

"Yup. There are some killer Korean barbeque joints out there."

"Well, I've never actually tried Korean barbeque, so maybe we should check it out!"

His enthusiasm made him even more charming. I had been so focused on his face when I first walked in that I hadn't really taken much time to observe what he wore. His leisurely dark jeans and a long-sleeved knit shirt in a chocolate brown color made him look completely normal and unobtrusive. It was almost as though we had been precisely in sync with regards to keeping things simple. I found it immensely reassuring.

"Well, we're going to need to drive. It's about half an hour away from here in Duluth."

"Thomas," Melissa interrupted. She stood beside me and listened to our planning with the look of a hawk circling above, waiting for her prey's misstep. "I don't think it's advisable to just go off on your own to God-knows-where with someone you hardly know."

Honestly, I agreed with her... though my eyes still narrowed in irritation at her insinuation. Preying Mantis was going to be a major pain in the ass.

"Melissa, you've made your objections clear... several times. I'll be fine. I'm also not interested in taking Jim or Marcus with me. I don't think it will be necessary."

She pursed her lips and shot me an excellent go-to-hell look. Not to be outdone, I responded in kind. Man, she had at least eight inches on me. Zorro covered his mouth to stifle a small burst of laughter, and Tom smiled crookedly at me with barely-concealed amusement.

"So, where's your car?" Tom asked as he moved around the sofa between us to stand closer to me. I felt a small adrenaline rush pulse through my body to see his face so clearly for the first time since the day I met him. As I attempted to quell my quaking nerves, my mind digested his words.

"You want me to drive?" The surprise in my voice was unmistakable.

"Well, you won't want me to drive. The whole left-side of the road thing has really mucked up my eye-hand coordination. Plus, I was never a very good driver to begin with."

"Okay. No complaining about my driving, though," I said firmly.

Preying Mantis let out an overtly audible huff of frustration as we passed her to walk towards the door. She probably was not used to having her concerns left so unaddressed. One of the bodyguards rode down the elevator with us to the parking area and walked to my car to make sure we were both safely situated before he silently 47 turned around to return to his post.

As I put my key in the ignition, I realized with a sudden jolt that this was the first time we had ever been alone. He must have come to the same conclusion as I had because we just sat there for a moment and stared at one another. The smile on his face spread slowly and made its way over to me with infectious effect until we both grinned widely. My cheeks flushed with pleasure at the warm look in his eyes.

"So, in case I forget to tell you later, I'm really glad you came." His soft voice held a note of shyness that further emphasized the surprising normality of the man sitting next to me.

"Well, in case I forget to tell you later, it's still shitty that I had to come and get my own iPod."

"I'll try to make it up to you. Shall we?" He gazed pointedly at the wheel with a smile.

I backed out of the spot and peeled onto Peachtree Street. We drove in silence for a few minutes until we reached the freeway.

"Holy shit!" he sputtered as I merged into traffic. "You drive like an absolute lunatic!" He grasped the handle above the window so tightly his knuckles turned white.

I snorted blithely. "Relax, Grandpa. This is Atlanta; you won't get anywhere if you don't make a break for it. You haven't even seen crazy yet… ride with my cousin in San Juan and allow her to redefine the term 'lunatic' for you. You'll never complain about me again."

"Do all Puerto Ricans drive like they have nothing to live for?" he teased.

"That's the problem with you prudish Brits. You think that anyone figuratively coloring outside the lines must mean they have some dark desire to inflict harm. Don't read into mundane things like driving, Lord Tennyson. I haven't killed anyone yet, and I don't necessarily break rules… I just like to bend them."

He laughed loudly as he released the handle. "All right, Chip. I'll attempt to overlook your psychotic driving. You'll have to answer some questions to distract me from pondering the meaning of my life as it flashes before my eyes."

"You know, my friend Gita theorizes that people drive the way they live," I mused in an attempt to stop him from asking me questions.

"If that's the case, you live life recklessly and entirely too fast." He chuckled to himself.

"Well, that theory is incredibly flawed if that's the case. I could probably stand to live life a bit *more* recklessly. I'm the furthest thing from being a risk taker," I admitted.

"All evidence to the contrary…maybe the way you drive is more of an outlet for the way you live—like a chance to exist on the edge for just a moment."

"Hah! How do you drive?"

"Atrociously! I'm extremely cautious, and I drive very slowly It's probably because I have very little experience with it. I keep feeling like I'm going to kill someone every time I get behind the wheel. Learning to drive a car in L.A. was probably a piss-poor idea…I never actually had to drive in London."

"I'll bet all those Beverly Hills speed demons love having to drive behind you," I joked.

"Honestly, that's one of the reasons I'm so nervous when I drive. Yanks are unbelievably impatient. It's effing hilarious to watch the guy behind me go bat shit because I didn't gun the engine so he could make the light. I can see him shouting about my mum like his life depends on it." He laughed again, and I realized how much I liked to hear him enjoying himself.

Ugh. Further proof I was in over my head.

"I've noticed that you like being an observer," I said with a half-smile.

He raised his left eyebrow in my direction. "I've noticed that you like avoiding questions."

"See, now I just want to switch on the radio. I hate it when you're right."

He chuckled good-naturedly. "I'm a very patient man when I choose to be. You can switch on the radio if you'd like."

Not wanting to look a gift-horse in the mouth, I flipped stations until I found something I recognized that didn't antagonize my awkwardness. I placed a mental ban on anything sappy or interlaced with sentiments of love.

Radiohead. Perfectly innocuous.

As *Planet Telex* blared from the speakers, a comfortable silence developed between us. I peered at him from behind my sunglasses and realized we both mouthed the words to the song in perfect synchronization. He glanced in my direction, and when he noted the same thing, we smiled at each other again. I saw his left hand turn over in his lap and his fingers curl slowly into his palm. It was as if he were holding an invisible hand. I begged myself not to look into it at the same time that my stomach warmed over at the thought of him touching me.

49

"This is my favorite Radiohead album," I blurted aloud without thought.

"Mine, too. Your iPod brought back a lot of fond memories of me in high school listening to this band obsessively and wishing I could be Thom Yorke." He ran his fingers absentmindedly through his shaggy mop of hair. Whenever he felt uncomfortable, he spoke incredibly fast. I had a hard time breaking apart the words and turning them into coherent thoughts.

"Well, I think you're probably cuter than Thom Yorke, so I wouldn't lament the fact that your dream didn't come true."

"So, you think I'm cute?" He grinned crookedly again, and his eyes glittered with amusement.

"Passably. Don't get cocky now. I'd still pick Thom Yorke over you any day." I pursed my lips mockingly.

"It's okay if you admit it. I think you're quite pretty."

My face flushed, so I reverted to my trustworthy habit of making a wisecrack to avoid feeling self-conscious. Basically, I uttered the first thing that came to mind when I returned his careful gaze.

"Actually, your nose is a bit crooked." *Damn! I'm such an idiot!*

He barked a short guffaw of surprise. "Your eyes are a little small," he deadpanned subsequently.

"Your eyebrows are way too bushy."

"Your teeth take over your face when you smile," he retorted without missing a beat.

I bared my teeth in a Cheshire cat grin and squinted my eyes simultaneously to enhance their smallness. My nose wrinkled with the effort, making the overall effect propitiously unattractive.

That did it. Both of us hooted with amusement as we continued to mock the "flaws" in each other. I was surprised at how self-aware he appeared to be for a movie star. His unabashed laughter reminded me a bit of a child being tickled—it was incredibly charming.

We were still insulting each other under our breaths as we prepared to walk into the Korean restaurant in Duluth. He temporarily conceded the match when I brought up his hobo-inspired hair again. Before we left the comfort of the car, he pulled the cap he'd held in his hand onto his head and lifted his collar to conceal his face as much as possible.

"Hey, Dick Tracy…are you going to eat in disguise?" I asked.

"I don't know if we made it here without anyone following us. I'll take off the coat once we're inside."

"Are you serious?" I asked in surprise.

"Unfortunately."

I frowned to myself. In the half-hour drive to Koreatown, I had managed to forget that Tom was a well-recognized celebrity. For the first time, it occurred to me that unflattering photographs of me in my Che shirt stuffing my mouth with *bulgogi* barbeque might make it onto the net. Instinctively, I pulled the collar of my coat up around my face and lowered my head into it.

Tom chuckled under his breath when he saw me.

Thankfully, the bored Korean girl at the front of the restaurant didn't look closely at Tom's face as she led us to our table. His posture was tense, and he took a deliberate look around the restaurant before his shoulders relaxed and he removed his coat. I followed suit.

"I guess this is what it would have felt like if I had joined the CIA," I joked nervously.

"You wanted to be in the CIA?"

"I toyed with the idea when I first graduated from college. Thankfully, that whole Valerie Plame thing happened, and I decided against that career. I don't actually want that much attention." I smiled in an attempt to make both of us feel more comfortable.

"If your recent attempt at subterfuge is your best effort, it was a good decision on your part," he jibed with an easy grin.

"I'm sure all of your career dreams when you were younger made total sense."

"Of course. I actually aspired to be a ninja when I was a little boy. I would dress up in black and tie my mother's scarf around my head. Then I'd hide behind doors and scare the piss out of my sister. I even went as far as to create completely useless ninja stars out of kitchen foil," he chuckled at my responding laughter.

We began talking about other careers we had contemplated as our food was brought to the table, and the grill turned on in between us. The smell of garlic, soy sauce, and green onion filled my nose and brought memories of my friends to mind. I tried to teach him how to use chopsticks properly, and soon I had forgotten yet again that we were anything but a guy and a girl out to dinner.

I was regaling him with a story about my friends when I noticed he stared at me with a contemplative look on his face.

"What?" I asked point blank.

"I'm sorry. It's just that … I really like you. You're very easy to like."

*Don't worry. You'll find someone else. You're very easy to like.*

Ryan's words echoed through my mind and caused my entire 51

body to freeze in place as though I had been doused with an unexpected stream of cryogenic fluid.

Tom's face took on a look of extreme confusion as he watched the rapid change in my demeanor.

"What's wrong?" he asked quietly.

"Nothing," I said under my breath.

He exhaled in frustration and leaned his upper body over the table. With his left hand, he gingerly wrapped his fingers around my right wrist and lifted it from its resting place by my plate. The knuckles in my clenched fist were highlighted in white. He stared for a measured moment at the tension in my hand and then looked back at my face with concern.

"Look, this is much more than 'nothing.' All I said was that I liked you. It shouldn't have prompted that kind of response." His voice was kind and completely devoid of accusation.

I just looked at him. Did I owe him an explanation? I didn't think so... but the look on his face was so worried that I knew I had to say something.

He smiled gently. "Now, if I had told you a tarantula was poised on your shoulder sharpening its fangs, your response would have made total sense." I really appreciated his cheesy attempt to lighten the mood.

I curved the right corner of my lips with effort. "You didn't say anything wrong. I'm sorry I overreacted. I was... hurt... recently by someone I cared a lot about. He told me I would get over it and find someone else soon because I'm easy to like. It's just difficult for me to hear it again."

I looked down and away as my gaze focused on his hand wrapped around my wrist. It was the first time he had ever touched me, and a feeling of warmth traveled up the length of my arm and into my stomach. Sensing my line of sight, he released his grasp on my hand and immediately pulled away.

"I'm sorry. I must say that he sounds like a bit of a wanker."

"He probably was... I hope you don't think I'm some kind of freak now." I realized as I was saying the words that Tom's perception of me had begun to matter... a lot.

"No. Not at all. Things are beginning to make more sense, though. I'll keep being patient. Eventually I hope you trust me enough to tell me what happened."

"Thank you." I was genuinely touched by the fact he didn't try to pry more information out of me.

"Always." He grinned lightly.

"Just so you know ... I like you, too." I couldn't hold back the words. They were frighteningly true.

That night in my hotel room at the Ritz, the nightmare returned with an alteration ... proving money doesn't always buy you the right to have beautiful dreams.

The cold finality of Ryan's words pounded into my heart with the force of a Mack truck, the same as always. He turned to exit through the front door, leaving me in frigid darkness to crumble in my requisite heap of agony and loss on the floor. As my pitiful form grasped at the carpet pilings and my cheek began itching from the pressure of being smashed into the rough fibers, I noticed a small glow in the foyer.

It was extremely faint.

I did not have the strength to investigate it further.

# SEVEN

I exhaled another metered breath of anticipation as I circled slowly past the Arrival gates at Charlotte/Douglas International Airport.

I was looking for a man in a grey sweatshirt and dark jeans with polarized sunglasses and a blue baseball cap. He was roughly six feet tall and slender, with unkempt hair.

I perused carefully through the crowded mass of people waiting outside to be picked up. It was incredibly important that we move quickly and not draw any unnecessary attention to ourselves.

Soon, I saw my target breeze through the sliding glass doors towing a small rolling suitcase behind him. He moved fast and hunched his head towards the pavement in an effort to hide as much of his face as possible. The hood of his sweatshirt lay bunched against his neck to assist in this endeavor. He glanced quickly upward through the line of cars, refusing to pause for even a moment. He saw me in my Civic and shifted his trajectory in one smooth movement. Wordlessly, I popped open my trunk, and he tossed his suitcase into it. In less than thirty seconds, he had slid into the passenger seat of my car, and I pulled away from the curb.

As we sped down the exit ramp towards Billy Graham Parkway, I turned to face my silent passenger. He pulled the sunglasses off his face and grinned at me with unabashed glee.

"I think we may actually get away with this!" he murmured in disbelief.

Without warning, he reached over and yanked me into a bear hug.

The car swerved in its lane as I reacted to the electrified shock of his touch and the scent of his skin assailing my senses. His hands burned on my arms, and he smelled like a combination of sandalwood and maple syrup. I had to stop myself from inhaling deeply.

"Would you quit it! I want to make it back alive!" I teased as I elbowed out of his embrace with a playful swipe.

"I'm used to flirting with death when you're driving, remember?" he responded.

"Hah! I'm not the one who got pulled over by the cops at one in the morning last week!"

He groaned. "Don't remind me. It's a good thing I didn't actually drink anything that night."

I laughed. "What a lame reason to be pulled over too! Forgetting to turn on your headlights? Who does that?"

He mock punched my arm. "I already heard an earful of that from you last Friday. It's getting old, Cris."

"Not to me. Plus, you only heard an earful because you woke me up at four in the morning to relate the tale of being forced to take a Breathalyzer test. By the way, if you ever wake me up that late again, I will *end you*."

"I guess a lot of people leaving parties in Hollywood after midnight are usually smashed. I didn't think you would actually wake up and answer the phone. I thought it would be a funny message for you in the morning. Most people don't answer their phone in the middle of the night!" he responded without missing a beat.

I didn't reply as I chewed on my lower lip thoughtfully. The reason I had picked up the phone at four in the morning was simple: I couldn't wait to hear his voice. Ugh.

The hole I started digging for myself one blasted text message at a time grew rapidly in both size and capacity.

"What are you thinking about?" he demanded softly.

I shook my head to prevent a pensive cloud from noticeably settling on my disposition, then aimed a carefully constructed smile filled with carefree radiance at Tom.

He stared back at me with an appraising look on his face. "You're not fooling me," he murmured.

"Damn." I sighed. It was alarming how Tom could read me so well. "I guess I'm just a little nervous," I admitted in a small voice. It was true, even if I didn't actually answer his initial question.

"I am, too. But it gets easier each time I see you."

*Must change the direction of the conversation . . . right now.* "How did everything go on the flight? Did anyone recognize you?"

He frowned knowingly at my pitiful attempt to deflect. After pausing an excruciating moment more, he decided to play along.

"They let me on the plane before anyone else. I buried my face in a magazine while the other people boarded, so I don't think anyone noticed. The flight attendant tried to say something to me once we were airborne, but I pretended to be asleep."

"I knew that whole acting thing would come in handy someday," I teased.

55

He chuckled as he reached over to change the song playing on my iPod. Two emotions dueled inside my head at his subtle display of comfort in my presence. It warmed my spirit at the same time that it absolutely terrified me.

For the last two months, we had been in constant communication. My email inbox was filled with messages from bobdylan85@ yahoo.co.uk, and every other night my phone would ring at odd hours, prompting conversations filled with hushed laughter and insightful discussion on things as mundane as what we had for dinner, and issues pertaining to the economic crisis. Tom had quickly become a very close...*friend*. There was no other word for it. The tenor of our communications never blatantly crossed the line, nor did it ever clearly indicate that the relationship was moving in a romantic direction. Unfortunately, I was both troubled and comforted by these seemingly incontrovertible facts.

I wanted to kick my own ass.

The fear and hurt that had spent nearly a year lying hidden in the deepest reaches of my psyche caused me a great deal of mental anguish as they reared their ugly heads in the forefront of my mind with growing frequency. The residual pain I felt whenever my long-dead heart stirred at the thought of Tom stopped me from consciously cultivating anything meaningful when it came to him. And yet...he was so kind. So smart. So patient. So funny. So incredibly... down-to-earth. It was harder and harder for my fickle heart to listen to the constant warnings of my mind.

"You're doing it again, Cristina," Tom muttered next to me. I glanced over at him. He carefully studied my visage with narrowed eyes and a set jaw. He tried hard to stop his mouth from uttering the words he instinctively wanted to say as he shifted his pressed lips slowly from side to side. The stern expression on his face made the definition of his features even more pronounced...it actually looked ...incredibly sexy. ¡*Coño!*

"Doing what?" I said breathlessly.

"Driving me insane."

"Huh?" The tempo of my heart increased.

"You're thinking a lot of things and trying to hide it. I wish you wouldn't," he stated simply.

I opened my mouth to respond with a lighthearted quip, but he stopped me before I could say anything.

"Please, don't make a joke. You belittle your feelings and insult my intelligence at the same time." His voice was soft, direct. Shaming.

My cheeks flushed. I clamped my teeth together in anger and embarrassment.

He sighed and took off his hat to run his fingers rapidly through the shaggy mop of hair on his head. "I'm sorry. That was stupid. I've really been looking forward to seeing you... I shouldn't give you a hard time," he said apologetically.

"It's okay," I whispered.

"It's not, but I hope we'll deal with it properly one day."

I stared straight ahead and let the music fill the void of silence in the car for a while. I hated that he understood me so well as to see through the shell I showcased to the world. I wasn't going to get away with merely being witty and lighthearted in his presence much longer.

"You're really brave to come and meet my friends," I stated good-naturedly with a kind grin of forgiveness in his direction.

He returned the smile. "I feel like I know them well already because you won't shut up about them." His eyes flashed with thankful mirth.

"I can't help it. I wouldn't worry too much though. Hana is going to love you. Gita... might take a little while, but she'll come around."

He chuckled. "Well, so much for not worrying... It's a pretty city, by the way." He gazed at the skyline in the distance to our left. The lights of uptown Charlotte twinkled with flashing effervescence. It *was* a pretty city... even if it couldn't compare to a New York or a Los Angeles, Charlotte had a charm and grace that was all its own.

"I love it here. You can experience city life when you want to, but Charlotte hasn't lost its grasp on its roots... sometimes in a bad way, but more often in a good way," I remarked honestly.

"What do you mean?"

"I mean, we *are* in the south. People are generally warm and hospitable, but it's not nearly as progressive as... London, for instance," I responded.

"London is not as warm and hospitable as it could be, so I suppose there are pluses and minuses to each." Tom had a way of being obscenely diplomatic and fair-minded. I often teased that he should have gone into politics rather than the movie industry. He usually remarked that the two weren't very different anyway. Of course, on top of everything else, he also had to have a quick sense of humor.

I pulled into the spot in front of Naz and Hana's home while Tom hid behind the hat and sunglasses once more. I saw Hana peeking through the blinds in the front and stifled a giggle. She had probably waited there, wearing a perfectly pressed apron for the last twenty

57

minutes. I made sure no one else was around us before we moved silently from the car to the front door, unseen. It opened soundlessly before us, and my nostrils were inundated by the delicious scents of the Middle East: cumin, cinnamon, coriandor, nutmeg, turmeric. I breathed in deeply. In a past life, I think I must have been from this part of the world. The food and the music always called to me with an inexplicable familiarity.

"Well, it's about time!" The lyrical voice of my best friend echoed peevishly around us.

As I foretold, Hana Fateri stood in front of me wearing designer jeans and a turquoise *kurta* blouse from India covered with a carefully pressed apron bearing the words "Chef de Cuisine." Her waist-length hair was knotted in a loose bun at the nape of her neck. She stuck her hand out towards Tom before I even had a chance to say anything.

"I'm Hana. It's really nice to meet you, Tom," she chirped. The look on her face was preciously mock-worthy. She was trying so hard to remain calm and treat Tom as though he were merely an average human being instead of a famous celebrity whose face emblazoned the magazines and blogs she loved so much.

In stark contrast, Gita Talukdar was still seated in her chair with her arms crossed over her chest, staring warily at Tom the Movie Star. In one fluid motion, she rose to walk towards us with the graceful lope of a stalking panther. She waited patiently to be introduced. From the corner of my eye, I saw Tom smile quickly when he realized how enlightening a testament the differences in a mere introduction were to their personalities.

He put out his right hand and smiled awkwardly at Gita. "I'm Tom. You must be Gita."

Wordlessly, she held out her hand and shook his firmly with a nod of assertion. She ran her gaze over his tall frame with a shameless look of open judgment.

"Jesus, Gita! Can you be any more obvious?" Hana cried as she smacked Gita's arm.

"Shut it, Fateri. I can't help who I am," she muttered as the color rose in her neck.

"I like it. No bullshit. It really doesn't bother me," Tom responded genially. He began pulling off his shoes as I had directed him to do earlier. No shoes were permitted in Hana's house past the front door. Halfway through awkwardly removing his left sneaker, he teetered perilously to one side and would have crashed to the floor if I hadn't grabbed his arm just in time. So much for not being bothered.

The chuckle of a male voice echoed from the staircase landing off to the side. Naz strolled down the stairs with a huge grin on his face. I wasn't the least bit worried about Tom and Naz getting along. Everyone loved Nazir. I couldn't articulate exactly why that was the case without oversimplifying his personality—you just had to meet him to understand.

"Really, you could have kept on your shoes. You just need to wash the floors before you leave," Naz jested warmly as he approached Tom with his hand extended in welcome.

Tom smiled gratefully at Naz. See what I mean? "You must be Nazir. Thanks so much for letting me stay here this weekend."

"Call me Naz. Yes, like the rapper. Don't even bother making up a joke…I've heard them all, man. Can I get you something to drink?" Naz successfully pulled Tom into the kitchen and away from the studious gaze of feminine eyes.

"Damn, he's cute!" Hana whispered loudly as they disappeared from view.

"He's a little skinny, Cris. Does he eat?" Gita murmured disapprovingly.

I ignored both their comments and linked my elbows through their arms as we made our way to where Tom and Naz leaned against the cabinets, drinking beers and chatting.

"Something smells amazing," Tom said in an appreciative tone.

"Do you like Moroccan food? I've made a tagine," Hana beamed with pride at him.

"If it tastes like it smells, I'm sure I'll love it."

"Hana's a fabulous cook. If I lived here, I'd weigh two hundred pounds," Gita stated in an imperious manner that dared anyone to challenge her assertion.

"I would too, but she beats the weight off me," Naz deadpanned. Hana threw the kitchen towel at him while we chuckled in response.

Soon we had taken a seat around the table where plates of couscous and an exotic concoction of chicken, chickpeas, tomatoes, pine nuts, and eggplant steamed in each of our faces. As the food disappeared and the wine Tom brought as a gift began to flow more freely, the sounds of jibing and laughter echoed around me in a manner that lent itself to a deep sense of peace. All was right in the world as long as I could be with the people I loved. Tom immediately fell into sync with Naz's sense of humor and showered so much praise on Hana's culinary prowess that she flushed with pleasure. Even Gita's initial 59 frostiness began to thaw at the sound of his boyish laughter. I was so proud of how elegant and worldly my friends were.

After the food faded into memory, Naz walked over to the stereo to switch on some music while we all cleared the table. The evening had progressed flawlessly.

*"Ass and titties, ass and titties, ass and titties … and big booty bitches!"* were the booming words that screamed their way out of the Bose speakers before a mortified Naz Fateri managed to silence their insolence.

The total stillness of shock permeated the room.

Naz stared in complete chagrin at Tom for a split second … until Tom began shouting with unbridled laughter. I guffawed along with him and turned to see Hana's hands clapped over her mouth and her wide eyes shining with an unmistakable glint of humor. Soon, Gita was clutching her stomach in pain while her shoulders shook with the silent strain.

"Honey?" Naz began as he looked at Hana with utter embarrassment. It just elicited another bout of laughter from Tom.

Hana set her face unrepentantly. "I'm not going to apologize or offer explanations for my taste in music … however, I'm sorry if the language offended Tom. Oh well, I guess I'm officially the crazy friend!" She sniffed.

"You're not sorry, at all!" Gita cackled.

"I actually think it's pretty fucking hilarious, and I'm the furthest thing from offended. It completely fits the picture I had of you," Tom said once the latest fit of mirth had died down.

"Meaning?" Hana asked with curiosity.

"I knew you had to be incredibly interesting because Cris never runs out of things to tell me about her friends. Sometimes, the 'crazy friend' is the best of the bunch. This just proves there are many layers to you, and I think I'm going to have a great time getting to know them all."

That did it. Gita Talukdar smiled in earnest for the first time at Tom the Movie Star.

My heart. My beaten heart shuddered under the strain of feeling alive again.

"Do you want to go with me to rent a movie?" I asked Tom around eleven that night.

"Sure!"

60    I was a little dismayed by how quickly he leapt to his feet.

"Cris, why do you need to go rent a movie? There are tons here!" Gita asked automatically.

Hana shot her a dark look. "Get something funny!" she said with a smile at us.

"No problem."

We walked outside to my car. The crisp April night was filled with the intoxicating smell of earth and rain blended circumspectly to fashion one of nature's most perfect perfumes. I breathed in deeply. The sound of grasshoppers and cicadas created a symphony in the flowering azalea branches and completed the sensory experience of a typical spring evening in North Carolina.

"It's beautiful here," Tom stated as we pulled onto the street. I lowered the windows to allow the sounds and smells to enter the car.

"I think so, too."

"Your friends are really great people," he remarked in a suspiciously husky voice.

"I can tell that they like you a lot. Thanks so much for being so.. wonderful," I said quietly.

He stared at me for a moment with a gaze that made my pulse race. I looked straight ahead and focused on the road in front of us as a pitiful excuse for my avoidance. The moments ticked by at a languorous pace. I pressed on the accelerator, mentally cursing myself for being such a chickenshit.

He exhaled slowly with the beginning signs of frustration. Thankfully, our destination loomed in the distance, providing temporary refuge for my cowardly self. I pulled into the parking lot of Blockbuster and slid from my Civic in an obvious hurry.

He followed me and lowered his hat onto his forehead while he looked around us with the careful study that had become a necessary habit. No one else appeared to be inside Blockbuster, and the teenage boys manning the desk in the front were completely disinterested in us.

We strolled around the New Releases section without any real purpose. I paused when I saw one of his movies lining the shelves before us. He played a minor role in the film since it was made before his catapulting claim to fame as a sexy specter lusting after a teenage girl.

"You know," I whispered, "I've never actually seen your work."

He groaned under his breath when he saw the film I was eyeing with a wicked gleam of expectation.

"And you won't…at least, not tonight."

"Aw, come on. It could be fun!" I teased.

He opened his mouth to protest—

"OH…MY…GOD!" A shrill voice rang out from behind us.

"Bloody hell," Tom muttered in a barely audible register.

The girl appeared to be about eighteen years old. She smacked on her gum furiously, and her eyes were about to pop out of her head with shock.

"You're— You're—" she stammered as she pointed a trembling finger at Tom.

He turned to her quickly and plastered an idiotically fake smile on his face. "Not again! I get mistaken for him all the time!" he replied with a thick southern twang that made my jaw drop. "Again" sounded like "uh-geen" and "get" sounded like "git." There are no words to properly describe the experience of hearing a British man speak like a redneck.

"No—no…you're…there's no way. You look…" she continued.

"Just like him? I've heard that everywhere. I should probably go along with it to pick up the chicks. Really though, why in…tarnation…would he be at a Blockbuster in North Carolina on a Saturday night?"

I could barely contain my laughter as I bit my lower lip in an attempt to remain silent.

"Uh, I guess you're right." She still didn't believe him completely.

"I bet my britches he's in Hollywood at a party right now walkin' some red carpet." Tom winked at her like a fool, and she smiled weakly back at him.

"Uh, yeah. Sorry to bother you…uh, man you look like him, though!"

"No trouble at all, darlin'. You take care!" he said quickly.

As soon as she disappeared from sight, I grabbed his arm and yanked him out of Blockbuster and back to the car.

I barely had time to shut the door before I started shaking with silent laughter.

"Tarnation? *Seriously?* Britches?" I gasped as hilarity-induced tears welled in my eyes.

"I thought I did a pretty good job," he responded petulantly.

"If you were in the Appalachian mountains circa 1950, maybe!" I choked out as another fit of giggles washed over me.

"I'll admit I was inspired by reruns of the Andy Griffith Show. Well, you did say you wanted to see my work," he smiled crookedly as he watched me try to regain control of myself.

"Tarnation!" I barked again. The tears spilled over and down my cheeks. I leaned towards the glove compartment to find a tissue as I continued half-sighing through small aftershocks of glee in the traditional dénouement that followed a damn good laugh.

He caught my wrist as I reached over his lap. My laughter stopped immediately. His grey eyes held a look of focused, warm intensity that caused me to feel my heartbeat pound in the tips of my fingers as though I had placed them too near a raging fire moments before. He raised his right hand and slowly wiped the tears on my cheek with his thumb. I sensed every motion of his body in the stillness of the car. Every action had an equal and opposite reaction. He placed his palm on the side of my neck when he was finished drying my tears. I could feel his fingers curl in my hair as he leaned towards me. His intention was clear and his lips parted ever so slightly as they drew nearer. Using the tip of his nose to brush against mine, he tilted my head upwards for a kiss. A highly charged current of energy ran through me. The smell of his skin so close to my face....

"No!" I gasped involuntarily as fear gripped perilously tight onto my soul. The pounding in my chest and the roaring in my ears drowned out everything else.

Tom released me and pushed his head into the headrest. He glared at the roof of my car for a moment, struggling with what could only be irritation and disappointment.

"I'm sorry," I whispered.

He turned to me abruptly. "I know. Unfortunately, that's not good enough. Not tonight."

I pled silently with him. In the rearview mirror, I saw my eyes were filled with dismay. "Please. I ... don't know ... I'm—" I tried.

In one quick motion, he grabbed my face between both of his hands.

"No. I can't continue to guess what's hurt you this badly. I care too much for that. Even as nothing more than a friend, I'm missing something very important about you."

He was right.

"Why do you want to hide it from me?" he whispered.

"I don't," I murmured back without thought.

He let go of me, leaned back against the window, and waited for me to talk with a soft expression that nevertheless demanded answers.

"I want to tell you. I think ... I'm just afraid of seeing you when you're armed with the truth," I said quietly.

"Why?"

"I . . . hate it when people feel sorry for me . . . or do things just because they think I'm . . . pitiful . . . or something." I struggled to find the right words.

"I could never think you're pitiful, Cris. Being hurt doesn't automatically make you pitiful. Letting the hurt consume you does."

I nodded slowly and took a deep breath. "I've only been in love once in my life so far. He's also the only man I ever seriously dated. I met him in college through mutual friends. Ryan was . . . is . . . a very intelligent man with a voracious thirst for knowledge. His intellect drew me to him, and we were friends for a few years before we started dating. I thought everything about us was perfect. His dark sarcasm and emotional depth reminded me a lot of my father. After a few years, I never really considered a world where we weren't together. Last year he proposed to me, and I thought my life was made. No matter what happened to me, I had Ryan by my side to share the good and the bad. He bought a house for us. Everything was perfect. . . ."

Tom leaned towards me instinctively when I shuddered at the thought of what came next.

"He began growing distant. It was almost like he only brought half of himself home to me. I tried to ignore it—pretend nothing was wrong in my perfect world. One night, he . . . told me we were through. He told me to leave. He didn't want me anymore," I whispered so that the trembling in my voice wouldn't be too apparent. I cleared my throat and began again with renewed conviction. "He had found someone else. I guess . . . she was better than me in some way. He never really told me why.

"I was kind of in a haze after that. Nothing could provoke deep reactions in me. I already told you about my father; the cancer hit about two months after Ryan broke up with me. My father was gone a month after being diagnosed. It was a lot to deal with, but I think life isn't about living with ease . . . it's about finding the easiest way to keep living when you're dealt a shitty hand. I was just given two really heinous hands back-to-back."

Through the last bit of my sob story, I chose to focus my gaze on the gearshift. For some reason I couldn't look at Tom. It wasn't shame or embarrassment . . . it was something more.

"Cristina," he murmured in a soothing voice.

I exhaled slowly and raised my eyes to his face. I expected to hear the same reactionary stammering I received from dozens of people following the drawn-out explanation of why I was single and suddenly down one parent. "I'm so sorry!" or "You poor thing! You didn't deserve that!" or "Don't worry, everything will be okay!"

FYI: everything was not "okay," you effing moron.

Tom said nothing. He carefully brushed away the wispy tendrils of hair that had fallen into my face. His eyes were so filled with caring that I looked down before my emotions were pushed over the edge. His warm lips pressed carefully onto my forehead for an instant. Poignant. Electrifying.

"Look at me," he said softly. I shifted my sight upwards.

"I won't tell you that everything will be okay. It's not my responsibility to do that. There is something I *will* tell you though . . . I've never met anyone better than you."

He pulled me into his chest and placed his chin on top of my head as he wrapped his arms around me. I rested my face against his cotton shirt and breathed in the scent of him. My heartbeat slowed with comfort.

At that moment, I couldn't have asked for more.

# EIGHT

"Next!"

I dragged my rolling suitcase towards the ticket counter at RDU and momentarily placed my paperwork in my mouth while I rummaged through my purse for my driver's license.

"Name?" the bored Delta employee intoned.

"Cristina Pereira. My confirmation number is MCZ209," I replied after glancing at my paperwork and handing her my identification.

"Round trip to LAX?" she chimed.

I nodded.

Her fingernails tapped rapidly against the computer keys from behind the desk as she glanced at the screen with an expression akin to mild hypnosis. I heard the printer fire up and spit out the boarding pass below the computer. Damn. I wanted to ask for a seat in the exit row. Five hours trapped in the Economy Class "sardine can" would be a bit more bearable with the additional legroom.

"Um, are there any seats left in the exit row?" I asked with a bright smile, hoping my cheerful attitude would spur her to help me out.

She looked at me with a puzzled expression.

"Uh, I don't mind the responsibility. A bulkhead seat would be great, too," I stated in mild confusion. Why was she staring at me with such a weird look? I couldn't be the first person in the world to ask her for a seat with more space!

She glanced surreptitiously at my petite form from narrowed eyes. Jesus! Is it so wrong for short people to want more legroom?

"The bulkhead seats are already taken, and there isn't exit row seating in First Class," she replied humorlessly.

My eyebrows shot up in surprise. First Class? I groaned inwardly. Even though it would be amazing to steal someone else's expensive seat for the trip, it would probably be better for me to avoid tickling my karma so early in this venture.

"Not that I'm complaining or anything, but you must have made a mistake. I purchased an Economy Class ticket last month," I stated with a wry smile.

She sighed with the weight of the world on her shoulders as the patter of her nails against the keyboard resumed.

"No, ma'am. There's no mistake. Your ticket was upgraded to First Class just this morning."

It took me exactly two seconds. Tom! I pursed my lips together in irritation. After I explicitly told him not to do this!

"I suppose it would be idiotic for me to ask you to change it back," I mused sardonically.

She nodded at me with a look that clearly said "Yes, you moron."

I stuck out my hand for the boarding pass with a huff. As soon as I cleared security, it was on like Donkey Kong. After I passed through the metal detectors and underwent minor infringement on my sexual dignity, I marched purposefully towards the gate and sat down in a flurry of papers and bags.

I proceeded to dial the number stored under the solitary moniker of "Z." It rang several times and cycled predictably to voicemail. That sneaky Brit was avoiding my call!

"Yeah. You're not getting away with this. I'm actually coming to visit so I can secretly steal your toothbrush and dirty laundry. I will then sell them on eBay for an obscene amount of money so that I can buy *you* a First Class ticket to Antarctica. I don't think the penguins have heard of you yet."

I clicked the phone shut. Oh well. I'd never flown First Class before. Since cocktails were free on the other side of the curtain, maybe I should drink a lot and show up in L.A. completely wasted! I laughed to myself at the passing thought. With my kind of luck....

For the first time in my life, the glowing letters on my boarding pass permitted me to get on the plane with the "Elite-Medallion-Platinum-I'm-Better-Than-You-Are Club." I proceeded to settle into my absurdly large, leather-clad lounge chair and take in my surroundings like a monkey given toys to play with for the purpose of scientific observation. Oh, miracle of miracles! I had my own TV with a touchscreen!

My phone vibrated in my pocket with a new text message.

**Blocked ID (5:06 pm): fyi there is actually a penguin fanclub**

I grinned idiotically before typing out a response.

Me (5:06 pm): In that case, hope your ass can swim.
Blocked ID (5:06 pm): lol. i'll be waiting out front at 7:30
Me (5:07 pm): No! Srsly! I can take a cab!
Blocked ID (5:07 pm): srry, that txt didn't come thru right. looked like a load of bs
Me (5:07 pm): Tom! Don't risk it!
Blocked ID (5:07 pm): get ur phone fixed, look for a white merc with a bad tint job
Me (5:07 pm): Ur ridiculous! It's completely unnecessary!
Me (5:08 pm): Hello?
Me (5:10 pm): THOMAS?

I held the phone in my hand and waited for a response until the flight attendant glanced at me pointedly. Ugh. I don't know why Tom insisted on making his life harder by personally coming to pick me up! Initially he had managed to hide this obsessively stubborn streak from me by utilizing the disarming wiles of his cute accent and charming wit. In all truth, Tom was incredibly obdurate once he made up his mind about something. This dogged determination to behave as normally as possible when I came to visit was both heartening and problematic.

When he first asked me to come to L.A., I had struggled a great deal with the decision to sequester myself in his apartment for an entire weekend, even if he did have two bedrooms. The Blockbuster Debacle from the last visit in Charlotte had proven that this relationship was not simply on a course destined for mere friendship. It seemed ridiculous that nearly five months had elapsed since that fateful encounter in a Raleigh mall, and I still remained unsure of how to handle the burgeoning rush of emotions that continued to wash over me with increasing frequency each time I received an email, text message, or phone call from Tom.

I liked him—way too much, way too soon.

I sat back in my chair as the plane took off into the skies and decided that I had five uninterrupted hours to do an extended reality check. It had been a while since I had to do one of those.

In spite of the fact that Tom appeared to be one of the nicest guys I had ever met, I was still not entirely sure how much of the bravado was for real and how much of it was merely his "representative" on its best behavior. Sometimes he seemed a little too good to be true...and thinking this way made me invariably want to flog myself. Women complain when men are too bad, and then we proceed to do the same thing on the flip side. It's like our gender conspires to force its collective entirety into being twisted versions of Goldilocks (I abhorred that fairy tale). We want one that's *juuuust* right. Utterly ridiculous.

I hated the next thoughts that ran through my mind, but knew they needed to be dealt with instead of conveniently stored on the upper shelves in my brain's closet, which now had more crud crammed into it than I cared to fathom. I really wasn't sure I wanted to date someone famous. I felt like a girl with a lower than average IQ aspiring to make merry with the likes of Albert Einstein. The unflattering comparisons in my mind were endless...and humorously cruel. I heard once that you never see a really good-looking guy with a homely girl, but it didn't seem terribly unusual to witness a beautiful woman with an aesthetically forgettable man.

I might get thrashed for saying this, but I think that many women are so focused on their sense of self-image that they can't stomach being the question mark in a couple; they prefer to be the exclamation point. Now, don't get me wrong, I know I'm not hideously unattractive, but a large part of the way we, as a culture, define what is visually desirable is centered on the packaging in its *complete* form. Thus, it is not good enough to have a beautiful face, one must also have an absurdly tight body poured into the right clothes, accented by the right haircut, the right car, the right makeup, the right shoes, ad nauseum. Exhausting.

And...drumroll please...on to the Extended Reality Check! Cue cheesy gameshow music.

Fact: Tom is a movie star.

Fact: You're a social worker.

Fact: Tom is very wealthy.

Fact: You're a social worker.

Fact: His career takes him to exotic places where he meets people of influence.

Fact: You're a social worker.

Fact: He wears Prada sunglasses (I saw the label myself).

Fact: The Chinese man in SoHo knows your sunglasses are by

Fooey Vuitton.

I stopped to chuckle at the rapid degeneration of my thoughts and vowed to begin again with renewed focus and direction. Deep breath.

Fact: He lives in Los Angeles, California and London, the United Kingdom.

Fact: You live in Raleigh, North Carolina.

Fact: His career is unpredictable and takes him all over the place.

Fact: You can't be a social worker "all over the place."

Fact: You have to get on a plane just to see each other.

Fact: He's surrounded by beautiful, accomplished women everywhere he goes.

Fact: You were hit on twice yesterday by the security guard named Cletise.

Fact: Keeping your sanity and self-esteem intact will take gargantuan effort.

Fact: It's impossible to have a normal relationship with this man.

I sighed painfully at the last fact. Given all of these rather cringe-worthy issues, it probably made no sense for me to be flying five hours on a plane to spend time with him. *Really stupid move, Cristina.* I definitely should have insisted on getting a hotel room instead of letting him guilt me into staying at his place since he stayed at Hana and Naz's in Charlotte. It was definitely true that getting around unseen would be easier if we could stay within his comfort zone rather than try to coordinate field ops from unfamiliar territory. Divide and conquer doesn't really work when one of you is a beacon of light in a sea of darkness…or maybe more like a marked man with an unwavering red laser pointed his head at all times. This was moot anyway. I had already agreed to be a guest in his "flat."

And there we have it: as should be expected, I was now forced to deal with my biggest hang up. My biggest hang up? All sarcasm pushed temporarily aside…it had to be…sex.

Being a real estate broker caused Hana to look at a great deal of things from that rather unique vantage point. She always joked that having sex with someone was like painting bricks on a house. Once you go there, you can't go back…the color of the paint forever marred the surface of the bricks in a way that was impossible to eradicate. The paint seeped indelibly into every nook and cranny. No amount of thinner or scrubbing would make a marked difference. The only way to remedy a bad choice in "paint" was to paint over it with another color.

I had one layer of paint on my bricks already. Only one. It had basically stained them irreparably. Even steadily chipping away at the surface with the wide assortment of tools available to my overly analytical mind hadn't made a dent in the project. I wasn't sure I was ready to slap on a different color in a sad attempt to hide the trauma of the first. Staying at a man's "flat" for an entire weekend, and childishly assuming sex wouldn't be an issue, was completely laughable.

About three months after Ryan tossed my love out the window and drove away like a bat out of hell, my colleague Jennifer had set me up on a date with her cousin Jake. She had assured me he was a wonderful guy with a good job and a great sense of humor. Pushing aside my reflexive desire to gnash my teeth at becoming one of those girls who appeared to need a matchmaker, I agreed half-heartedly to go to lunch with him. I was now a character in *Fiddler on the Roof.*

He was everything Jennifer promised. Cute and charming... and a lawyer, to boot! We shared a plate of nachos and chatted seamlessly for an hour. He asked me to dinner the following weekend and I didn't hesitate to accept. Maybe it wouldn't be so bad after all! Even after four years out of commission, I still knew how to wade into the waters of dating.

Little did I know how shark-infested those waters had become.

After dinner, he asked me to come back to his place and watch a movie. I remembered being in college and going to see movies in the room of my freshman crush. It was so innocent! Popcorn, some harmless teasing, and perhaps some sexually repressed tickling and pinching here and there. Completely passive-aggressive... and controllable. Thoughtlessly, I acquiesced to Jake's request. I still felt as though I had the upper hand.

We didn't even get to the movie. Jake poured me a glass of wine as I walked over to his extensive DVD collection to select the closest thing to a romantic comedy that I could find. Before I knew it, he had wrapped his arms around my waist and begun groping me while nuzzling my neck! I whipped around awkwardly and pushed him away. The look of confusion on his face shocked me. He honestly thought he had done nothing wrong!

When I demanded an explanation, he furrowed his brow at me and said, "Look Cris, I know you haven't dated in a while, but I like you... and I'm pretty sure you like me. What's the problem?"

In my four short years in Coupleville, men had apparently decided that the only prerequisite for getting laid was the mutual understanding that you "liked one another." I liked plenty of people;

hopping into the sack with every one of them was not the logical next step. I had wordlessly collected my things and left.

The following day at work, Jennifer wouldn't talk to me. When I finally couldn't stand it anymore, I asked quietly why she was shooting daggers at me from her cubicle. She pressed her lips together and perused me with an expression that suggested my presence forced her to suck on figurative lemons before replying.

"Jake told me that he had a great time with you, and you agreed to go back to his place. He said you freaked out when he tried to kiss you. What's the deal with you anyway? Why did you even say you would go back to his place if you were going to go all prude on him? It's not nice to lead a guy on."

I hadn't even bothered to respond. Apparently, my behavior was distasteful to women as well. How shitty was my life at that moment? Pretty shitty.

So, if Jake the Rake thought the mere existence of likeability led to an inevitable dance of the horizontal mambo, I had no idea what Tom thought about me staying in his apartment for the entire weekend.

The scariest thought of all when it came to my "biggest hang up" was that he would write me off as soon as he discovered what an apparent prude I was. It had stung a bit that Jake lost interest in me after he learned that I wasn't going to have sex with him anytime soon—if ever. It would be devastating to realize that this was the case with Tom as well. It briefly made me wonder how many lonely girls had smiled through their teeth at men like Jake and let them get what they wanted to ensure a phone call the next day from the hormonal predators. Men are essentially wanton degenerates.

Part of me desperately wished I lived in a different time and place where issues like having sex on the second date were not even a consideration. Like, for instance, Jane Austen's era. Polite letters and stimulating dialogue laced with mildly suggestive innuendo would be all that were expected of me. Fans of Austen were always obsessed with Fitzwilliam Darcy and his angst-ridden love for Elizabeth Bennet. I honestly had a stronger passion for George Knightley, erstwhile critic of Emma Woodhouse. I loved how he constantly confronted her and forced her to see beyond the limitations of her own ego and circumstance. I'd take a Knightley over a Darcy any day. I didn't want to be rescued…I wanted to be challenged.

Of course, I doubted a woman in the world of Jane Austen had ever been inundated by the scent of sandalwood and soap emanating from the skin of an incredibly sexy man...or felt the stubble on his chin brush against her forehead as he held her rather shockingly tight in his arms. Yeah, Austen might have reworked some of her tales, at least in her head, if she could have witnessed the glorious evolution of men in Britain as they moved ever closer to their zenith. Tom was getting pretty damn close, if you asked me.

I sighed as the simple truth washed over me. All I could be was myself, for better or worse. If he didn't like me for my prudish self, then good riddance. I would deal with the pain later. Alone.

Not wanting to dwell inordinately on those bitter thoughts, I decided to switch on my nifty personal television and find something to watch. Since fate often manages to take hold of situations like these, I found my finger poised ironically over the movie that had recently launched Tom's stardom. Tom as a brooding ghost in love. Wasn't that movie already made back in the 80s? With a sly grin, I decided I should probably check it out.

Tom on the silver screen was utterly charming...and even more unattainable. He acted with the ease of a man completely devoid of pretense. The fact that he portrayed a spirit experiencing the pangs of unrequited love only served to mock me further. Ugh.

Right before I arrived at LAX, I drank a really strong cup of espresso. The plane was landing a little bit before 7:30 at night in Los Angeles, but it was 10:30 back home. I didn't want to fall apart in a few hours and snore unflatteringly on the sofa. Popping a piece of gum in my mouth to hide the traveler's breath and espresso remnants, I collected my things to deplane.

Before leaving, Hana had insisted that I arrive at LAX in the true fashion of a celebrity. She wanted me to wear her insanely large sunglasses and loop scarves around my neck to shield myself from the unbearably cold weather that California was famous for having. I chuckled as I remembered her tongue-in-cheek description of the ideal ensemble and took a final look at my dark leggings and thigh-grazing tunic to make sure everything was where it should be. Not glamorous, just comfortable. Tom already knew that my love of fashion was relegated to the racks of Target and T.J. Maxx. If I had the money to afford better clothes, I would probably buy them; I just didn't have the money. So I made do with what I could afford and spruced it up with jewelry and a sunny smile. Hah.

The sun was just beginning to set as I walked through the glass doors leading into the warm night air. I took a deep breath and scanned the line of cars and taxis waiting with blinking lights and craning necks. White Merc with a bad tint job, and then I saw it. Hidden near a bend in the queue, an old, beat-up white Mercedes with windows so dark they appeared to be completely black sat noticeably silent and still in the mix of cars and people. It was trying painfully hard to remain unnoticed. I grinned to myself as I walked carefully towards the automobile. It had to be him or else I was about to scare the hell out of some random person taking a nap.

I tapped my knuckle against the windshield. The passenger door swung open with a grating sound that made me wish I had a spray can of WD-40 in my pocket. I tossed my suitcase and carry-on bag into the backseat, slid quickly into the car, and pulled the door closed behind me.

As I turned to smile broadly at Tom and say something sarcastic about his ride, the words died on my tongue when he leaned in swiftly towards me and pressed his warm lips right below the base of my left ear in a heart-stoppingly seductive move.

Speechless, I merely stared at him with wide eyes and my mouth slightly ajar.

He chuckled warmly as he sat back up and pushed the key into the ignition. "Welcome to L.A., beautiful."

# NINE

I see now why you were so appalled by my driving. It's incredibly frightening when you're *actually getting somewhere*," I teased.

"Sod off!" He grinned.

"Yeah, I'm not sure what that means. I'll assume it means you agree with me. Seriously… how old is this piece?"

"I bought it for three thousand bucks two years ago. I think it's from the early nineties. I hate cars. Well, I like looking at them. I hate driving them," he replied with a bemused expression on his face.

"Three thousand bucks? Dude, you were had!"

"It's diesel. I actually felt pretty damn smug when no one could find gas in L.A. for less than twenty bucks a gallon," he said.

He continued moving slower than molasses in January down the expressway. Cars zoomed all around us and hands flew out their windows, gesticulating inappropriately in our direction. If they only knew who was driving this P.O.S. My thoughts made me snicker quietly in my seat.

"Look, if I push the car and it falls apart, I have no idea how to fix it," he admitted with a sheepish glance towards me.

"That would really be a travesty, wouldn't it? Then you might actually have to buy a car that works!" I let out a silvery peal of laughter before continuing. "I do need the story on the ghetto-fabulous tint job. It really takes the fugification of this car to a whole new level!"

He chuckled at me merrily. "When I first came to L.A., no one recognized me, and it was completely fine driving around to the store or to get some coffee. About six months ago, things started to get a little dodgy. I was at a stoplight and this car full of girls noticed me. They started screaming and honking and tried to get me to pull over. I nearly had a bloody accident trying to get away. The next day I drove the car to the nearest garage and asked them to put the darkest tint they could on the windows. I think it might actually be illegal to have tint this dark."

I smiled with irony as I considered his words. "You know, most guys would be flattered to get noticed like that by a bunch of girls. Instead, you freak out and try to hide behind tinted glass that would be the envy of a foreign dignitary."

"Most guys. I was never that suave with the ladies."

I laughed at his wide eyes and utter seriousness. "I doubt you have much trouble with the girls now."

He pursed his lips together morosely and glanced at me with eyebrows raised to contradict my statement. "I still have trouble. One girl in particular...."

I crinkled my nose at him and said nothing.

About forty-five minutes later, we pulled up to a large white building espousing modern architecture. Directly ahead of us were two iron doors that slid aside with a groan after Tom typed in a security code. We proceeded to enter a well-lit, subterranean garage and parked in a numbered spot sandwiched between a Maserati and a mean-looking BMW with blinding rims. The butterflies that had shaken from their cocoon after he kissed me in the car began to flutter frenetically in my stomach when he paused in front of the entrance to his apartment.

What was I thinking!?

He held open the door for me and grinned as I walked warily past him. The first thing I noticed was the way the sound of my shoes echoed loudly with each hesitant step I took into the darkness. Nothing cushioned the noise of the reverberations. I heard him shuffling behind me as he rolled my suitcase into the apartment and fumbled to turn on the light switch.

I gasped involuntarily at the sight before me. I heard him laugh to himself as he moved to stand nearby.

"You...have no furniture!" I whispered in shock.

"That's not fair. I did buy a proper bed for the guest room since you were coming. It worked out well because I was forced to move the manky futon into my room. I still can't bear to throw it away even though it's utterly disgusting."

"But...you don't even have a real sofa! It's just a bunch of cushions thrown on the floor!" I murmured.

"I told you before that I'm really minimalist. If I don't need it, I don't buy it."

I frowned a bit.

"You look troubled. Why?" he asked with curiosity.

I thought for a moment before responding. "It's not that I'm incapable of appreciating your perspective. I think it's great that you're so economical. I guess I'm troubled because...I want you to feel comfortable at home. Honestly, this isn't really a home. It's cold and empty. No wonder why you feel lonely here!"

He just stared at me with an unreadable expression on his face.

Crap, I must have pissed him off. "I wasn't trying to insult your place, Tom. I just—"

"You didn't insult me. I didn't think you'd have such a strong reaction to my lack of stuff. I'm surprised that it would bother you so much."

"I guess it's because I always feel like home needs to be a sanctuary," I said quickly as I tried to cover up the dismay that had settled onto my face at the sight of his empty "home." It was so barren and joyless! "This is...not."

He chuckled. "This isn't really home for me. London is my home."

I decided to change the subject because I was off to a horrendous start. *Epic fail, Cristina. You walk into his house and all you can do is criticize his austerity. Thumbs up, dumbass!*

"Well! What can we eat? I'm starving!" I stated with a huge smile. I was trying to save him as much as I was trying to save myself.

"Really. Tell me why it upsets you," he persisted.

I exhaled loudly and thought I heard the sound resonate off every corner of the empty living room.

"Don't laugh. If you insist on hearing my thoughts, I'd appreciate it if you didn't mock them. I was upset because...no one takes care of you here. Not even your house takes care of you."

He smiled crookedly at me. "I'm a grown man. I can take care of myself."

"You know what I mean. Everyone deserves to be taken care of on occasion."

"Including you?" he queried.

"Don't turn this around on me! You wanted to know what I was thinking. It looks like you're consciously trying to prevent yourself from cultivating any roots here...like having an actual sofa."

"Ouch. Is it that obvious?" he teased.

Not wanting the conversation to continue moving in an introspective direction, I shoved his shoulder jokingly. He caught my hand and swiftly pulled me into an embrace. My heart pounded in my eardrums. I breathed slowly as I buried my face into his shoulder and allowed the comfort of his scent to wash through me and banish the reactionary panic. I was determined not to freak out for any reason. We were past the point where it was excusable...and I didn't want to be excused anymore.

"Thank you for caring," he whispered.

I pulled my face away and smiled up at him. There was something I wanted to do, so I gritted my teeth and demanded that my mind cease its senseless mutterings as I allowed my heart to take tentative control for the first time in nearly a year. Slowly, I leaned forward and placed a small kiss on his chin. He inhaled sharply and, when I pulled away, I saw that his eyes were closed and the left side of his mouth was curved upward in contentment.

"You're welcome," I said unwaveringly. "Now ... let's figure out what we're doing for dinner!"

He hesitated a moment. "We can go out someplace," he suggested as he released me. The look on his face made me think that this was not his first choice.

"We can cook something, too," I suggested.

"No. If I cook something you'll likely never want to see me again ... and I didn't ask you to come visit so that you would cook for me."

I laughed. "Takeout or delivery?"

"Delivery." He smiled to himself and walked over to the kitchen to collect a bunch of takeout menus.

"Uh, Thomas ... you have no table," I stated wryly as I took a closer look around.

"Christ!" he said in mock frustration as he handed me the menus. "I'll get a table before you come next time. I promise. Chairs, too."

Unable to control the giddy child within at the thought of him already planning a future visit, I stuck out my tongue petulantly in his direction.

"God, that's sexy," he teased.

This was how I spent my first evening in Los Angeles with a movie star ... eating Chinese food on the floor in pajamas and laughing until my sides hurt. Blissful and unpretentious ... not at all what I would have expected. Tom never failed to surprise me.

After we finished eating, I walked over to one of the only things that took up space in the living room—a full keyboard that had been pushed up against the wall near the large flat screen TV sitting forlornly on the floor amidst a jumble of cords.

I switched on the keyboard and began running my fingers quickly across the keys in a scale and then transitioned into a series of arpeggios.

"I didn't know you played piano," Tom murmured as he pulled the rickety metal stool towards me.

"If I get tetanus from that thing, you're in a lot of trouble," I joked as I sat down carefully on the stool. He chuckled in response. Feeling particularly confident, I launched into a movement of my father's favorite piano work: Franz Liszt's Piano Sonata in B Minor. Soon, I was absorbed as I remembered the way my father loved to sit on the sofa and listen to me play. He would close his eyes and nod in affirmation as the lyrical lines rose from the strings within our piano at my persistent prodding. I had never been a ridiculously good performer, but watching my Dad as he listened to me play would have caused the casual observer to believe that Emanuel Ax himself was the one eliciting music from the cold ivory keys. I had not played the piano since the day I held my father's hand in the hospital and watched as he fell peacefully into a forever sleep. For some reason, I felt as though he would have found my choice to play at this moment appropriate.

As I finished the last series of soft, repetitive notes, I glanced up and smiled at Tom. He was sitting amongst the cushions thrown haphazardly on the floor with his mouth agape and his eyes unblinking.

"Oh, come on!" I said as I tried to hide the flush creeping into my skin. "I made tons of mistakes! Don't stare at me like you're amazed!"

He cleared his throat. "I can't believe you never told me you played that well," he muttered.

"It wasn't important."

"It's important to me. How long have you been playing?" he asked.

"Since I was five. When I was in high school, I played fairly well … but I squandered the ability when I stopped practicing regularly. Now, I can only play slow pieces … I don't have the technical aptitude to play anything seriously demanding. That's why I chose the *Andante Sostenuto*."

"I'm sorry. I don't know what that means," he said kindly.

"It's my father's favorite piece by Liszt. The movement is known as the *Andante Sostenuto* … it means … um … slow and sustained? I guess that's the best translation I can come up with!" I giggled nervously. Tom still stared at me with glowing admiration.

"He must have loved you so much," Tom replied with a smile.

"I loved him … so much," I whispered as I grazed my hands slowly over the black keys. The tenor of their tones rising into the air was intentionally melancholy.

I stood up to walk over to the cluster of cushions where Tom was sitting and plopped down gracelessly into the hodgepodge. He stared reflectively at my face.

"I didn't mean to go melancholy on you," I said with a sad smile.

"You didn't. I was just thinking about how unfair life can be."

"How so?" I asked.

"You shamed me just now. I can see how much you love your father, and he was taken from you. My father is alive and well...and I haven't spoken to him properly in over a year."

I looked at him questioningly.

He sighed and ran his fingers through his hair while choosing his words. "I've always been really close to my sister Anne and my Mum. They've been really supportive of me. My father...is really critical. He thinks I have some kind of complex or something...like I need a crazy amount of attention just to be happy. It's so far from the truth. I really feel passionate about acting. Whenever I see him, we argue constantly." He exhaled in frustration. "I don't know what to do about it...so I gave up about a year ago."

I reached over and took his hand. "Not talking to him won't help the situation," I said as gently as possible.

He squeezed my hand and nodded simultaneously. "It's not easy."

"I hate to sound insensitive, but life in general is not easy. There was a lot about my father that ticked me off, but at the end of the day I always felt he knew how much I loved him. That's all you can really do. Love earnestly...love fully...or not at all. "

He leaned towards me and put his hand on my cheek. "Do you ever feel surprised that you still believe in the importance of love?"

I thought for a second. "No. Not at all. Love was never absent in my life...even in the darkest moments I never doubted its presence." I smiled at the comparison forming in my mind. "One bad wine doesn't mean all future wines are destined to taste awful."

"That's a terrible metaphor," he teased huskily. I noticed that he was moving in closer as he positioned himself to sit crossed-legged in front of me.

My breath caught as he cautiously brushed my hair behind my shoulders and ran his fingertips down the side of my neck. I felt his thumb graze my chin with a feather-light caress. He inhaled as he leaned closer. A lock of his unruly hair fell onto his forehead, causing me to feel this involuntary desire to brush it back. I looked for a place on his head to put it, but the chaos there didn't lend itself to this gesture, so I tried to ignore it.

"God, you smell fabulous," he whispered.

I smiled as calmly as possible. "You do, too." The air was growing warmer around us, and my senses shifted ostensibly to place all emphasis on the man sitting before me. His eyes narrowed slightly and a look of determination filled their grey depths as his hands rose once more to my face. "I want to kiss you."

My heart leapt into my throat, and the panicked musings of my brain tried in vain to stop the yearning from coursing through my body. Enough was enough.

I reached up and took hold of the errant lock to put it back where I thought it might belong. The vision of me tangling my fingers in his soft hair caused my heart to palpitate erratically. I took a deep, steadying breath and softened my expression with the calming salve of resolute awareness.

"Then kiss me."

He grinned in triumph before closing the gap between us. Stopping a hair's breadth from my lips, he held my gaze with his piercing grey eyes. I could see that they were flecked with bits of green and gold, and the way they thoughtfully searched my face for any sign of resistance destroyed the last remaining doubt in my mind.

Without hesitation, I closed my eyes and pressed my lips to his. He was caught off guard by my kiss, and it took him a moment to regain his bearings. Tom's lips were soft and careful as they began to move against mine with slow deliberation. He placed my lower lip between his, and his tongue brushed against it tentatively. His hands slid from my face to my neck, and my palms moved instinctively to his shoulders. When I parted my lips as the kisses grew more fervent, I felt him rise to his knees and clutch me against him. My arms clasped behind his neck as he lowered our forms onto the cushions surrounding us. My mind told me to stop this insanity before it progressed beyond the realm of reason, but his scent assailing my nostrils and his taste lingering on my lips would not allow it.

We kissed for a solid ten minutes. His hands never strayed, and I never felt for a moment as though he was trying to test my limits. The fervor died down as he reverted back to kissing me tenderly and cautiously. He smiled through a final kiss. "I'd rather not push my luck," he whispered as he pulled away.

I pouted in jest at him as relief flooded through my tingling form.

"Don't even look at me like that. You have no idea how hard it is for me to actually stop, and when you stick out your lower lip at me ...you drive me mad," he said in a low voice as he pulled me into his arms and held me.

"Thank you for caring," I whispered as I hugged him back.

"Of course. *Andante sostenuto*," he murmured with a grin. Slow and sustained.

I sighed contentedly.

# TEN

S o, where are we going exactly?" I demanded for the fourth time.
"I didn't tell you the first thousand times you asked me, so
what makes you think I would tell you now?"

"What if I opened the window and stuck my head out to tell the
whole world who was driving this car? Would you tell me then?" I
teased.

"I seriously doubt the whole world waits to hear what you have
to say." The grin on his face caused the corner of his eyes to crinkle
in an absurdly cute way.

"You're right. I think I'll leave the gigantic ego to the *movie star*,"
I jeered.

"I guess I deserved that."

The combination of our laughter mixed in with the sounds
emitting from the old CD player in Tom's car. His beat-up copy of
Metallica's *Black Album* was definitely worse for the wear. Many of
the songs skipped intermittently, and the damage to one track in particular was so severe that it refused to be heard at all. This was clearly
a loved CD.

"You look beautiful, by the way," Tom said as he glanced over at
me appreciatively.

I couldn't stop my girlish smile of response.

Earlier this afternoon, he had announced that he was taking me
out tonight. When I asked where we were going, he merely told me
that I should dress festively. I donned a sleeveless, fuchsia-colored
jersey dress with a skirt that flared at the knee. Copper heels and
accessories completed the ensemble, and my unmanageable hair fell
in torturously coaxed curls to my shoulders.

Tom looked quite sexy in his slate grey button-down shirt and
dark blue jeans. Both were a bit wrinkled, but I didn't think we were
at the point where I could force him to iron his clothes (hah!). It was
funny to me that I found him so attractive now; when I first met him,
I had not been that impressed. He was good-looking for sure, but not
drop-dead gorgeous. His personality and charm made him look far
more appealing than his mere physical attributes, which already gave

him a decidedly unfair advantage to begin with. Damn, I was hooked.

I bit my lower lip as I studied his face in a scouting attempt to glean our destination from him one last time.

"No," he stated firmly when he noticed my expression and added, "You're truly incapable of relinquishing control, aren't you?"

"It's not one of my stronger character points."

"Relax. Let go of the reins. It might not be as awful as you think."

"Ugh. We'll see."

Nothing could have prepared me for the sight I was about to behold. My jaw dropped to the floorboard of the white Mercedes at the music pounding from the two-story tan building he pulled up to. The bright neon lights and rolling sounds of Spanish dialogue filling my ears only enhanced the effect. I sat in the car completely speechless.

Tom the Movie Star . . . had taken me to a Latin dance club in LA—a *real* Latin dance club.

"Wha—how . . . are you freakin' serious?" I whispered.

He laughed heartily. "Hana told me you loved to dance."

"But, you're a white guy . . . a *British* white guy!"

The laughter continued. "Yes, I'm white. Yes, I'm British. Sometimes, British people like to dance."

"Whether they *can* dance remains to be seen," I muttered skeptically as I glanced over at his impish expression of triumph at being able to render me momentarily at a loss of words.

"You can teach me. I'm sure you'd love to have that control anyway."

He pulled on dark sunglasses and placed a black-knit cap hastily onto his head. The overall effect reminded me of a cross between Boho and Euro chic.

"Are you sure this won't be a problem?" I asked as I glanced around at all of the smiling faces raucously laughing and carrying on in the queue forming by the entrance of the club.

"No. But I don't intend to let it rule *all* our decisions."

I took a deep breath, swung myself out of the car, and marched over to the end of the line. Tom followed swiftly behind me. His hand held lightly onto my elbow as we took our place in front of the club and waited patiently to gain admittance.

As we stepped into the pulsing nightclub, the stress that had induced the rapid beat of my heart began to subside. It was dark, and many of the people were slightly inebriated. I kept hoping we would escape any undue notice. Thankfully, this would be one of the last places anyone would expect Tom to be on a Saturday night. No one around us paid a great deal of attention to the tiny Puerto Rican girl and the tall *Inglés* trying to make their way through the throng of mulling people.

A particularly bass-laden tune thudded from the speakers, and a resonating cheer arose from the masses. I listened carefully to the lyrics of the reggaeton song…invariably, the artist was sure to pompously announce himself. I smiled as the name echoed off the walls. Pitbull—a Cuban, like my father.

"Do you want to dance?" Tom shouted above the music and into my ear.

I grinned humorously. "I always want to dance…but it's okay if you want to wait." I stood on my tiptoes to speak by his ear.

He tugged playfully on my elbow to pull me even closer. "Stop thinking I'd rather slit my wrists than dance. Who knows, I may dance better than you do." He wagged his eyebrows and pursed his lips with a smug certainty that begged to be soundly trounced.

"Riiiight." I snatched his hand and pulled him onto the dance floor.

The music thumped all around us as though it had taken possession of the walls and the floors down to the very studs of the building. I could feel the reverberations jostle my nerve-endings. The beat rose from the ground into my frame, and soon my feet and hips developed minds of their own. Tom watched approvingly as I shook what God and country had given me.

In my past, I had been granted numerous opportunities to witness the horror of an uncoordinated white man trying to dance to music not of the "Cotton-Eyed Joe" or "Journey" persuasion. There were several styles I had stored in my psyche for reference. The first was undoubtedly the most horrific: "The Pelvic Thrust of No." In essence, aforementioned white boy would pantomime the act of intercourse in full view of the public and wonder indubitably why he wound up going home alone that night. The second was "The Stupor Shuffle." In this more pitiable routine, the feet would drag listlessly across the dance floor from side to side while the hands remained at chest level desperately trying to ascertain the beat. The eyes would dart around in a panicked fashion wondering what moron thought going to the club was a good idea. The final one was the most fun, but still not praiseworthy: "The I Can't Dance and Who the Hell Cares." In this scenario, body parts were all over the place, and the joyful semi-awareness of the individual almost overrode the visual onslaught of gracelessness. Essentially... it was a disaster of gleeful proportions.

Men like Justin Timberlake were genetic aberrations. Mutants... like the X-Men. It was just that simple.

You can imagine my shock and dismay when I discovered that Tom might actually necessitate a fourth category: "The I Can Dance ...Sorta."

Seriously, he moved better than I ever would have imagined possible given my preconceived notions. No awkwardness, just a reasonably on-target demonstration of semi-prowess. He tried to imitate my motions, and soon we were laughing uproariously at his slightly modified take on my dancing. The unabashed smile on his face as he turned my hand in mid-air to spin me in place made me feel a joyful abandon I had almost forgotten existed.

A couple nearby proceeded to get down on the dance floor as the girl leaned her backside into the guy and slowly rotated to the ground with their hips gyrating in synchronization.

Momentarily distracted by the pseudo-sex act occurring to our right, I hadn't noticed the girl behind me moving towards me in an attempt to create more space for herself. A sharp elbow poked at my lower back with clear intent to usurp my position. I exhaled and tried to ignore it as I took a step to stand even closer to Tom.

One could imagine my growing irritation when the errant elbow steamed full ahead once more with even more force behind it. I turned to glare momentarily at its conductor before I planted my feet on the dance floor in a silent protest that refused to cede any further ground. Tom chuckled at the look on my face.

"I swear," I muttered in his ear with a warning note to my voice.

As if she heard my hidden threat and wanted to call my bluff, she pushed her elbow jaggedly into my shoulder for the third and final time. I nearly lost balance as I was pitched forward into Tom's waiting embrace. I spun around and tried to maintain a jovial attitude in spite of the impending flare of my temper hovering behind my smile. I decided to opt for a teasing comment that would hopefully impress upon the girl that I was neither amused nor willing to take any more of her shit.

With a forced grin, I turned and stated loudly, "*¿Oye, corazon, es que te estas secando las uñas? ¡Porque ya mismo me quedo sin costillas!*" I rubbed my left ribcage to illustrate my words. Tom hovered nearby with a grim look on his face.

As soon as she opened her mouth, I knew I should have known better than to attempt to disarm a drunk Latina with a few smart-ass comments. *Coño.* She was Dominican. *"¡Oh, oh! ¡Ere' tu que estas tomando to' este espacio con tu blanquito!"* she spat.

Now, why did she have to go and play the race card? Poor Tom stood next to me completely unaware of this girl's vocal disdain for the presence of a *blanquito*—even one as good-looking as he. If she only knew what she was saying... what an idiot. Sure enough, the flare lying dormant in my throat rose to barrel out of my mouth with uncontrolled vigor. A dragon spitting fire... ya gotta love a pissed off Puerto Rican.

*"¡Mejor blanquito que borracho!"* There! Take that! I'll take my *blanquito* over your drunk-ass anyday!

I heard a muted groan emit from Tom's throat as the Dominican girl's well-muscled boyfriend stepped forward to glare down at me threateningly.

*"¿Quien esta borracho? ¡E' que a la carajito esta le gusta hablai'!"* he slurred.

The fool called me a bitch! Oh, hell no! I advanced towards him and raised my index finger to his face while trying to harness my wrath behind eyes squinted in fury. Before I could utter a word, Tom had stepped between the inebriated mammoth and me.

"Oy, you two..." he began in a calming tone. He placed his palm against the guy's huge chest warningly. Ugh. This was not good.

At the unwanted presence of Tom's hand on his chest, a roar emitted from the mammoth's lips. *"¡Mira, flaco 'e mierda!"*

Before I could yank Tom to safety, the mammoth's hand reared back and shot forward to connect with Tom's nose in a resounding crack. He landed on the floor into a jumble of legs.

"BLOODY HELL!" Tom screeched as he clutched his nose between his hands. Blood spurted from underneath his chin. My sight flashed red with rage.

Before I had a chance to pounce on the mammoth and begin beating the ever-loving crap out of him, the security guards yanked him towards the door with his loudly protesting girlfriend in tow. I crouched down and tried to pry Tom's hands away from his face to ascertain the damage.

"Fuck!" he shouted as I unwittingly jarred his nose once more.

"I'm so sorry!" I cried. "I think it might be broken. We need to go."

I grabbed his elbow in an attempt to hoist all six feet of him back into a standing position. A guy watching on the periphery came forward to mercifully assist. Before anyone realized whom the broken nose belonged to, I yanked Tom towards the exit in a fluster.

His eyes were blurry and squeezed shut in the pain that accompanies a nose thrashing, so I dug into his pockets to retrieve the keys to his car. I took a deep breath after shoving him into the passenger seat. God, please help me drive this thing! I pushed the key into the ignition and listened to it turn over with a roar.

A muffled groan of pain echoed from behind his hands. "He broke my bloody nose," he muttered acerbically.

"Tilt your head back! Do you have any tissues?" I said with extreme concern. My brow was creased with worry as I scrounged around the car for some Kleenex. After finding a handful in the glove compartment, I pressed them to Tom's face.

When he removed his hands, I saw that his nose had begun to swell grotesquely. Stifling a gasp, I bit my lower lip in horrified awareness. "Uh…I think we need to go to a hospital."

"You think?" He cocked his left eyebrow at me humorlessly and grimaced at the effect the motion had on his nose. The tissues stuffed onto his face became spotted with blood.

I put the car into Drive. "Where do I go?"

"iPhone." He leaned forward so I could pry his phone from his back pocket.

"I don't know how to use this thing!"

"You'd better sort it out! I certainly can't do it!" he groaned once more.

"There's no need to be snippy!"

"I'm sorry. I must have been mistaking myself for someone with a *broken nose*!" he shouted. I could see a spark of annoyed humor flash in his eyes.

"Pansy." I fumbled once more until I was able to reach the Menu part of the phone.

"There's a mapping function in the Apps." His tone was muffled under his hands and many layers of tissues.

"Why the hell are there so many things on this phone?" I demanded as I flipped through what appeared to be hundreds of Applications.

"Christ, I'm bleeding to death with each passing second!" he moaned exaggeratedly.

Soon, I was pressing my foot down to the floor on the accelerator as I tried to coax the car to move as quickly as possible towards our destination. The Mercedes lumbered obstinately onward like a battered tank.

Approximately one hour later, we were behind a hospital curtain in the emergency room waiting for a doctor to give us directions on how to mitigate the pain and swelling. Tom sat on the edge of the hospital bed with a cool compress against his face and stared at me through narrowed eyes that warred with varying degrees of irritation and amusement.

"You just had to pick a fight, didn't you, Cristina?"

I pursed my lips together and lowered my gaze stubbornly. "I don't do well with people when they're disrespectful."

"Pick your battles, love. Next time, I'd prefer if you didn't pick one with a man twice my size."

"You didn't have to get involved. I had things under control... for the most part," I murmured as an element of shame clouded my tone.

He jutted his lower lip forward mockingly and then exhaled. "Only a total wanker stands by and lets a drunken fool threaten his girl."

I couldn't help it. I smiled at him as I reached up to brush back his hair and check on the swelling.

"I'm sorry, Tom. I wasn't thinking. I've gotten used to watching out for myself... and I didn't think about what that would mean for you in this situation."

The right side of his lips curved upward slightly. "I'd like to watch out for you too, if you don't mind."

"I don't mind," I said in a small voice.

"So... do me a favor next time and look out for me as well." He chuckled good-naturedly as he gestured towards his bruised nose.

I leaned forward to press a light kiss to the compress.

"I'll do my best," I said with a grin.

We returned to his apartment at nearly three in the morning. After administering all of the pain meds the doctor prescribed, I took a seat on a disgusting-looking futon in Tom's bedroom.

"Seriously, you don't have to play Florence Nightingale," Tom murmured from his bed.

"You wish. I just want to make sure that you're okay before I go to sleep."

He groaned inwardly. "God, I think this is the worst headache I've had in a while. He smacked me with a club, not a hand!"

"This futon smells gross."

He chuckled. "I was thrashed today on account of you, and I'm completely knackered. Let's not say anything about the futon, eh?"

I laughed with quiet amusement. "This may be totally inappropriate given the fact that your nose is broken and you're hopped up on drugs... but I had a really good time this weekend."

He smiled with a bemused expression on his face. The bruises surrounding his nose were beginning to turn interesting shades of purple and green. "It didn't go exactly like I planned, but... I'm glad you had a good time." He yawned quickly before refocusing his gaze on me. I saw the faintest sign of a grimace cross his features right after he yawned.

I studied his battered face again and frowned in frustration. "I wish there were something I could do to make you feel better."

He smirked at me knowingly. "I can think of a few things you could do...."

I grabbed the pillow at the end of the futon and swung it towards his feet. "Again... you wish."

He laughed outright. "Honestly, you walked right into that one." He stopped chortling long enough to narrow his eyes in utter seriousness. "You do realize... I'm completely falling for you."

I inhaled sharply as he stared at me with an intense expression that caused adrenaline to course through my body. I pulled my knees under my chin to bide some time. The response of my heart never gave my mind a chance. "You do realize... I've already fallen for you."

"I'm not staying here tonight. When I come back on Sunday, you won't be here. Take whatever you think is yours."

His eyes narrowed as he watched my world unravel with the gaze of a detached observer. "Don't worry. You'll find someone else. You're very easy to like."

He turned around quickly and walked down the shadowy hallway towards the door. I forced my feet to stay glued to the carpet.

*Please Ryan! Don't do this to me! Don't destroy us!*

Alone another heart-wrenching time with my anguish, I fell to the floor and dug my nails into the carpet to prevent them from clawing at my skin. Cold. Dark. Suffocating. Again, as I attempted to pry my fingers from the pilings, I felt a warmth emanating from the foyer. I tried to shift my gaze towards it and saw the light glow brighter than before... it reminded me of a candle flickering faintly in the wind, but refusing to go out.

The vision blurred....

I breathed in swiftly to stop the pounding of my heart as I opened my eyes in Tom's shadowy bedroom. My legs were cramped from their odd angle on the futon, but I didn't want to risk the action of stretching them out and waking him in the process. I also didn't want to draw any attention to myself as the tears coursed mercilessly down my cheeks with no chance of ceasing anytime soon. Frustrated, I squeezed my eyes shut and tried to stop the pain in my core from inhabiting all of my soul as it usually did. Carefully, I turned around on the futon and buried my face into it, bad smell be damned. My shoulders shook minutely with the force of the soundless sobs.

Wracked with the concentration of remaining quiet, my senses did not initially pick up on the movement around me. I felt warm hands push aside the hair cloaking my face. Soft fingers wiped at the tears, unbidden. Soon, strong arms moved under my knees and behind my neck to lift me from the futon. Blessedly, no words punctuated the silence. I was lowered into the bed, and the same sinewy arms wrapped around me like a cocoon. The scent of sandalwood and maple syrup filled my nostrils... the steady tears of only moments before began to fall intermittently. Lips pressed against my temple and below my ear. I hid my face in the cotton T-shirt in front of me and breathed with a semblance of normalcy. Sometimes, the strongest words are the ones left unsaid.

We were awakened to the harsh light of day by the screaming cell phone near Tom's head.

"Hello?" he groaned. The swelling had diminished, but the ghastly bruising marred his features with stains reminiscent of an eggplant.

"Christ. Are you serious?" His eyebrows furrowed with aggravation.

"I didn't call you because it was after one in morning!" he continued.

His teeth snapped together angrily as he listened to the ranting female voice on the other end of the phone.

"Fine. It wasn't done with the intention of causing you trouble, Melissa."

"I understand. No, I'm not mad. I just…she's not ready for this."

"No. Thank you. It's fine. The doctor said the bruising would be gone in about a week."

"Do whatever you need to do. Thanks. I'll call you later."

He lowered the phone from his ear and turned to look at me with a strange expression on his face.

"What's wrong?" I asked hoarsely.

Deep in thought, he shifted his mouth to one side and brushed his thumb across my chapped lips.

"It's all over the net."

"What?" I muttered in confusion.

"Someone took pictures of us in the hospital, Cris. There are pictures of you with me all over the internet." He kept stroking my face soothingly with a look of grim acceptance and tacit concern.

My mind processed his words slowly…and a gasp of shocked comprehension filled the air.

"Holy shit," I whispered in horror.

# ELEVEN

I never really paid attention to blogs or gossip before. I knew myself very well, and I had a tendency to exhibit obsessive behavior when it came to outlets for wasting time. My Facebook FarmTown in its heyday was a thing of glory. Thus, I attempted to temper these propensities by refusing to indulge them unnecessarily. Hana Fateri followed gossip rags and the blogosphere with a fervor that made me jokingly refer to her as the female reincarnate of William Randolph Hearst. Whenever I wanted to know who dumped whom and who was seen with whom, all I had to do was ask her. I knew that if I allowed myself to humor these inclinations, I would spend way too many precious moments scouring the net for cheaper versions of Emmy Rossum's sweater or Jessica Alba's jeans . . . whatever struck my fancy at that moment. I cut it off at the pass by never giving it a chance.

Little did I know that "yellow journalism" was more in vogue than I ever would have imagined.

Tom warned me: "Don't look at the net. Ignore it. If you don't, you'll get sucked down a black hole of shite and then it's impossible to surface for air."

Silly rabbit. . . .

I'd like to take a moment to share a few of the standout news blurbs accompanied by grainy photographs (obviously taken with a cell phone) that shot across the World Wide Web with the speed and ferocity of a forest fire. I never thought I'd come to a place where I felt relieved at being referred to as nothing more than an "Unidentified Companion."

Page Six: "Reigning British Heartthrob Tom seen in hospital at 2am with unnamed Latina. Could he be off the market? Horror of horrors!" Perez Hilton: "Sexy Tom Sucker-Punched? Seen in the ER with as-yet unknown goldigger girl. The bitch better not have ruined that beautiful face!"

LaineyGossip: "Brooding Eurotrash Actor Bitch-Slapped by Nameless Famewhore. Pictures taken of the cub in the hospital nursing his wounds while the lioness watches from the sidelines. Does anyone know who she is? I have cookies."

People's StarTracks: "Bloody Nose? Rising star Thomas Abramson seen in hospital with unidentified female companion. Treated for nose injury that forces the hunk to cancel several photo shoots and appearances."

I'm guessing I don't need to further iterate how craptastic this was. The entire plane ride home, I kept mentally replaying that throatily crooned line from Amy Winehouse's song "Me and Mr. Jones": "What kind of fuckery is this?"

The worst development of technology and "blogsip" was the advent of the public's facility to comment in real-time on the "news."

Let's just say that "famewhore" and "goldigger" were some of the less virulent comments made about me by the fawning masses claiming to "love" Tom. I was truly thankful that they had yet to learn my name or anything of import beyond my existence. How could they hate me that much based on a few pictures? Why did everyone assume I was the one who hit him? Whatever happened to responsible journalism?

And now... for the cherry on the crapbomb sundae:

From: Melissa T. Nash <mnash@venturemngmt. com>
To: Cris Pereira <7crisp@gmail.com>
Date: Mon, May 18, 2009 at 9:28 AM
Subject: (no subject)

Cristina,

I hope this message finds you reasonably well. I do not have an endless supply of time, so I think it would serve us both if I get straight to the point.

Thus far, I have managed to loosely conceal your identity from the press. I did not necessarily do this as a service to you—given our past encounters, I know you will appreciate my candor. It will not be possible to stave off the media for an extended period of time, especially if you insist on publicly broadcasting your relationship with Thomas.

94    In most careers, it should not matter what an

individual chooses to do in their own time. Unfortunately, this luxury is not given to those in Thomas's industry. At the moment, public interest is high in what he is doing in all facets of his life. His affiliation with you may produce far-reaching ramifications, and it is difficult to anticipate if they will have anything but negative repercussions–for both of you.

Given the incident from this past weekend, and its ever-growing consequences, I can only assume that you would be willing to assist me in my attempts to keep your relationship as private as possible.

As distasteful as it might seem for you to take my advice on these matters, I can assure you that I share it with the dual purpose of preventing public relations nightmares like the one from this weekend from occurring again and moving Thomas's career forward in the best manner possible. I would prefer that he remain "single" in the eyes of the entertainment industry. He is too young, and his career is too fresh for him to risk a public display of attachment to any one woman.

Please do not go out in public with him as much as can be avoided. If you must go out in public, please do not walk with him. Please do not attempt to speak with anyone in the media about anything in your life. If you have Facebook, MySpace, Twitter, or anything of this nature, it might serve you to remove pictures of yourself from these accounts. Unflattering personal statements should be purged as well. The abuse of photos and information existing in these mediums is rampant and quick.

Passwords on email accounts should be changed frequently. Please do not use the same password for multiple accounts. Do not distribute your phone number or contact information to anyone unless it is absolutely necessary.

Your quick attention to these matters would

be much appreciated.

Melissa Nash

---

I called in "sick" the Monday after I returned. Honestly, I *was* sick... sick to death of feeling paranoid that someone would recognize my blurry face in the pictures and proceed to inform the salivating hyenas of my anticlimactic identity. The day was spent deleting every photo I could find of myself online. I subsequently shut down my MySpace page and placed every privacy restriction I could discern on my email and Facebook accounts.

However much I wanted to punch Melissa in the kisser for just being... her... I had to be thankful for whatever magic she conjured that prevented people from gleaning any more knowledge about me or my affiliation with her client.

After a week passed without any further incident, I began to breathe normally. It was just a flare in the world of blogsip... quickly lit and short-lived. As long as I followed Melissa's directions and stayed out of the way, I wouldn't have to worry about feeling... I don't know... I was very surprised that the criticism of people possessing absolutely no information or credence to their claims would bother me so much. I guess when you read that people halfway around the world are calling you a "bitch" and a "slut" many times over it starts to have an effect. How original.

What I wouldn't give to take it all in stride. Tom's cavalier attitude about the whole thing irked me as much as I envied him for possessing it.

"How can you be so... cool about all of this?" I demanded one night.

"Practice. Desensitization... and the realization that this is just how it is. It used to bother me a great deal. I would stay up at night reading all of this rubbish and obsessing over who thought I was a shit actor and needed to lose weight, gain weight, bulk up, cut my hair, whatever. It's total crap, Cris. They love to hate you just as much as they love to love you."

"I just... You're right. I guess I have to develop a thicker skin," I mumbled.

"What were you going to say?"

"Uh, what do you mean?" The rising pitch of my voice only lent further credence to his query.

"You were going to say something else... and you stopped yourself."

I exhaled loudly. "Tom…I stopped myself because what I was about to say wasn't helpful."

He paused for a moment. "I'd like to hear it anyway."

"Stop being difficult!"

"You're being difficult. There's no reason for you to edit yourself with me," he said curtly.

"Look, it's not about editing. It's about being constructive. What I wanted to say served no purpose, but if you have to hear it, then don't bitch about what I say after the fact…I'm just pissed that I had to fall for someone whose life is an open book. This means that my life will eventually have to be an open book as well…and I hate it." By the time I finished my rant, I was definitely on the brink of shouting. Yep, deflection of irritation rarely resulted in a positive outcome.

Dead silence.

I groaned loudly. This was the first time we had a noticeably harsh exchange, and the feeling of anxiety that came from poking a hole in the shining bubble of a new relationship began to creep into my throat.

"See? Editing is necessary," I cried.

"No, it's not."

"You're pissed off at me…and I hate that, too," I stated earnestly.

"If I'm pissed off, it's not at you. This is my reality. I want you to be a part of it. I think you're strong enough to handle it."

"I wish you wouldn't force me to say things that might upset you," I said gently.

"One of the things that attracted me to you was your honesty. Don't hide it from me in a sad attempt to save my feelings. You hate my job. As long as you like *me*, then it doesn't matter." His tone was matter-of-fact.

"I don't hate your job…and you know it's not that simple," I murmured.

"I want it to be. If and when it gets more difficult, we'll deal with it then."

"That's not my style, but I'll go with it…for now," I acquiesced.

That conversation had left a bad taste in my mouth for several days. It seemed asinine to dismiss something that was becoming so increasingly troublesome, but thus far in our relationship it had not made a big difference, so I clung fast to the childish hope that ignoring the problem would eventually make it go away.

Four weeks had passed since an angry Dominican man broke Tom's nose and my blurry mug had made its way to blogs all over the world. Thank God I worked with people too engrossed in their own lives to recognize that their colleague was a "goldigging famewhore." The blessings of working for the state of North Carolina definitely showcased their attributes from time to time.

I stood in the kitchen with my mother and surveyed the spread. The *pernil* sat in the center of the table ready to be carved. The smell emitting from the plate filled the air with the scent of roasted pork stuffed with whole cloves of garlic and a seasoning rub that had infiltrated the meat over four long days marinating in the refrigerator. A mixture of traditional dishes from both Cuba and Puerto Rico surrounded the *pernil*, along with the requisite beans and rice. Tom had said that he wanted an authentic, home-cooked meal. It didn't get any more authentic than this.

Mami fidgeted for the fifteenth time with her outfit while waiting nervously for the doorbell to ring.

"Stop! You look beautiful!" I murmured in Spanish.

"I don't know . . . maybe I should have worn the dress," she mused.

"No. That color is perfect on you."

She continued muttering to herself about her appearance and the "humble" state of our home. I had heard these comments for the last two weeks since telling my mom that Tom wanted to meet her. Our house was certainly not a Hollywood Hills McMansion, but it was cozy and filled with memories on every wall and in every corner. I grew tired of listening to my mother speak as though Tom were an overlord coming to visit the peasants living on his fief.

"He's just a boy," I said again in irritation.

She opened her mouth to retort, but the doorbell rang. I took a deep breath as she ran to check her makeup a final time in the mirror hanging in the foyer. It would have been nice to pick up Tom from the airport myself, but after the Preying Mantis's email about the recent debacle in the hospital, we decided to play it safe and utilize taxis.

I threw open the door with gusto.

"Hello," I breathed as a silly smile made its way onto my face at the sight of the lanky British man gracing our doorstep.

"Hi."

My mother rushed over and nearly elbowed me aside in her attempt to get a good look at Tom.

Apparently, the many conversations I had shared with Tom concerning my mother's effulgence had made a lasting impression. He grinned and bent down to sweep her into a bear hug that caused her to turn bright red and giggle like a schoolgirl.

Even I was rendered speechless by this simple gesture. I didn't know how Tom instinctively came to the conclusion that my mom was a sucker for a good hug, but she was officially a stalwart fan after that. She rambled on and on at him in a mixture of English and Spanish that even I had troubled breaking down at times. In between piling his plate with a ridiculous amount of rice and telling him her entire life story, I saw her reach over to pat his hand indulgently and preen at his compliments with unabashed pride.

"*Mira*, you need a haircut, Thomas," Mami said sternly as she perused his appearance with a critiquing eye while we put away the dishes. She pronounced his name with the stress on the second syllable instead of the first.

I tried not to smile knowingly. "Mami! I think he knows what he's doing with his hair!"

He barked a quick chortle of laughter as he winked at me. "I've heard this before. Maybe I should just shave it off."

"*Noooo*. Not too much, *tu sabes*...just a little. It's too long," Mami replied. "*Oye, pero tu eres guapo*. If you fix your hair, it's perfect."

"I'll keep that in mind." His eyes twinkled merrily as my mother launched into another tale without end. She was so happy that I couldn't stop myself from watching her with a silly expression of contentment on my face.

After my mother had exhausted herself and marched up the stairs to bed, I sat down at the table and stared silently at Tom until he took the seat near me with a look of quizzical amusement. I placed both palms under my chin, propped my head onto my elbows, and narrowed my eyes at the movie star sitting at my tiny dining room table as though he belonged there.

He arched his left eyebrow at me and waited.

"Why are you still single?" I demanded simply.

He chuckled. "Why are *you* still single?"

"Listen, Socrates...I asked you first."

He shrugged.

I exhaled loudly. "Seriously. You were so amazing with my mother. I can't tell you how much that meant to me. I haven't met many men as thoughtful and aware as you are. Compounded by the fact that you're incredibly easy on the eyes and a member of a profession most lay-folk can only aspire to be a part of, I just don't get it. *Why are you still single?"*

He continued studying me as I spoke. "Tell me why you're asking me this, and I'll answer the question."

This time, I shrugged in response.

"You really don't see yourself, do you, Cris?" he asked me softly.

"This isn't some pitiful fishing expedition for half-assed compliments. I see myself pretty well."

"I think if you saw what I see, you wouldn't ask me this question." The warm look in his eyes made me stare down at the table for a moment to collect my jumbled thoughts.

"Fine then. I'm not going to insult your priorities by saying you can get a hotter girl. I just don't understand why you would go through the trouble of taking on a relationship that has so many obstacles when you could have your pick of girls with much less baggage and far easier situations." I felt ridiculous saying this, but the dubious seed of doubt in my heart needed to hear a response that made a semblance of sense.

"I don't want easy. I want you."

I flushed, but refused to back down. "That's very poignant, but it isn't a real answer."

He leaned over the table closer to me. "You're right. I could probably find something easier . . . someone that doesn't exasperate me as you often do. Honestly, I just want to be around someone who sees me as nothing more than a guy with a weird job and a strange sense of humor. Most girls I meet are nice enough, but they can't get passed what I am and how it makes them feel about themselves. You didn't care. That made you the sexiest girl I'd ever seen. You were also completely disinterested in me. Even as a kid, I loved a challenge."

"I was disinterested because I live in the real world!"

"I live in the real world, too. Many of the girls who would love to date someone famous don't realize that most of us are nothing special. I find myself insanely boring. It's a lot of pressure to be someone's dream. Is it too much to ask for me to have a girl who lives in the same world as I do?" he posited softly.

I wanted to tell him that he didn't live in the real world. I wanted to point out that he existed in a realm that made him virtually untouchable to 99.9% of the world, but I said nothing.

"Plus, you're incredibly smart and effing hilarious," he added with a smile.

100    I grinned reflexively. "Hah."

"I've come to realize how important it is to surround myself with people who don't take the world too seriously and can always be counted on to see the humor in things. In my experience, there aren't too many people like that. You don't know how many times your humor has improved my day."

"Glad to give you a measure of what you've given me," I murmured.

"That's the way it's supposed to be. I'm supposed to make your day better, and vice versa."

"You succeed. You've also made my mother's day better, and I can't think of words strong enough to thank you for that. She's not going to shut up about you. Your efforts were a slam dunk," I stated appreciatively.

"She has an amazing daughter…worthy of such efforts."

"God!" I cried.

"What?" He was startled by my mini-outburst.

"Now, I just want to jump your bones so that you stop making me feel so self-conscious!"

He laughed loudly.

I narrowed my eyes at him. "I'm serious."

He wrinkled his brow mischievously. "I'd let you."

"I'm sure you would, but we're at my mother's house. Simmer down now."

He reached his hand over to me and ran the back of his fingertips down the side of my face to my exposed collarbone. I released a shaky breath.

"Watch yourself," I murmured as I stood up and moved closer.

Leaning down, I ran my hand through his hair before pressing my lips to his. He stood in one fluid motion to pull me into his arms without breaking the kiss. Soon, we were tugging at each other's faces with a fire that threatened to burn caution into oblivion. He wrapped his arms around me and lifted my small frame off the ground so that he wouldn't have to strain his neck. Thoughtlessly, my hands traced the taut muscles of his back. I had to stop my fingers from grabbing his shirt and yanking it over his head.

"I want you," he whispered hoarsely in my ear.

I smiled impishly as my heart pounded in my throat. "I know you mentioned that you don't want this kind of pressure, but I'm going to dream about you," I teased.

He chuckled. "Just tell me that dream can actually become reality sometime soon, and I'll deal with the pressure."

I gazed at him for a moment with an expression of mock indecision. "Hmmm. There's a good chance you might get lucky very soon."

"I'll take it. Dream away."

Don't worry. I will.

# TWELVE

I n order to understand the events moving forward, it is necessary to take a small step back to the beginning . . . to the time of the Email Question Blitz. It was amazing how much insight I obtained about Tom and his life through these simple exchanges. Often, his questions alone would shed a great deal of light onto his personality. His responses to mine were always a quirky mix of humor and fact that drove me to laugh to myself in recollection. Honestly, I must have looked crazy as I pumped gas and chuckled about something he mentioned while answering my off-the-wall queries.

The email below highlights my answer to a question he posited to me on a random Sunday in March. The question was: "What is something completely harmless that no amount of money could ever force you to do?"

From: Cris Pereira <7crisp@gmail.com>
To: Tom A. <bobdylan85@yahoo.co.uk>
Date: Sun, March 18, 2009 at 5:41 PM
Subject: I wanna rock your gypsy soul

Z:
I'm listening to INTO THE MYSTIC as I write this. It makes me want to sit outside on a porch and watch the rain fall. Damn. I need a porch.

There are quite a few harmless things that money could never entice me to do; the second that anyone offers to pay me for something stupid, my suspicious nature takes hold. It's like when someone says, "Ew, this tastes gross! Try it!" Uh. No. WTF?

When I first read the question, one thing in particular flew into my head, so I'll just go with that. When in doubt, always answer a question with your gut instinct—or choice C.

Camping.

Yep. No amount of money could force me to go camping. I know, I know . . . you're sitting there thinking to yourself, "What? I'll bet she doesn't like it when her hair gets wet, either! (I don't.) What a boring little priss!" I like being outside. I like having the sunshine on my face. I've been hiking several times before, and I had a pretty good time.

So, what it boils down to is this: I am not going to the bathroom outside. No. Never. I'll hold it until my bladder explodes . . . and don't even talk to me about the deuce. NEVER GOING TO HAPPEN.

Thus, money will not make me go camping as the demands of my bodily functions cannot be avoided in that scenario. I had a friend in Puerto Rico that I grew up with, and he went camping once with a bunch of his buddies. They probably didn't cook their food properly, and he got sick . . . as in major gastrointestinal issues. He forgot to take toilet paper with him into the forest and used some leaves instead. Turns out . . . he used poison ivy. I still call him "Ass on Fire" when I see him.

It's Celebrity Deathmatch Sunday. Don't forget, you must make a serious argument for your pick. Miss Piggy vs. Optimus Prime. Go.

Chip

---

The morning after Tom first met my mother, I woke up early and put on comfortable clothes and tennis shoes, as he directed the night before. Grabbing my packed overnight bag, I met him at the bottom of the stairs in my house and knew I sported a markedly suspicious look on my face.

"I hate it when you won't tell me what we're doing," I grumbled.

"I know." He flashed a close-lipped grin at me with unabashed smugness.

"You're sure I don't need to bring anything except water?" I asked for the fifth time.

He rolled his eyes exaggeratedly and gathered his things.

"Are you going to play for me?" I teased as I took note of his guitar.

"No. I don't go anywhere without my guitar. It's my version of Linus's blanket," he bit back smarmily.

"Gotta love that British sarcasm. It just reeks of too many sunless days and secondhand smoke," I retorted with a half-smile.

After giving my mom promises to return safely, we walked out the front door to my car. He wordlessly handed me a piece of paper with an address on it, and I proceeded to type it into my Garmin GPS. Twenty minutes later, we pulled up to a car rental place in Raleigh. He stepped out of my tiny Civic after directing me to sit still (if possible) for a few moments, and then he carefully concealed himself behind large aviator sunglasses and a worn baseball cap. Soon, he came out with paperwork and a set of keys.

"No. You're wretchedly adorable, but I have nothing to say yet," he stated flatly when he saw the look on my face.

Taking his lead, I removed my bags from my car as he took down my GPS from the windshield and walked over to a gunmetal-grey Jeep Cherokee that had just been moved out front by an employee. He loaded our things into the backseat and took position behind the wheel.

"You're just going to have to trust me. Give up. You're not going to suss it out anytime soon," he jibed.

I glared at him for a moment before climbing into the passenger seat.

"I'm the planner!" I sputtered as I watched him type a destination into my newly muted Garmin. How childish did that sound?

"What are you talking about?"

Might as well embarrass myself fully. "I'm the planner. Ask my friends. Anytime we go someplace or do something, I plan everything right down to carpooling. I don't know how the responsibility always fell onto me, but it's just been that way for a long time," I muttered.

"I know how it fell onto you. You're a total control freak. Most people don't want to fight with a woman who's gone mental and takes her inspiration from Mussolini."

I shoved his shoulder lightly. "Seriously, though. I can't remember the last time I felt so utterly out of control."

He paused a moment. "The wanker never surprised you with a trip?" His jaw always set with slight tension whenever Ryan was brought into the conversation.

"No," I answered honestly. "I usually did most of the planning."

"I told you he was a wanker."

"So, when are you going to tell me what the hell we're doing today?" It was never a good idea to dwell on an ex-file.

He smiled, but it didn't reach his eyes as it usually did. "Hopefully, I won't have to tell you. The closer we get, the more obvious it should become. I'm counting on your natural intelligence just as much as I'm counting on you liking me enough to forgive me."

My mouth fell open a bit as I narrowed my eyes at Tom. "So, you think I'm not going to be happy about it."

"I'm living dangerously right now. You should try it."

I refused to answer as I wracked my brain for possibilities. From the corner of my eye, I could see him studying me.

"Cristina, you really need to live outside your head more," he said gently.

"Meaning?"

"Exactly that. I can see the wheels turning. Have you ever considered spending a day every once in a while where you don't think… you just do?" His tone was introspective and slightly prodding.

I thought for a moment more. He laughed outright. "What?" I asked in confusion.

"You can't even answer that question without stopping to think first!"

"Hah, hah."

"I believe I have my answer. Well, my goal is to make you live outside of your head. This is only the beginning," he stated with satisfaction.

"I might not like it."

"How would you know?" He wagged his eyebrows at me in an absurdly cute fashion.

After a few hours of traveling in a westerly direction, the Appalachian Mountains loomed majestically before us. When it became clear to me that we were heading intentionally closer to them, I cleared my throat in an attempt to stifle the slew of questions bubbling precariously in my chest, just waiting for an opportunity to burst forth.

Soon, he parked the Jeep on Main Street near a Sporting Goods store in a sleepy town that emerged from the endlessly winding roads slicing their path through the rolling terrain. I stepped out of the Jeep and stretched my arms over my head as I breathed in the clean air and watched a soothing breeze ripple through the trees around us. Armed with his hat and sunglasses, we proceeded to walk up and

106

down the quiet street and peer into the windows of the shops along the sidewalk. I was fairly certain we didn't have to worry about the paparazzi in this quiet haven. Tom reached over to take my hand as we paused in front of a gallery to look at the clay pottery lining the window. About an hour later, we walked back towards the car, intent on getting something to eat. A delicatessen was attached to the Sporting Goods store, so we went inside to order some sandwiches for a picnic lunch. I grabbed more water and a few granola bars in preparation for what I felt certain was an impending hike.

Holding our selections, we walked to the register located between the deli and store to pay for our food. The grey-bearded man nodded at Tom with a patient smile as he rang up the few incidentals in our hands.

"That will be $421.67," he announced in a kind tone.

"What!?" I cried involuntarily.

Nonplussed, Tom handed the man his credit card. "Thanks, Jim."

"Are you crazy?" I demanded. "There's been a mistake, sir," I said to the man as he proceeded to slide Tom's credit card through the machine.

"The maps and manuals are sittin' on the driver's seat. You call me if you need anything," Jim said to Tom as he reached over to shake his hand.

"Of course. You've been a lifesaver. Thanks again. Say hello to Janie for me," Tom said with a big smile.

"Will do."

Tom took my hand and led me outside. My face still registered nothing but complete confusion...until he opened my door for me, and I saw that the trunk was filled to the brim with...

Camping gear.

"Priceless. You look utterly gobsmacked. It's perfect," he crowed as he nudged me into my seat by prodding on my lower back.

"You...no...I...THOMAS!"

"Just wait, just wait. Before you verbally berate me in multiple languages, let me explain," he began.

"*¡Este hombre esta del carajo!*" I wailed.

He started the engine of the Jeep while snickering to himself, obviously proud of his successful gambit.

"I found a campsite right next to public toilets. Relax. You don't have to piss in the woods," he teased.

While slightly mollified at hearing this news, I still felt as though 107

I had a right to some important information. "Have you ever been camping?" I demanded.

"No."

"Um . . . two idiots alone in the forest with no prior camping experience doesn't sound like a recipe for a fun time," I stated dubiously.

"It can't be that hard. You're intelligent, and I'd like to think I'm reasonably smart. Isn't camping essentially sleeping and eating in the woods? I don't think we're going to die trying it out."

"Famous last words. I think they probably said the same shit to each other in 'The Blair Witch Project' before a psycho in the mountains killed them all. Just so you know, I can't be counted on for much, but I'll give it a try." I snatched the manuals from the floor in between us and tried to set a course of action in an attempt to assuage my fears.

We found the campsite and parked the car nearby before yanking the accoutrements out of the trunk and laying it all out on the ground to begin devising a scheme for assemblage.

"All these fucking poles look the same," Tom announced in dismay as we still struggled to erect the tent an hour later.

"Because you're not even looking at the directions! How predictably male!" I pried the papers from under the rock employed by Tom to keep the instruction manual from blowing away. The afternoon sun grew hotter on my back, so I rolled the sleeves of my T-shirt and the bottom of my jeans higher to fight back against the heat.

"This shite is doomed," he stated as he looked at the ragged excuse for a tent that was beginning to take "shape" under our inexperienced guidance. "One strong breeze and we're done for." He opened a bottle of water and dumped it onto the back of his neck to combat the rising temperature.

"Don't look at me! Didn't you tell me you spent your formative years in London's West End? I guess they don't offer tent-building classes or Boy Scout training in Leicester Square!"

"Piss off! I suppose you didn't take much time from obsessively organizing your life on Microsoft OneNote to learn anything useful either!" he mocked as he tossed the empty water bottle in my direction.

"Dude. If some cataclysmic event befalls the earth anytime soon, we're done for. It's Darwinian. We can't even put together a place of refuge from the elements."

108 "No. It would only be Darwinian if we were unable to propa-

gate." He winked suggestively in my direction.

"Don't hold your breath, you perv. I won't 'propagate' with anyone unless I have shelter."

"So demanding. I think you need to lower your expectations."

"I think you need to stop talking and help me put together this friggin' tent!" I said with exasperation.

An hour later and we were both dripping sweat. A ramshackle excuse for a campsite surrounded us. The tent had a decidedly fuck-it-all look to it, and the cooler filled with our food sat next to a pile of twigs surrounded by a circle of misshapen stones that comprised a miserable parody of a fire pit.

"I smell terrible!" I proclaimed as I tugged on the sleeve of my T-shirt again. "Good call on the camping, genius. I feel incredibly sexy right now."

"Against all odds, you do manage to look quite sexy. Damn, it's hot!" he announced loudly before yanking his sweat-soaked shirt over his head.

"That's not fair. I hope you get chewed to bits by the bugs." I pretended to study the manual again to hide the flush that flared onto my cheeks at the sight of his semi-nude form. *Ugh...so...unfair.*

He laughed at me. "No one's stopping you from doing the same."

I raised my head and wrinkled my nose at him. "You wish. This campsite didn't come with a pool by any chance, did it?" I pulled at my sticky shirt to increase the airflow onto my skin.

"No pool... but... there's a lake about a quarter of a mile that way." A gleam had come into his eyes—a gleam that spelled trouble for me.

"No way."

"Come on. I'll race you." He wagged his eyebrows at me in anticipation.

"Um. I—"

"Don't think. Just do." He grabbed my hand and took off towards the lake with me in tow.

"What about our stuff!?" I yelled through the trees.

"Run, you idiot! You don't want to lose, do you?" he shouted back through his laughter.

*Don't think. Just do.* I pushed aside the concern for my purse and our food. I forgot about worrying that I might trip over tree roots or get smacked by a branch in the face. Soon, I only worried about keeping pace with the tall man ahead of me. I had no idea where we were going...and for some reason I didn't feel compelled to ask as 109

I placed one foot in front of the other and willed my legs to fly. I dodged roots and trunks in our path. The mirth rose from my stomach and into my throat, eclipsing the exhaustion that had overtaken me only moments before.

I smelled the lake before I saw it…as though the hedonistic run through the forest had heightened my instincts. Tom curved the trajectory of our sprint in the direction of the lake's center and grabbed my hand once more as we approached it.

"I'm not just going to run into it!" I yelled in dismay as I tried to slow down.

"Oh yes, you bloody well are!" He yelled a nonsense word I didn't understand as he plowed ahead into the murky lake water.

"*Ahhhhh!*" I screeched as I closed my eyes and followed after him. The shock of the cool water drowned my scream as it mixed in with our laughter.

"Bollocks, it's cold!" he yelled.

"What you said!" I shouted back.

He pulled me to him and placed his bare arms around my torso as he waded into even deeper water. My feet no longer found footing, and only our heads remained above water.

"There better not be leeches or weird blood-sucking creatures near the bottom of this lake," I warned as I brushed my water-soaked hair out of my face. He chuckled as he slid his palms down my thighs to lift and wrap my legs around his waist.

"I'm saving you from the leeches," he explained as I arched my left eyebrow at the suggestive stance he had just created by intertwining my limbs across his back. "But…I can't in good conscience save you from myself."

I fixed a gaze of acid-laced humor on him, and then a delayed burst of mirth escaped my lips.

"What's funny?" he asked with amusement.

"This is so cheesy. It's reminding me of that scene in 'Dirty Dancing'…I heard once that every girl deserves at least one 'Dirty Dancing' moment. I guess this is mine."

"I don't think I've seen that movie," he stated.

"Loser! What kind of man doesn't watch Patrick Swayze save Baby from being put in the corner?"

"What the hell are you talking about?" he teased.

"I guess you're just going to have to see it."

"I guess so," he replied as he ran the tip of his nose along my
110   forehead.

"You're not trying to take advantage of this situation, are you?" I sighed as I felt his hands move from my waist to rub seductively on my lower back.

"I most certainly... *am*," he jibed.

I crossed my arms behind his neck and leaned forward to take his lower lip into my mouth with a smile of jest. He dragged me against his bare chest with a quiet rumble of laughter and kissed me back unabashedly. His hands moved under the hem of my shirt and began a tentative exploration upward. My heart took off at a crazed pace as warmth collected in my stomach and stunned me with its force. I positioned my fingers to grasp the tight muscles of his forearm as our embrace grew increasingly more inappropriate. His body did not have the hugely protruding musculature that I thought was requisite of a Hollywood actor... rather, it was completely devoid of fat and had sinewy muscles that showed their definition in movement—so incredibly sexy.

"Mommy!" A child's voice punctuated the tree-lined edge of the lake behind us.

"Shit," Tom muttered as we broke our embrace.

"Good Lord! This is a family camping ground! Take it someplace private!" A highly irritated female came into view as she gesticulated wildly for us to leave.

"I'm sorry!" I gasped back as shame washed over me. Tom had already turned back towards the embankment and tugged at my arm as he tried to keep himself from laughing out loud.

"It's not funny!" I stage-whispered back at him. In truth, I was trying really hard to ignore my own mirth.

"Whatever you say," he retorted through his pained attempts to stave off his amusement.

We walked leisurely back to the "campsite" in spite of the fact my heretofore- immaculate tennis shoes were soaked and covered with mud that sloshed in my socks with each step.

"My shoes are ruined," I lamented as we arrived back at our shiteous shelter.

He shrugged. "We'll get you some new ones. Frankly, I think our shoes are a small price to pay for that memory."

I couldn't help the quick smile that brightened my face.

We changed, wrapped ourselves in our sleeping bags, and placed our wet clothes on tree branches to dry. Utilizing the combined efforts of the two most pathetic excuses for campers the woods of North Carolina had ever seen, we managed to start a fire and skewer 111 some hot dogs for dinner.

After we ate, Tom pulled out his guitar and strummed chords listlessly. His face expressed he was deep in thought as he stared at the dwindling embers.

"Can we trade questions?" he asked and abruptly stopped playing.

"What?" I replied, startled out of my own reverie.

"You can ask me any question, and if I choose to answer it, I have the right to ask you a question in return."

"Why do we need a game to do that?" I queried.

He narrowed his grey eyes at me in consideration. "It's too easy to avoid difficult topics in regular conversation."

I sighed knowingly. "Do I get to start?"

"Yes."

I thought for a moment. "Have you ever been in love?"

"Yes. The first girl I ever dated. I was sixteen. We were together for almost a year, and we broke it off because we grew out of it. I thought I was in love with another girl about two years ago, but I think it was more infatuation than anything else."

I nodded. He was being forthright, and I was certain he expected nothing less from me. I had to admit that my curiosity had been the driving force behind my acquiescence to this exercise. Deep down, I knew nothing good could come out of delving too deeply into the past.

"What made you cry that night in my room?"

*Ugh. Ugh. Ugh.* I knew it. I would be dying of curiosity, too. He had never once brought up the incident, and it must have been really hard for him to let it go for this long.

"Well, you don't mess around, do you?" I said nervously.

He waited patiently with his arms linked around the guitar.

"Sometimes, er . . . I have nightmares about the night Ryan left me," I stated with biting simplicity. I really hoped he wouldn't ask me for details I couldn't vocalize.

His gaze hardened. "I thought as much. At first, I wondered if it had anything to do with your father, but nightmares don't usually come from things we're at peace with, and you've always had open dialogue with me about your father."

I stared down at the ground for a moment while I dragged a twig through the dirt. Was my answer sufficient?

"Your turn," he murmured. *Thank you.*

I glanced up at the handsome movie star next to me. His tousled hair fell into his face, and the light from the fire made the flecks of green and gold in his eyes even more noticeable. I had a question I'd been dying to ask him for several months, but it was a question an insecure person would ask … oh well, he was going for blood, so I might as well get this answer while I had the chance.

"How many girls have you slept with?"

He couldn't stop himself from smiling as he glanced down into the fire. "I guess I brought that one on myself." He paused momentarily.

"I've slept with six women. Two of them are the women I mentioned earlier … one was from a drunken night in London where loneliness overcame me. It wasn't a one-night stand, and I tried to make it work afterwards, but it was mostly out of a sense of guilt. I've found that relationships created from guilt are rarely destined to work out well. Another woman was someone I dated for about six months, but she moved away and wasn't interested in long distance. I'm particularly embarrassed about the last two. In a nutshell, I had sex with them to see if I could. One was this rich party girl in L.A.—a regular fixture at the clubs. Anyway, she threw herself at me and told me she wanted to have sex … so one night I did it. I kept telling myself that this was what I was supposed to do. Young Hollywood. How boorish, eh? I was terrified afterwards that she would want more, but that appeared to be it. I guess she just wanted to see what it was like or something … then I was scared shitless that she would start spreading rumors about me. 'Tom Abramson's a lousy lay' or some shite like that. The other girl was actually someone I was attracted to in L.A., but she just wanted to have a good time. I was pretty uncomfortable with that experience as well."

"God, you're honest," I murmured.

"There's no reason to lie … Do you think about him often?" The piercing way his eyes bored into mine showed me that this question meant a lot to him … a lot more than his seeming nonchalance indicated.

I shifted uncomfortably in my space. "Yes," I whispered before taking a slow breath. "Mostly because it's impossible not to. He was so much a part of my life, and everywhere I go there are memories. Usually when I think of him, it's because I feel bitter … bitter that he got away so easily, so unscathed. I never contacted him after that night, and I just … I just don't understand why he did that to me. I don't know what I did that drove him to treat me like that. When I'm left to think about it, I can't help but feel bitter." I paused a moment. 113

"Does this bother you?" I asked carefully.

Now I watched as he warred with himself. "Yes, it does."

I waited while he searched for the right words.

"When I first met you, you were so...guarded. I knew it was because you'd been hurt before. I thought I would just wait for you to tell me what happened. I'm not sure why it bothers me so much, but I swear if I saw the wanker, I'd be really conflicted as to whether or not I'd thrash him or shake his hand in thanks. After all, if he hadn't treated you so abominably, we wouldn't be here."

He took a deep breath, and for a moment I saw a much younger boy sitting next to me—a boy anxious about something. "Would you take him back?" He was extremely careful not to show emotion in the words he spoke, and his effort belied his objective. In that instant, I realized something that frightened me almost as much as it astounded me: Thomas Abramson cared deeply enough to be afraid of losing me.

I shuffled closer to him in my sleeping bag.

"No," I said without hesitation. "I would never take back a man who cheated on me. I can't love freely without trust. It might be a weakness on my part, but it's who I am...so take note," I stated with a small smile as I rested my cheek on his shoulder.

"Noted," he replied as he kissed the top of my head affectionately.

He strummed his guitar again, then proceeded to launch into a mellow version of the song *Use Somebody* by Kings of Leon. He was a very talented guitarist, and I watched as he settled himself to play in earnest. His voice was raspy, and he was honestly a more gifted player than he was a vocalist, but the passion conveyed in his performance negated any discrepancy in skill. This man loved music, and it only made him even more attractive to me. As he sang the last line of the song, he immediately shifted his technique from strumming to fingerpicking. As he played the first few notes of the next song, I sat up in surprise.

"Explosions in the Sky?" I stated incredulously.

"You know this band?" He was impressed.

"Know this band? I love this band."

He continued playing the melodic line of *Your Hand in Mine*, and I wrapped my arms around my knees inside of the sleeping bag. No matter how cheesy I would have judged this scenario to be as an outsider, I could not deny that there was a deep-rooted sense of peace pervading the space around us as Tom played his guitar by the fire and the stars lit the night sky above our heads. The glowing embers from the waning flames still managed to pop and fizz intermittently.

"This is nice," I said softly.

"It is."

One of the things that I loved about being around those closest to me was the ability to sit in complete stillness with them and not feel an irresistible urge to fill the void with conversation. There was a closeness in comfortable silence that even the most carefully chosen words failed to enhance.

When the last few notes resonated into the night air, Tom moved to the tent to put the guitar away in its case. I stood up to stretch and then began to collect the remnants of our meal so we wouldn't attract the attention of any animals in the area. I was holding a plastic bag full of garbage when...

"OH BUGGER!" Tom came crashing out of the tent with a look of horrified shock on his face.

"What?" I demanded.

"There's...a SNAKE in the tent! It slithered across my bloody foot!"

"*AHHHHH!*" I screamed as I proceeded to jump backwards in terror. "There are SNAKES here?" I yelled.

As he managed to regain control of himself, I wasn't too surprised by his next outburst...of laughter.

"You're totally going to take the mickey out of me for that one, aren't you?"

"If you mean mock you endlessly, then yes, but first we need to figure out what we're going to do...because I'm sure as hell not sleeping in that tent with a snake in it," I managed to bite back.

"You think *I'm* going to sleep in there?"

"Get rid of it!" I gasped.

"You get rid of it! Prior snarky comment regarding Leicester Square ring a bell?" He was still chuckling uncontrollably.

Fifteen minutes later, we were sleeping on top of each other in the backseat of the Jeep, covered up in our sleeping bags.

"Well, this didn't go exactly as I planned," Tom said with mirth.

"Whatever made you think that?" I teased.

"I was hoping to get some action tonight, but seeing as how I can barely stretch out in the backseat of this car comfortably, I'm assuming that's not going to happen."

I shoved his shoulder. "Between that, the snake, and me smelling like old lake water, it's a pretty safe assumption...but you're welcome to give it a try. I figure once you hit your head on the roof of the car in a moment of passion, some sense will be knocked into you."

"Promise me something," he said with a smile.

"What?"

"Let's never go camping again," he murmured as he pulled me even closer.

"Amen, brother. Amen."

# THIRTEEN

The second flight to LA was decidedly more stressful than the first. In retrospect, I can't place *all* of the blame on Hana. We were both uber-paranoid about this particular kind of problem. After all, a man had cheated on me once before with far fewer temptations dangling in his midst.

As I waited to board the plane at ten o'clock that Friday morning, I received a phone call from my best friend.

"Cris?" By the sound of her voice, something bothered her a great deal.

"What's wrong?"

"Uh, look . . . I really struggled with whether or not to call you about this, and I might be completely out of line, but—" She hesitated.

"They're getting ready to board, babe. Just say it."

"Naz doesn't want me to tell you because he thinks it's ridiculous, but has Tom ever mentioned someone named Jenna Morrow?" she asked.

"Are you talking about the actress? They're filming a movie together right now," I responded patiently.

"Yeah. Well, there are pictures on the web of him with her at some party this past weekend. She's—she's all over him . . . and it looks like he doesn't mind one bit."

I was silent.

"Cris? I mean, it's probably nothing . . . but three days ago there were also pictures of him hanging out with that heiress girl, Brooklyn Beresford."

"The reality TV chick? The one who argued that Africa was a country, not a continent?" I sneered pejoratively.

"Uh, yeah . . . all these sites are clamoring to suggest that Tom Abramson is 'sowing his oats,' and he's enjoying his newfound fame in the arms of California girls. There's a paparazzi picture of 'Tom-Tom,' as they call him, allegedly leaving Jenna Morrow's house later that same night—around three o'clock in the morning. An unnamed source says they're seeing one another."

"Unnamed source, my ass. Some idiots are just trying to drive traffic to their site," I spat.

"You're probably right. You're not mad at me, right?"

"Of course not," I stated in a much kinder tone. "Don't worry about it. I'm sure it's nothing."

"Definitely. I just thought I should tell you before you got to L.A. I didn't want there to be any nasty surprises."

I knew exactly what she meant. For the first time in many months, I could feel that strange tearing sensation in my heart again.

"Thanks, Hana. Love you," I murmured.

"Love you too."

For the next five hours, the left side of my brain fought the right side with unceasing vigor.

Of course the "spin doctors" would try to attach an attractive actor like Tom with someone equally fascinating. It was nothing to be surprised about. If Tom fails to give them enough media fodder to suggest that his love life is red-hot and full of sin, the next step would be to challenge his sexuality.

But... Why was he at Jenna Morrow's house in the middle of the night? *Why didn't he tell you about it?* Was Jenna one of the girls he mentioned by the fire last month? *You never asked him any of their names. Oh, God...*

*He's not cheating on you.*

*You shouldn't have waited this long to have sex with him.*

*Come on, Tom's not just in it for the sex. He's not that kind of guy.*

*Didn't Brooklyn Beresford have a sex tape?*

*It's not a big deal... just a few stupid pictures.*

*Pictures don't lie.*

Back and forth. Back and forth. The angel and the devil continued their war.

*He's an actor... you're nobody special.*

*Tom is not Ryan.*

A jolt of adrenaline shot through me as I considered the last, and most resonating, thought.

*Tom is not Ryan, and you shouldn't believe Tom would do something that repugnant just because Ryan did.*

I tried to focus on that for the remainder of the flight and the subsequent taxi ride to Tom's apartment.

I was just so... afraid, and I hated Ryan even more for making me this frightened of a few wayward photographs taken by people trained to make something out of nothing.

I punched in the security code to get into the apartment building and hauled my suitcase into the elevator. My reflection stared back at me in the mirrored doors, troubled and uncertain. I tried to quell these feelings as the elevator opened onto Tom's floor. He was too observant, and he would definitely notice something was wrong if I didn't do a better job of concealing it within the next few seconds.

The apartment door opened soon after I tapped tentatively on its surface. I plastered a smile on my face and walked inside, actively trying to conceal my mental siege. Tom yanked me into an embrace and pressed his lips to mine with breathtaking effect. I kissed him back as though I were trying to banish any trace of another woman's touch from his memory—which is, all things considered, nothing more than an emotionally destructive form of branding. Desperation, thy name is Jealous Female.

He pulled away from me to catch his breath, and his eyebrows furrowed in puzzlement as he stared carefully down at my face.

I averted my gaze and strode further into the living room.

"What's the plan?" I asked cheerfully as I gazed at nothing.

"Look at me."

I took a deep breath and spun around to smile at him with forced merriment.

"Awful," he sighed. "Just awful."

"What's awful?" My voice sounded shrill and manufactured.

"I think I should be asking you that question," he said as he looped his arms across his chest and waited. I stared back at him in complete silence. There was no way on earth he would force me to admit how scared I was of "TomTom" and his California girls.

"What happened between last night and today to prompt that ghastly performance?" he demanded quietly.

"Nothing." I cut my eyes and wordlessly asked him to leave it alone.

He walked over to me in two strides and grasped my chin between his thumb and index finger so he could tilt my head upwards and peer unobstructed into my face.

"Don't play these silly games with me, Cristina. You're far too self-assured for this. If you want me to beg you for the next hour to tell me what I did wrong, we can do that, but either way I'll find out. Save us the time and just tell me so I can start to make it right."

My heart jerked to a sudden stop as I gazed earnestly into his grey eyes. They were filled with an intense concern that leveled me. In that instant, I realized something even more terrifying than the news Hana had divulged to me hours before. I looked away as awareness washed over me.

I knew I was finished. My struggle was done. Every effort I had made to prevent myself from having to undergo further heartache in my life was now immaterial. I was in love with Tom Abramson. There was no way to deny it to myself any longer.

A revelatory moment that should have brought pure joy instead brought with it unadulterated fear. If I loved him, he could hurt me. Irrevocably. I couldn't take it. Not again.

"Jenna Morrow," I choked out pitifully as I forced myself to look up at him.

His shoulders sagged a bit, but his face relaxed considerably as his mouth curved into a wry half-smile.

"You were looking at the net again. I warned you about that," he said sardonically.

"Look, I hate myself for this, but if I don't ask you…it will just get worse. I'm ill-equipped, shall we say, to deal with this shit again," I whispered.

"I understand," he responded.

"I just need to know: what were you doing at her house in the middle of the night?"

"Firstly, Jenna is a really sweet girl, and I don't want you to be mad at her for any of this. Her boyfriend broke up with her that night, and she had a lot to drink. She just needed a friend, and I wanted to make sure she got home safely. The same morons who said I left her house in the middle of the night also knew I was there for no longer than fifteen minutes, but that information isn't racy enough, so they neglected to report it." He waited patiently for me to digest the facts.

My cheeks started to flush as I absorbed the foolishness of the situation in its entirety, but I still needed a moment to come to terms with the fact my fears were unfounded. "Those who cannot remember the past are condemned to repeat it."

"Not good enough?"

"I guess you were too much of a gentleman to tell her to take her drunken paws off of you. I just need a minute to banish the image of what I was planning to do with her angelic blonde hair if I got my hands on it," I mused acerbically.

He pulled me into his chest, and I felt a rumble of laughter against my cheek. "Don't hurt her. The poor girl's been through hell this week."

"I'm sorry," I said in a muffled tone as I buried my face against him.

"Don't be. It's a little ridiculous that everyone thinks I'm shagging every girl I talk to...if only I could be that lucky," he joked.

"Hah!"

"At least you didn't mention the blurb about that reality star, Brooklyn Beresford. I like it when women know basic geography... it's sort of a small pre-requisite," he continued.

"God, you're picky. If basic geography is a pre-requisite, I think I should know the proper way to refer to your country on a map. England? Great Britain? The United Kingdom? I have a suggestion: How about 'Island of Scones and Bangers'?"

"I like it...since you've already taken 'Island of Twice-Fried Fatback.' "

I laughed loudly as he leaned in to place a kiss on my forehead. "I still don't know why you're single, Abramson. You're a riot," I teased back at him.

"Just so you know, I'm not actually single, and maybe it's time the public knew that."

"Because that would be such a good idea," I stated dryly. I could not help the smile that made its way onto my face to hear he no longer considered himself single.

"Eventually they have to find out...why not now?"

"Want me to hold a press conference?" I said with bright sarcasm.

He didn't respond. Instead, he merely grinned knowingly before glancing at his watch.

"Are you supposed to be someplace?" I asked.

"*You're* supposed to be someplace after lunch. Let's get something to eat, and then I'll take you there."

"What's going on?" Suspicion laced my words.

"You know better than to ask, but I'm taking you out tonight, and I forgot to tell you to bring something to wear, so we need to take care of that."

"I brought a dress," I said carefully.

"Humor me...and that's all I intend to say on the subject." He ruffled my ponytail affectionately before turning towards the kitchen to find our trusty delivery menus.

After lunch, I followed Tom to his car, and he proceeded to drive us to the back entrance of a red brick building off a highly trafficked thoroughfare.

"Is this a dress shop, or am I being questioned by the police?" I 121 asked in confusion as he held open the door to a small flight of stairs we climbed.

"You'll see," he said with mirth.

At the top of the stairs, Tom swung open another door to a brightly lit room with scuffed hardwood floors.

"You're late." The testy, accented voice of Esteban Alvarez rang from the opposite end of the space. Tom merely shrugged glibly in response.

Racks of clothes spanned the perimeter of the room, and Esteban was next to a large mirror with makeup and other styling products strewn about him. Another individual patiently stood and waited while studying me with an unabashed gaze of curiosity.

"Dude, I know you didn't like my clothes last time, but I didn't come here to be a contestant on 'What Not to Wear,' " I stated firmly to Esteban.

He rolled his eyes. "*¡Callá y vení, monstruito!*" How nice... *Shut up and come here, you little monster.*

"Someone needs to tell me what's going on," I demanded.

"Do me a favor and trust me," Tom replied with a smile.

"And do *me* a fucking favor and just obey for the next three hours." Esteban motioned for me to hurry the hell up. "I don't have time to deal with your emotional issues *and* your appearance at the same time."

I took a deep breath, shot Tom a look of frustration, and marched to Esteban's side to "obey" with Tom closely in tow.

"There are a couple of things I need to take care of for tonight. Do you mind if I run out for a bit?" Tom asked as he rubbed my shoulders soothingly.

"Thanks for asking this time, Thomas," I said with snide irritation. It really did drive me bonkers that he wasn't the consultative type. He was really trying to drive home the point that I couldn't control my life so implicitly. One of these days I would let him have it.

He grinned at me and leaned down to plant a lingering kiss on my neck. Esteban's eyebrows shot up at Tom's open display of affection.

After Tom left, Esteban yanked my hair out of its ponytail unceremoniously with little concern for my resounding "Ow!"

"Look at this hair." He groaned and ran his fingers through my wantonly misbehaving waves. "It will never stay put for an entire night!"

"Tell me about it," I agreed.

"We could just put it up, like this." The other man wrapped his fingers in my hair skillfully to wind it into an intricate twist. "By the way, my name is J.D."

"Hi J.D. I'm Cris." I reached over to shake his hand.

"I know... I've heard a ton about you. He's so incredibly into you," J.D. gushed with enthusiasm.

I blushed in response.

"Oh, how adorable. Looks like you're really into him too. Oh my God, Esteban. Did you see how he kissed her? Completely in love," J.D. continued.

"*¡Callá, por favor!* Focus!" Esteban yelled as he fidgeted with my hair and prodded at my face studiously.

"Ugh, can I at least find out what I'm wearing?" I asked with imploring eyes.

Esteban opened his mouth with the clear intention of refusal before J.D. shot him a look.

"Fine," Esteban groaned as J.D. blurred into the next room excitedly.

A moment later, he rushed back to our sides. I turned as he held a dress out with gusto.

"Isn't it gorgeous? Tom picked it out himself. The man has terrible taste when it comes to his own clothes, but this is impeccable. You can't go wrong with *Marchesa,*" J.D. pronounced.

I honestly had no words. The dress was gorgeous: strapless with layers upon layers of tissue-thin, bright turquoise fabric draped from a gathering at the bust line into an elegant flare that pooled spectacularly on the floor. The sweetheart neckline had a row of intricate crystal work woven between threads of silver and gold that reminded me of Indian embroidery. It was the most beautiful dresses I had ever seen.

"Where is he taking me?" I whispered in undisguised horror.

"Someplace nice; so we need to get to work, if you don't mind," Esteban retorted with finality.

For the next two and a half hours, Esteban and J.D. argued as they nitpicked over the slightest details. With deft hands and Esteban's artful direction, J.D. swept makeup onto my skin and tortured my hair into the elegant up-do he had envisioned when he first saw me. They slid my feet into strappy, gold heels by Rene Caovilla and placed thin gold and silver bangles on my left wrist.

"Thomas left these for you." Esteban handed me a small velvet box.

I opened it to find teardrop-shaped, blue sapphire earrings encrusted with pavé diamonds. The color of the sapphires matched the dress with thoughtful intention.

"He didn't buy these, did he?" I stated in a near-whisper.

J.D. handed me a small index card. "Of course. Esteban forgot to give this to you." He rolled his eyes at Esteban.

It was a simple, hand-written message:

*I hope this gift helps you forgive me for what I've done ... and what I'm about to do.*

*Tom*

"Jesus Christ. These are huge!" I muttered in awe as I held them up to the light.

"Give them to me, sweetie," J.D. said and plucked the box from my hand.

After he carefully looped the earrings through my earlobes, J.D. and Esteban took a step back to admire their handiwork.

"I think I see it now," Esteban announced with the first smile I had seen on his face all afternoon.

"See what?" I asked.

"Why he thinks you're so beautiful."

J.D.'s grin was enormous as he led me to the full-length mirror hanging on the wall at the end of the room.

I looked at my reflection and felt my knees begin to shake under the layers of silk and organza. With each tremor, the dress rippled elegantly as though the fabric were made from the waters of the Caribbean. My mahogany hair was piled onto my head in a manner that accentuated the line of my neck and highlighted my tanned collarbone. The earrings flashed with wild abandon at the slightest movement.

I saw the door to the room open as Tom breezed in looking sinfully handsome in a tuxedo and a thin black necktie. When he saw me, he stopped short and stared at my reflection. His eyes roved carefully from the floor to my face as he took everything in with the discerned eye of an artist. A flush crept into my skin at the appreciative smile that spread onto his aristocratic visage and made the corners of his eyes crinkle in an absurdly cute way.

"Absolutely breathtaking," he murmured into the silence.

"I'm forced to agree," Esteban said.

"Honey, you look perfect," J.D. crowed.

I turned to face Tom. He moved forward and took my hand. "Let's go," he said with a half-smile.

He held my hand as I gingerly walked down the stairs and outside to an idling stretch limousine.

I stopped momentarily to narrow my eyes at Tom before I stepped into the limo.

"If you didn't look so annoyingly sexy in that tux, I would definitely refuse to get in until you told me where we were going. There's something about a man in a tux—I think it makes me stupid," I announced as I settled into my seat.

He grinned. "You look really beautiful. Honestly, I always think you look great, but that color is stunning on you."

"I heard you picked it out, so you should really congratulate yourself. By the way, remind me to yell at you later for spending so much money on these earrings. I've never seen jewelry like this up close, let alone owned anything like it. Thank you." I leaned forward to kiss him with careful remembrance of the painstaking efforts needed to make me look like a princess. Esteban would kill me if I messed up my makeup.

"I'm afraid to touch you," Tom joked as he nuzzled my nose with his and chuckled under his breath.

"You'd better not. I might start melting like the Wicked Witch of the West…and Esteban will have words for you later."

"To be sure." He toyed with the bangles on my arm in a nervous fashion that heightened my suspicions.

"So, are we going to prom? If so, I don't have a boutonniere for you."

"No, we're not going to prom," he answered carefully.

"I hope we didn't get this dressed up for takeout!" I was pushing him, but my curiosity was nearly at its breaking point.

"Not exactly … although we probably will need to eat again later," he mused.

"Please, just tell me where we're going!"

"Give me five more minutes, and I'll tell you. I promise."

The minutes ticked slowly by as the limousine made its careful progression down the streets of L.A. The limo slowed as it encountered what I believed to be traffic congestion ahead, and we inched towards the far right lane.

"So…I'm taking you to a party," Tom stated plainly.

I took that in for a moment. "What kind of party?"

"The kind I have to go to. I really don't have a choice. I considered skiving the entire thing, but Melissa would kill me if I didn't go."

"Is the host a friend of hers?" I asked.

"Not exactly."

The limo stopped by the sidewalk, and Tom moved towards the door.

"Whose party is this?" I demanded quickly.

The car door swung open...

...and camera bulbs flashed maniacally.

"Vogue."

Tom stepped out of the limo, and a general uproar sounded as the masses struggled to get a glimpse and a picture of my movie star boyfriend.

"Thomas! Thomas! Look here!" The shouting fervor grew in pitch.

He reached back into the limo with his hand outstretched for me.

I was frozen in horror.

"I...I can't," I stammered.

"Kill me later. You look beautiful."

I took his hand, and he grasped it tightly in his as he directed me onto the red carpet and into a sea of flashing bulbs. The waiting vultures clamored over one another to see me. I wanted to shrink back into the shadowy depths of the limo, but Tom held tightly onto my hand and smiled at them forcefully. Even though he appeared a great deal more comfortable than I felt, I still detected a trace amount of awkwardness in his stance and attitude. He looked the part but still didn't fit in.

"Who is she, Thomas?" A photographer yelled as the cameras flashed with even more vigor. The media started to digest the fact that Thomas Abramson brought a date.

"Who are you? Are you dating each other? Is that your girlfriend? What about Jenna? Thomas!" Variations of these statements rang out around us as we made our way down the red carpet. Movie crews followed our movements watchfully. Movie cameras? Oh God! I could feel my knees shake even more tremulously from underneath my *Marchesa* dress.

Before I collapsed into a heap of pitiful shock on the ground, I did a quick mental pep talk.

*Cristina, pull yourself together. They're just taking pictures. If you think it's bad now, imagine how crappy you'll feel when you see photos of yourself look-*

126

*ing like a stunned ferret in a dress that probably costs more than you make in a month. Throw your shoulders back, stand proud, and smile at these morons like your life depends on it.*

I tightened my calf muscles to control the shaking in my legs, took a deep breath, and lifted my chin to stare like an automaton in whatever direction Tom faced. He squeezed my hand again he pulled me down the seemingly endless stretch of red that led to the party's entrance.

A blitz of photographers captured every movement we made. Tom stopped to pause for a moment and put his arm around my waist as though he wanted to confirm their every suspicion. To take it a step further, he leaned in and planted a very deliberate kiss on my cheek. Flashes flickered responsively with blinding effect. I smiled like an idiot so I wouldn't lose my shit in front of a press army waiting to document my every faux pas with gleeful pleasure.

"What's your name, mamacita?" a particularly smarmy looking *gringo* shouted above the din. I narrowed my eyes a bit but forced myself not to react to the new onslaught of attention his outburst directed at me.

Blessedly, we managed to arrive at the party's entrance in one piece.

Or maybe not. Melissa Nash stood at the door with a glare of hatred that made me lose hold of my tenuous grasp on confidence, especially considering my slaphappy introduction into the world of celebrity. Tom was a dead man.

As soon as we made it through the front door, Melissa leaned into us and demanded in a harsh whisper, "What are you doing, Thomas?"

"I'm at the Vogue party, like you asked," he said nonchalantly. His eyes tightened minutely in response to her accusatory tone.

"I thought we talked about this...situation."

"You talked. I listened. I'd rather not try to hide my girlfriend anymore," he stated firmly.

She exhaled in a protracted huff. "We'll talk about this nightmare later."

Great...she thought I was a nightmare. Excellent.

I proceeded to follow Tom around the party like an idiot with only one friend in the world for most of the evening. Unfortunately, my "one friend" was in a hell of a lot of trouble once we returned to his apartment. I was completely out of place amidst the panoply of couture and diamonds. The glitterati mingled and praised one 127 another for their respective awesomeness. It felt as though they all knew I was merely playing dress-up, like the infamous scene in *My Fair Lady* where Eliza goes to the horse races decked out in her finest but couldn't escape the glaring truth of her humble origins. Hey, at least Eliza knew what she was getting herself into prior to showing up.

To make matters worse, Melissa continually snatched Tom away to speak with this producer or that director, and he tried to forcibly drag me with him so I wouldn't be left alone.

"It's okay, Tom," I insisted when Melissa shot me a particularly hate-filled look about two hours into the party.

"No. Just come with me," he insisted as he raked his fingers through his hair in a gesture I associated with frustration.

"I'm fine. Go do your thing. Network. I'll wait right here."

I stood by the table next to rows of Veuve Cliquot and distractedly observed the crowd while trying to quash my growing feelings of hurt at being placed unwittingly into an incredibly stressful situation.

In my periphery, I saw a slender woman with dark hair move to stand a few feet from me.

"*J'ai faim. Pourquoi les Américains n'ont-ils pas de nourriture à une fête?*" she exclaimed to herself under her breath.

"*Je ne sais pas, mais j'ai faim aussi,*" I responded automatically.

She turned to me in surprise, and I stared back at her, dumbfounded. She was my favorite French actress!

"Uh…uh…" I began in a panic.

"You speak French?" she asked with a smile.

"Ye-yes," I stammered back at her.

"You don't look French."

"I'm not. I majored in French. I'm originally from Puerto Rico," I blurted out awkwardly.

"Do you work for one of the studios?" she asked in rapid French.

I rotated my shoulders to release the tension before I responded in her native tongue. "No, I'm actually here with a…friend."

"A friend? I think you must mean your boyfriend," she said with a teasing smirk.

I grinned back at her. "*Peut-être.*" If I don't kill him later.

"Your dress is marvelous. I saw it on the runway in Milan not long ago. That color is a bit too much for my skin, but it looks lovely on you," she stated.

"Thank you! I hate to sound like a silly fan, but you're an amazing actress. La Môme Piaf is one of my favorite performers, and I thought you did a beautiful job portraying her." I tried not to gush too overtly as I spoke.

"Thank you so much."

We continued speaking animatedly to one another, and soon the conversation slipped into casual comfort. She was so charming and witty I almost forgot who she was and where we were. The minutes passed much quicker in her sharp-tongued company, and I was grateful to have someone to talk to. Before I realized I had been monopolizing her time, a gentleman I didn't recognize came over to speak with her.

"It was so nice to meet you, Cris," she remarked as she leaned in to kiss both of my cheeks fondly.

"Thanks! It was great meeting you, too!" I just stood there like a star-struck idiot while she danced into a circle of elegantly attired people nearby.

I still grinned foolishly to myself when Tom approached me with an apologetic look on his face.

"I'm so sorry. I had no idea I would be gone that long, but from the looks of it, you didn't seem to notice. I knew you'd have a good time. Have I been replaced with someone richer and better looking? Is it Brad Pitt or Zac Efron?" he joked.

I narrowed my eyes at him.

"That mad? I promise to let you thrash me later, but I couldn't bear the thought of leaving you home alone while I came to this thing. I'm a selfish ass. I hope you forgive me," he stated in a blithe manner that led me to believe he was significantly less sorry for this transgression than he should be . . . would be.

I sighed quietly.

"Do you want to go?" he asked. "We don't have to stay much longer."

"Do what you need to do, Thomas. Melissa already hates me enough," I bit back grimly.

He furrowed his brow in concern. "You're really mad, aren't you?" It was a statement, not a question.

"We don't need to talk about this here. Please. It can wait. I don't want to be the cause of any more problems. Handle your business properly, and then we can go."

He exhaled through his nose with grim acceptance and proceeded to take hold of my hand purposefully.

"I won't leave you alone again. I promise," he muttered.

129

Half an hour later, we returned to the sanctuary of the limousine. He pressed my palm to his lips as the driver pulled into traffic to take us back to Tom's apartment.

"That's not going to save you."

He chuckled darkly. "I'm starting to believe you."

# FOURTEEN

In complete silence, we rode the elevator to Tom's floor and walked into the apartment. I slipped carefully out of my shoes and marched to the bathroom to remove the pins that had poked my scalp all evening. He stood in the doorway and watched me as he loosened the tie around his neck and unfastened the top few buttons on his white shirt. He sighed loudly as he tugged both hands through his hair in irritation.

"Cristina, I didn't do this because I wanted to piss you off," he began lamely.

I spun around to glare at his handsome face, brushed past him, and proceeded towards the kitchen to get a drink of water. He followed.

"Please, talk to me."

"Tom, if you didn't do this to piss me off, then please explain to me why you did this?"

He took a deep breath. "I didn't want to leave you alone here."

"I wouldn't have minded…and your argument about forgetting to tell me to bring something to wear is really the biggest bunch of bullshit I've heard in a while. You went to a lot of trouble to find a gorgeous dress for me, and I'm assuming you didn't just stop by the nearest jeweler and magically find earrings that matched it perfectly."

He waited patiently for me to continue.

"You obviously went through a lot to make sure I would go to this party with you. It would have been easier for you to tell me ahead of time and give me the choice of whether or not I wanted to go."

"You would have said no," he interrupted.

"Of course! *You* didn't even want to go to this party! What makes you think I would want to go?"

"I really wanted you to go," he said simply.

"So, you thought that the solution was to take away my choice? Normally, I don't mind too much when you negate the importance of my opinion by just asking that I go along with whatever you've planned. Tonight, you took it too far."

"I don't understand why you're so upset. I mean, I know that this was less than ideal, but you were amazing," he tried again.

"Amazing? I was terrified!" I shouted.

His mouth snapped shut in surprise. "Terrified?"

"Yes! I don't know any of those people! I don't fit in with them! I had one conversation tonight that didn't make me feel like a prize idiot! Even *you* looked uncomfortable there! Can you imagine if someone had dragged you to one of those parties for the very first time and neglected to tell you what to expect? Worse, imagine that they didn't even say where you were going?"

"Where did you think we were going in a tux and eveningwear, love?" he asked kindly.

"Don't patronize me, Thomas Abramson. Do you know what kind of shitstorm I'm in for tomorrow? You didn't even think it was necessary to consult me before you fed our relationship to the media wolves! I step into a limo thinking we're going to a fancy dinner or to see some show, and when I step out of it twenty minutes later, thousands of cameras are flashing in my face, and people I don't give a damn about are demanding to know my name."

He just stood there and stared blankly at me.

"How could you do this?" I wailed. "*Why* would you do this?"

"I was tired of hiding you from everyone."

"It's not just about you! I can't believe you would be this insensitive. Do you even care?" I yelled.

He cut his eyes and pursed his lips in the first gesture of anger I had seen in him all evening. "Now wait just a moment. I'm not going to listen to you say that I don't care."

"What about this situation shows that you care about my feelings or my opinions?" I demanded.

"Stop it, Cristina."

"No! You're just mad because you don't know what to say. You can't even answer my question about why you would do something like this because you don't know. It means that you never stopped to think about what it would mean for me…which then means, that you didn't care enough to consider it!" My anger consumed me as I ranted on thoughtlessly.

"I said, stop it!" he shouted. Irritation built up in him with each ill-advised word that passed my lips.

"Don't you dare tell me what to do! If you hate hearing me say that you don't care, then you'd better start acting like you do!" I bellowed as the angry tears welled.

That did it. Tom's eyes flashed furiously as he struggled to manage his temper. "You think I don't care? Are you really that mental?" he yelled back

"Mental? How dare you!" I raged as the tears streamed down my face.

"Do you even know what the fuck you're saying, or do you just like to hear yourself talk?" he demanded as his fury took over for one tense moment. Immediately afterward, I saw the dismay in his gaze as he realized what he had said and watched me cry in response.

"Don't you dare curse at me!" I choked pathetically.

He closed his eyes for a moment to regain control of himself. When he opened them again, he yanked me into a rough embrace.

"I'm so sorry. God, I'm a dick."

I was silent as I wrapped my arms around his torso, and he cradled my head in his hands.

"I'm sorry, Cris," he whispered into my hair.

"I know."

"I just—I can't deal with you thinking I may not care. It's like someone telling me I don't care about my family or something. I don't want to hear it. I guess I overreacted," he continued soothingly.

"You guess? I thought Brits were cool under fire." My voice was muffled against his chest.

"You're one to talk... you've got quite a temper," he said huskily.

"Pot, meet Kettle."

"Kettle, I'm truly sorry for being such an arse."

He placed each of his hands on either side of my face to direct my gaze towards his and smiled tentatively.

"I may not have a right to do this at the moment, but I want to ask you for a favor," he said as he brushed the hair out of my eyes.

"What do you want?"

"Promise me you won't say that rubbish again," he requested.

I stared up at him.

He inhaled carefully before proceeding. "I do care—very much. In fact... I'm in love with you."

I could feel my heart jump into my throat at his admittance. My mind was too filled with silly happiness to say anything. I merely smiled back at him as sweeter tears fell.

"Do you promise?" he whispered.

"I promise."

He pressed his lips to mine slowly... his touch was careful at first, but it quickly escalated in intensity as I tangled my fingers in his hair. His hands raked across my body, and our mouths locked 133 together as he lifted my short frame from the ground. He ambled back towards the bedroom, lowered me onto the bed, and his hand moved to the bottom of my dress to seductively slide from my ankle to hip. He rolled onto his back and pulled me on top of him. Electrified adrenaline coursed through my veins as I moved my mouth from his and brushed aside his tie to finish unbuttoning his shirt. I kissed his neck as I pulled the tie free and tossed it to the ground. He grabbed a handful of silk by my hip in an attempt to tug the hem of the dress upward.

"Thomas?" I breathed as I gazed down at him as my heart raced in anticipation.

His eyes were molten as they stared up at me with searing desire. "Yes?"

I Languorously dragged the tip of my tongue from the base of his neck upward to whisper in his ear, "I'm tired of just dreaming about you. Make love to me."

"Hell yes." His hands searched for the zipper of my dress as my fingers moved rapidly down the buttons of his shirt.

In mere moments, we had tugged free of our finery, and clothing worth thousands of dollars was strewn haphazardly across the floor. I was pretty certain Esteban would have a heart attack if he saw it.

"God, you're so beautiful," he said huskily as his eyes and palms sculpted across my skin. "Everything about you...."

I placed my hands on each of his wrists to momentarily interrupt his exploration. Slowly, I moved my fingers up his arms, across his chest, and past his neck to tangle in his hair. I grabbed his head roughly and pulled his face to mine.

"Are you going to recite poetry, or are you going to live it?" I demanded.

With a low chuckle, he wisely chose the latter.

Love is trust. Love is hope. Love is oblivion.

Inhaling with measured breaths, I attempted to control my pounding heart and the correlative tremble of my limbs. Each caress elicited its own unique set of responses. Each kiss took me further from reality. My ex had been a careful, deliberate lover. Everything was meticulously choreographed. Having no basis for comparison, I had relished in his consideration and tenderness for the four years of our relationship. By contrast, Tom was incredibly instinctual. Passionately unpredictable. Breathtaking.

Soon, the memories of my past burned to cinder in the blaze of my present.

If ecstasy could be adequately depicted in words...there would be little need for the imagination.

"You've officially missed...eighteen calls," I announced with glee as I looked at the screen of Tom's iPhone.

"And you've missed...seven calls." He tossed my cell back to the floor after a cursory glance.

"Ugh, I don't want to return to the real world," I groaned while pressing my face into the pillow dramatically.

"So don't. My bed will miss you if you do," he joked.

"It has been excellent company these last two days...and nights."

He grinned and gathered me into his arms again. Our behavior for the rest of the weekend following the Vogue party had been exhilarating...and slightly mortifying. We had not set foot outside the sanctuary of the apartment building, and I was embarrassed to admit I had failed to dress myself properly since donning Esteban and J.D.'s *Marchesa* masterpiece. Tom's T-shirts did not count as adequate attire.

"You realize I'm not giving this shirt back. It's way too comfortable. Plus, it smells like you," I proclaimed as I reached down to retrieve my weekend uniform from its resting place on the floor. Tom pulled me against his bare chest and trapped me in an embrace that made it impossible to move.

"I've always found it quite unfair how women can steal men's clothes, and we don't have the same luxury. Not that I envy you those string-in-the-arse panties. I still have no idea how the hell you wear those and manage to smile at the same time," he teased.

"You get used to it. Not that I'm a staunch supporter of the thong or anything. It's a necessary evil...like the government."

I attempted to sit up in bed so I could yank the shirt over my head, but Tom refused to relinquish his hold on me.

"I don't know where the hell you think you're going."

"I have to get ready! My stuff is all over the place, and I need to go to the airport in an hour!"

"Great. That gives us forty five minutes..."

"No!" I laughed as he rolled over onto me and tangled us amidst the jumble of sheets.

"That T-shirt is going to cost you...forty five minutes," he mur- 135 mured as he placed stupidity-inducing kisses on my neck and down my stomach.

"I'm not a hooker," I gasped back as his palms curved behind my back for leverage. I was losing…and he knew it.

"No one's calling you a hooker. I won't be the only one who profits from this," he spoke matter-of-factly as his hand moved behind my knee to angle my leg suggestively. His lips grazed tantalizingly above my midsection.

"When you put it that way…."

An hour later, I had managed to throw my stuff into my bag without pausing to organize any of it. My hair was a disaster, and I was worried that I looked like I hadn't left the bed all weekend (hah). But it was difficult for anything to mar our contentment as we rode down the elevator to Tom's car.

You can imagine my surprise when Tom's body tensed as we drove towards the security gate to exit the premises. As we rolled slowly past the sliding wrought iron, a small group of photographers aimed their large cameras at the vehicle.

"Have they been waiting there all this time?" I asked with dismay.

"Yes." His tone was begrudging.

"My God! Why?"

"Sometimes they get paid tens of thousands of dollars for just one picture of a celebrity. That kind of money is a big motivator," he stated grimly.

As we pulled up to the departure terminal at LAX, Tom grumbled an undecipherable string of expletives when he glanced in the rearview mirror.

"They followed us," he intoned after he completed his sotto voce rant.

Sure enough, two vehicles halted immediately behind us, and car doors swung open as shutters clicked simultaneously.

He half-smiled in a bemused fashion at me.

"I had a really good time…minus the fight and the party," I said softly.

"I had a really good time, *including* the fight and the party. You're quite sexy when you're mad," he mocked affectionately as he reached over to run his right hand through my hair.

"Just when I'm mad? That sucks. I think you're always sexy ... well, most of the time."

He laughed and leaned over to place a tender kiss on my forehead. I tilted my head upward and pressed my lips to the underside of his jaw before his mouth met mine in a lingering caress. For a moment, I completely forgot about everything else around me.

The noise from the photographers outside distracted us.

"Bollocks," he muttered as he pulled away.

"I'd better go," I whispered.

He unbuckled his seatbelt.

"You don't need to come with me," I said quickly.

"Yes, I do. Keep your head down, and try not to respond to anything they say to you."

I wrapped my fingers around the door handle and took a deep breath.

"Cris?"

I turned my head towards Tom. "Yes?"

"I love you." He opened his door and stepped out into the sunlight.

"Thomas! Look here! ... Cristina!" Oh my God, how had they figured out my name!?

Tom ignored them as he grabbed my luggage and wrapped his arm around me protectively. We walked towards the doors leading into the terminal.

"How long have you been dating? Come on! Thomas! Cristina!"

"Call me when you land," Tom whispered in my ear and released me just in front of the door. Everything had happened so hastily ... and he was gone before I had a chance to say anything in response.

I strode through the sliding glass and into the rush of hassled people with burgeoning suitcases in tow trying to make their way to a ticket kiosk or a gate.

Disoriented, I stood in place for a moment before I spun towards the nearby window to glance back at the curb. Tom was halfway to his car with the paparazzi crowding around him.

Yanking out my cell phone, I typed one word:

**Me (1:41 pm): Wait!**

He paused and pulled his cell out of his back pocket to check the message. He turned quickly and saw me through the clear pane. 137

Blocked ID (1:41 pm): ?

I smiled at him before responding.

Me (1:41 pm): I forgot to tell you
something.
Me (1:41 pm): I love you.

He checked the message and grinned back at me boyishly.

Blocked ID (1:42 pm): i know

# FIFTEEN

From: Lt. Ryan Sullivan <ryan.sullivan4@us.army.mil>
To: Cris Pereira <7crisp@gmail.com>
Date: Tues, July 28, 2009 at 9:42 AM
Subject: (no subject)

Cristina, I've left three messages on your voicemail and sent you several emails. It's not like you to act this way. I need you to call me back.

Since you don't seem to give a damn, I'll say my piece here.

I miss you. I love you.

Ryan

---

From: Lt. Ryan Sullivan <ryan.sullivan4@us.army.mil>
To: Cris Pereira <7crisp@gmail.com>
Date: Fri, Aug 21, 2009 at 4:54 PM
Subject: (no subject)

Since you still haven't returned any of my messages, I went to your office today—I got a pretty big surprise while there. Your boss said that you were in New York for a "movie premiere." Looks like you're having one heck of a rebound. Funny, I didn't expect you to go for a pretty boy. When you come down from that cloud and get serious, I really need to see you.

Again, I love you. I'm really sorry, and I miss you like hell.

Ryan

"We will begin boarding Flight 1732 to London Gatwick starting with our special needs passengers and those traveling with small children."

I hunched down in my seat and pulled the baseball cap lower onto my forehead as the crowd queuing by the gate shifted to allow the first passengers to board the flight. The desire to convey nondescript anonymity was behind each of my movements. Carefully, I picked up my purse and carry-on bag. As I stood in preparation to take a place in line, I saw a group of soldiers dressed in military fatigues walk past me towards their respective gate. The sight of their duffle bags and camouflage reignited a feeling of discomfort that had been growing in me for the last month—since the day I received the first of many messages from Ryan.

My curious side had been dying to know what he could possibly have to say after a year of trying to banish our time together from both his memory and reality. It was amazing that he still had the gall to contact me with anything sounding even remotely like a demand. Some people....

My practical side really didn't give a damn. Ryan had betrayed me. He had hurt me in one of the worst ways a lover could hurt another. It wasn't enough that he cheated and threw it in my face—he lied to all of us. He lied to my friends . . . my family. He promised my father he would love me as I deserved to be loved.

He wasn't worth the time it took to read those emails.

I had not responded to a single one of his messages, nor had I even listened to any of the voicemails. I simply deleted everything. If he could erase me from his life with such ease, then he certainly had no right to decide when and how he would reinstate my presence. What a selfish ass.

I considered telling Hana and Gita about his attempts to contact me, but quickly decided he didn't deserve even a moment more of our consideration. As a result, no one knew anything about it, and that was the way I hoped it would stay.

Unfortunately, I could not press the Delete key on my curiosity.

"We will now begin boarding Business Class passengers and Executive Club members."

I walked towards the end of the line and stood patiently in place with my ticket and passport in hand.

"He's just so freakin' cute!" the girl in front of me murmured to her friend as she held open her *People* magazine for their joint perusal.

140    Shit. They were looking at pictures of Tom at his movie pre-

miere in Manhattan last month. Guess which idiot stood next to him and looked as though she ate one too many Metamucil crackers before going out? Worse, my posture resembled an individual trying to furtively remedy a monolithic wedgie.

"I know! At first, I wasn't sure what all the fuss was about. Now, I'm like 'day-umn!' That accent just takes it over the top. Too bad about the girlfriend," her friend responded.

"She's kind of pretty, but I totally think he could do better. I mean, she's nothing special."

*Thanks. Really. You look like crap too.*

"I bet it doesn't last. She's probably a clinger or something. Once he realizes he doesn't have to settle for a J. Lo wannabe, he'll drop the baggage. Then he can have my number." The friend giggled.

"Please! He can have my number *now*. I'm much better than a J. Lo wannabe."

They continued to bicker amiably to one another as the line moved forward. Part of me wanted to tap their shoulders and sarcastically offer my thanks for their vote of confidence. I guess it was too much to hope that they might believe the "J. Lo Wannabe" had feelings … or ears. Oh well.

The irony of the situation before me temporarily faded from my mind as I thought again of Ryan and his comments. Pretty boy? He missed me? He loved me? God, he made me so angry! Did he really think I was that desperate?

Once on the plane, my eyes quickly scanned the back of the Business Class cabin. In the far corner, a rather lanky man in jeans and a T-shirt appeared to be asleep with a book covering his face. I didn't even bother to check my ticket as I walked straight to the seat next to him and stowed my bags. Without missing a beat, I pulled out my book and pretended as though it were the most engrossing thing I had ever been granted the opportunity to read.

"Oyi."

I ignored the muted sound from the person who sat beside me with a knowing half-smile.

"You—with the book." The whisper was further muffled under the pages still strategically hiding his face.

"Not interested," I grumbled without a glance, "engrossed" in my book.

"Pity. You smell amazing. So, if I were to say that you had a great body, would you hold it against me?" he whispered suggestively.

"That's just awful. Epic FAIL!" I shot back under my breath as

I stifled a giggle.

The book moved a bit as he chuckled quietly and then resumed his posture of faked respite. Soon, the line of people who walked past us dancing the luggage samba dwindled to a mere trickle. His left hand darted across the seat divider, and strong fingers laced through mine as the plane prepared for takeoff.

"Did you want the window seat?" he murmured after he removed his "disguise" so we could finally speak to one another properly.

"No. I'm fine." I grinned back at him in a nauseatingly saccharine fashion. Blech. As if I needed any more proof that love makes you stupid.

"Brilliant, I didn't want to give it to you anyway."

"In that case, get your ass out of my chair," I joked.

"God, I missed you," he teased in a husky voice.

I squeezed his hand. "I missed you too... Man, I hope I didn't forget anything important. I've been wracking my brain for the last hour. Oh well. It's too late now. Are you glad to be going home?" I whispered.

"Yes and no. I love being in London and spending time with my family, but there are always difficult moments to deal with when I go." He frowned in momentary introspection.

"Your father?"

He nodded carefully. "I think I'm most excited about introducing you to Anne. She's been driving me insane the last few weeks about meeting you. It'll be nice to get her off my case."

"I can't wait to see her too. I brought her something."

He smiled crookedly at me. "What is it?"

"I actually have something for your parents, as well. Don't worry; it's nothing too big or fancy. I just couldn't come to visit without bringing gifts. I brought your father a collection of short stories by Kafka, since you said he likes philosophy. I found this great Puerto Rican cookbook translated into English, so I ordered one for your mother. You told me Anne liked the clutch I carried to the New York premiere, so I'm giving it to her. I know it's ghetto to give her something I used, but I can't actually afford to buy *Prada*, so I hope she'll forgive me. Now that I think about it, I guess that means *you* gave her the bag... which kind of compounds my ghetto-ness. Sorry."

"Don't tell Esteban," I added quickly.

He just sat there for a moment, looking at me in reflective silence.

"What?" I demanded.

"You're too good for me," he murmured.

"Whatever! Don't give me any of that self-effacing crap. It's the least I can do. They don't even know me, and they're letting me stay in their home for a week."

"Thank you." He pulled my hand across the polished wood divider between our seats and pressed his lips to it.

"You're welcome." I settled into my chair and felt a wave of calm wash over me, as though his mere presence were an opiate. Ugh. I should know better. Oh well. Could something that had been charred beyond recognition still catch fire and burn? I didn't really want to find out, but it was too late for me.

Almost seven hours later, we rolled our suitcases to the curb and hailed a "hack" to take us to Tom's childhood home in London. The warm night sky was littered with the pulsing lights of the city, and the punctuated staccato of car horns improvised the music that accompanied the urban scenery flashing by my face.

I had been to London once before and had already confessed to Tom that the occasion drove me to hate it with an irrational amount of passion. To be fair, I was a poor college student at the time, and London was not exactly kind to people who lived on a budget. I remembered paying the dollar equivalent of "hella expensive" once at a McDonald's for some chicken nuggets—five pounds. At the time, I thought that amount equaled ten dollars. Seriously. I mean, WTF? For McNuggets? Additionally, the weather had been a major buzzkill for someone coming from a land frequented by sunrays. Finally, I had been robbed on the Tube somewhere near Covent Garden, and the combination of being poor, mugged, and constantly left to my own dreary devices formed a lingering bad taste in my mouth. I also travel to eat, and London left much to be desired in that department. I did drink an inordinate amount of beer while there, but that had less to do with my affinity for it and more to do with the fact I was desperate for some kind of an affordable distraction. All things considered, the week I spent in London made up the low point of my European "backpacking" adventure.

When I first regaled Tom with tales of my London escapades, he had laughed uncontrollably and vowed to change my mind about his beloved, sooty city. I dared him to, and before I knew it, he told me we were going to visit his family.

And now, here we were: standing at the door to his parents' townhome. Tom was definitely not a man who made blanket suggestions without the decisive intention of following through.

He had barely touched his hand to the doorbell when it was surreptitiously yanked open. I was snatched by the forearm and pulled over the threshold with unceremonious effort.

"Tommy!" squealed the girl before me as she threw her arms around his neck and kicked the door shut behind us.

He laughed as he hugged her back. She was tall, with reddish brown hair and a rosy complexion. I recognized her warm smile from Tom's photos.

"Anne, this is Cris," he introduced with a teasing flourish.

She turned and, without hesitation, stepped forward to embrace me as well.

"I'm so glad to meet you *finally*. Tommy talks about you all the time, and I was going mad not having met you. Blimey, you're even prettier in person, and that's saying something! A bit shorter than I thought, but I'd kill to have your skin color. If I even try to tan, I turn into a lobster, and they're not creatures known for their attractiveness, if you know what I mean. No one ever aspired to look like a lobster for good reason. Hideous. I think they're in the same genus or whatever as spiders."

I could not help the wide smile that spread onto my face at her bubbly vivaciousness. Anne Abramson had the potential to talk just as much as I did, I realized. No wonder why Tom never seemed to mind whenever I rambled incessantly. He had apparently developed an immunity prior to coming in contact with me.

"Christ, don't talk her head off!" Tom joked before I could even put together a coherent response.

"Honestly Anne, I don't know how you're nearing thirty and still have the manners of a hyperactive schoolgirl," a slender, middle-aged woman murmured with a smile as she walked towards us. Her features were similar to Tom's in their aristocratic bent, and her brown eyes sparkled with a distinctive mirth she had definitely passed along to her son.

"Thirty? I'm only twenty seven, Mum!" Anne cried.

Tom's mother outstretched her hand in welcome. I grasped it in mine momentarily and returned her kind smile.

"It's so nice to meet you, Cristina. I'm very glad you could come to visit, and I first want to thank you for putting up with my son for so long. Lord knows it's not easy."

"Thank you," Tom replied acerbically as he gazed down at her with a mixture of undisguised affection and clear amusement.

She arched her eyebrow at him for a moment before he bent forward to lift her off the floor and into a sweeping bear hug.

"Thomas Patrick Abramson, you put me down this instant!" She laughed as her feet dangled at least six inches off the ground.

"I trust the flight went well and no one harassed you too much," stated a gruff voice that I knew belonged to Tom's father. With the disadvantage of my sensory-overloaded mind, he appeared to have materialized from nowhere and leaned against the staircase. He watched me with studious appraisal. He was stocky, and his features were etched with lines that indicated a propensity for deep thought or raucous laughter. I was inclined to think it was the former rather than the latter.

"Yes sir," Tom replied brusquely.

"Well then, you must be hungry. Let's have some dinner." Tom's father turned and walked purposefully to the back of the house without pausing for any pleasantries. *Interesting.* Tom narrowed his eyes at the empty space his father had just occupied. Anger tinged his expression, so I wordlessly put my hand on his arm in a soothing gesture.

"Thank you so much for inviting me to stay in your home. It's very kind of you, and I really appreciate it," I said warmly to Anne and her mother. "I think eating dinner is a great idea. I'm starving! All I've eaten recently is plane food, and that's nothing to brag about, so I apologize beforehand if I eat so much that it's frightening."

Anne's laughter rang in the room like a bell, and it successfully cut through some of the tension that had crept into the space with dismaying ease. She linked her arm through mine, and we marched towards the dining room with Tom and his mother in tow. Soon we were seated around a rectangular table with piles of pasta and salad on our plates.

"So, Cristina, you've been to university?" Tom's father asked. This was the first time he had deigned to address me, and as luck would have it, my mouth was full of food at that exact moment. I had no time to contemplate the utter impossibility of impressing someone important while scarfing down food. I hoped he wasn't the jackass who intentionally waited to acknowledge you whenever you were sure to look like an imbecile.

"Yes sir," I managed to croak out before I grabbed my drink to help swallow my food.

"And what did you study?" he asked.

"I majored in French and minored in Music as an undergraduate, and I have a Master's Degree in Social Work."

He nodded slowly in obvious consideration. "French and Music 145 don't seem related to Social Work. Why did you choose those things?"

"Oh, come off it, Dad. Are you interviewing her for a job?" Anne said teasingly as she tried to deflect the strain.

"I'm merely curious."

Tom snorted sarcastically as he lifted his glass to his lips. The sound was not lost on his father.

"I chose French because it's very similar to Spanish, and it was relatively easy to learn. Languages have always interested me, and I thought it was a good idea to study something I was good at as opposed to something I would struggle with," I stated simply.

"What do you struggle with?" he queried on mercilessly.

"Patrick," Tom's mother admonished.

I smiled to show I wasn't fazed. "Math. I initially wanted to be a doctor but failed my first-year Math classes ... twice. I figured it was the higher powers telling me I shouldn't pursue it any further."

"So, you're bad with numbers and good with languages."

"Didn't she just say that?" Tom muttered spitefully. He was behaving like a petulant child, so I nudged his foot under the table in warning.

Tom's father focused his gaze onto his son's face then made an ill-advised decision.

"With all that education under your belt, does it bother you that Thomas barely finished high school?" he asked in a cutting tone.

"Patrick, please. They only just arrived here," Tom's mother requested with more force behind her words.

"No, it doesn't bother me," I answered firmly.

"Would it bother you if he were poor?" God, this man was merciless!

"Bloody hell! Have you gone completely mad? This is the first time I've ever brought home a girlfriend since I left London, and you can't even control yourself for half an hour!" Tom exploded angrily.

"Tom," I pleaded. "Please."

"You said she was important to you. If she's important to you, I'm entitled to ask questions that shed light on her character. If you have a problem with that, then perhaps you should consider whether or not you were actually ready to introduce her to your family. It's just typical of you, Thomas. You just do whatever you want, and you never stop to think about anything else." His father spoke slowly with ruthless dispassion. The muscles in Tom's jawline rippled under the strain of trying to remain silent.

146   "Patrick!" Tom's mother said loudly.

"Yes, it would bother me if he were poor," I stated in a clear voice.

That took everyone off guard. Anne dropped her fork into her plate, and Tom's mother stared at me in dismay. I could feel Tom's body go rigid next to me, and his father's eyes settled onto mine as though he realized he had struck a chord that resonated.

I knew how important it was that I choose my next words with extreme care.

"But not in the way people would assume. Being able to buy as many fancy things as you want is nice, but it's not important to me. If Tom were poor, it would mean he was struggling, and I would hate to see him struggle because I care a lot about him. He's a very hard worker, and I know he spends a great deal of time studying to become better at his craft. Going to college is one way of learning, but I don't think that a classroom is the only place where you can get an education. Unfortunately, I'm biased in favor of fancy university diplomas because I come from a poor country, and I know what hindrances poverty and a lack of an education can be. So, I guess my own cultural views pushed me in the direction of college. But I think Tom is very blessed to enjoy what he does and have the ability to make money doing it. He's also very lucky to be surrounded by people who support him."

Yeah, I probably shouldn't have said that last part. *So sue me, you disgruntled meanie.*

Tom released a drawn out breath and turned to stare at me with a flurry of emotions crossing his face. Amusement, appreciation, and ... shock?

"Well, is that sufficient?" Anne demanded bitingly.

"Could you pass the salad dressing, Cris?" Tom's father asked as though nothing of import had transpired at all.

Wordlessly, I picked up the bottle and handed it over to Tom's father. His mother winked at me, and Tom's hand squeezed my knee under the table. His sister's hazel eyes sparkled wickedly.

Half an hour later, Anne whispered, "Oh, my God!" as we stood alone in the kitchen after clearing away dishes. Tom had left to take our luggage upstairs.

"What?" I asked.

"That was bloody brilliant! You actually got him to shut up. Tommy would have just kept yelling at him, and Dad would never let it go. Priceless! You've got to teach Tommy how to do that!"

"I hope you don't mind me asking, but why do they fight so much?" I asked as quietly as possible.

"I dunno. They used to be so close. I think it's because Dad wanted Tommy to make a difference in the world and do something meaningful with his life. Tommy is really smart, and he did well in school until he decided he wanted to be an actor. It was really random. Did he ever tell you that I was actually the one who wanted to be an actress? He came with me to an audition because I was watching over him, and the little twit got a job! He was nine years old. Dad was furious when Tommy announced he wasn't going to university so he could move to the States and be an actor. I think he was disappointed in the waste. Dad wanted him to become a barrister. Can you imagine? Tommy would be miserable! My brother's just really sensitive about Dad too. He thinks Dad will never be happy with him, no matter what he does … it just makes for a bad situation all around. Dad knows how to piss him off, and Tommy can't control himself. It's funny because he's usually so patient and easy-going. It's like Dad brings out the angry little boy in him." She shrugged nonchalantly. "Really, I think they just need to talk."

"I think so too," I agreed.

"Think what?" Arms wrapped around my waist from behind, and warm lips pressed against my cheek.

"I think you need therapy," I joked.

"I'll get in line behind you," he jeered back. "By the way, you're absolutely amazing."

"Isn't she? I nearly died at the look on Dad's face! 'Can you please pass the salad dressing?' " Anne tittered to herself as she studied her younger brother who held me in a loose embrace with an expression of total satisfaction on her face. "Really, you did quite well with this one, Tommy. Dad thought you were bringing home an American idiot with big knockers and a small IQ. This is just perfect!"

"Instead, he got a Puerto Rican smartass with no knockers and something to prove." I laughed with Anne.

"What's Mum doing?" Anne asked Tom.

"Yelling at Dad."

"Perfect. So, now it's my turn to ask questions, but they're really easy ones. I'm just dying to know some of the basic things about you, Cris. Bare with me," Anne said beseechingly.

"Go for it!" I replied with a grin.

"Favorite color?" she inquired.

"Red."

"Favorite day of the week?"

"Friday."

"Favorite book?"

"I've got two. *The God of Small Things* by Arundhati Roy and Emerson's *Self-Reliance.*"

"Nice! Favorite place to go on holiday?"

"The beach."

"Favorite kind of music?"

"Unanswerable. Depends on the week."

"Favorite kind of food?"

"Probably Indian...or Italian."

"Favorite movie?"

I smiled wickedly before responding with "Anything starring Thomas Abramson." I batted my eyelashes at Tom with a look of groupie adoration that prompted Anne to guffaw loudly and Tom to shove me with a groan. After she finished laughing, Anne announced she would straighten up the dining room and discreetly left us alone in the kitchen.

"I can't tell you enough how much I appreciate you standing up for me," he murmured.

"It's what I'm supposed to do...plus, I think it sucks your Dad can't see the forest for the trees."

"He would most likely say the same thing about me," he muttered in response.

"You really need to talk to him. I think you two haven't had a chance to have a serious discussion in forever. It looks like all you do is pick fights with one another."

"You're probably right," he agreed. "I just don't know where to begin."

"Not knowing where to begin is not an excuse. Remember what you said to me about my father? How it shamed you? Don't forget about that, and try to be more patient with him. I think he cares a lot more than he lets on."

He didn't respond. Instead, he placed a tender kiss on my forehead.

"I love you, Bad-Tempered Tommy," I teased affectionately.

"And I love you, Ass-Kicking Cris."

# SIXTEEN

My eyes opened of their own volition at six o'clock in the morning. No matter how much I willed myself to fall back to sleep, my body refused to listen. Jetlag was the bane of my existence.

After I tossed and turned for fifteen minutes, I rolled out of bed, tentatively stuck my head into the hall, and padded to the bathroom to brush my teeth. I changed into jeans and a bright blue T-shirt and treaded downstairs as quietly as possible to find my purse and iPod.

"Good morning, Cris."

"Holy crap!" I cried, taken off guard by the presence of Tom's father standing a few feet behind me with a mug of steaming liquid in his right hand.

"I didn't mean to startle you. Do you usually wake up this early on a Saturday?" he asked. Man, this guy was addicted to interrogative dialogue.

"No, sir. I usually sleep in, but I think my jetlag had other ideas. I didn't mean to bother you. I was just coming downstairs to get my purse."

"You're not bothering me at all. Would you like to join me for a cup of coffee or tea?" he queried.

I thought to myself for a quick moment. As much as I wanted to avoid spending time with someone I'd already deemed unpleasant, I didn't feel as though I had a right to insist that Tom spend time with his father when I couldn't bring myself to do the same.

"I'd love a cup of coffee," I replied with a cheerful grin.

I followed him into the kitchen. I dropped two cubes of sugar into the mug of coffee he handed me and sat in the chair across from him in the small breakfast nook. A chessboard was set up between us, and the pieces were scattered around the board in mid-game.

When he noticed where I gazed, he smiled. "I was playing with Anne last night before you arrived. Chess is a hobby of mine. Do you play?"

"A bit. My father loved chess too, and he always pushed me to play with him. He used to say that you can tell a lot about people from how they play chess."

"He sounds like a wise man. You lost him last year to cancer, correct?" For the first time, I heard a hint of empathy in his tone.

I nodded and returned his introspective stare without hesitation.

"Would you rather not talk about it?" he asked gently.

"I don't mind. I love talking about my father."

"I'm surprised that you don't seem angered by the unfairness of it all," he continued.

"Death isn't fair…I think that's the way it usually works. Honestly, I'm kind of thankful it happened so suddenly, if it had to be because of cancer. He didn't suffer as much as he could have, and I'm grateful for that." As I spoke, I absentmindedly made the next move on the chessboard with the white knight before me.

He smiled crookedly, and, for a moment, I saw Tom in his expression. "That's a very mature response."

"To me, it's more about self-actualization. At the end of the day, I know I did everything I could think of at the time to help, and that was more important to me than dwelling on how unfair it all was. I miss him all the time, and sometimes it makes me angry that I can't hear his laughter or ask him for advice anymore, but I've never been mad about it being unfair." I watched as he removed one of my white pawns from the board and shifted one of his black pawns into its place.

"I hope you're not offended by what I'm about to say, but I'm very surprised by you," Tom's father remarked.

"May I ask why?" I made another move on the chessboard.

"I did not expect you to be so…composed and intelligent."

"Now it's my turn to hope you won't be offended. Your low expectations are kind of a disservice to your son. Did you really think he would like a silly, stupid girl?" It was probably too soon for me to be this candid with Tom's father, but he honestly brought it on himself.

He actually chuckled before replying. "I thought he would like someone that fit his job more appropriately." His bishop took position closer to my king.

"So you think his job is silly and stupid?"

"In a word: yes. He could have been so much more," he stated bluntly.

"But I don't think that detracts from what he is now. He's a success, and I'm always impressed by how well he handles it, even though he's not comfortable with his success, yet. I don't know him as well as you do, but I've never felt for a second that his job takes 151 away from the great person he is."

"You love my son. Sometimes love makes it hard to see the truth."

"And sometimes it makes us project our wishes onto those we love and ignore their version of success in favor of ours." I moved another chess piece.

He chuckled again. "You certainly are feisty. Check," he murmured as he threatened my king with his queen.

"I'm sorry if I was too forward. I just think you'd be pleasantly surprised by how down-to-earth and humble Tom is, even if you think his profession is vapid." I rescued my king and took a careful glance at my strategically arranged pieces.

"It would be nice to know that side of Thomas, but I haven't seen it in him for a while now."

"I apologize for being feisty again, but I think that it would help a lot if you both sat down and spoke with each other candidly. I know it's really presumptuous of me to say this to you, but I'm sure Tom wants to talk to you. In fact, he mentioned it last night." Inspired, I decided to go a step further. "I think he would love to have lunch with you today, just the two of you."

His eyebrows rose in surprise. "Really?"

I nodded emphatically. Of course, I hadn't consulted Tom yet, but he always told me I needed to live outside of my head and be more spontaneous. I was certain he wouldn't mind too much, and we didn't have any plans for the afternoon. We were supposed to spend time with some of his childhood friends in the evening.

"Check," he said again as he positioned himself for another attempt at my king. "I would like that very much."

I beamed at Tom's father. "I'm really glad." I prepared to sacrifice my white knight to save my king and finished setting up the stage.

"Thank you. My son is very lucky to have you in his life." He removed my knight from the board as he grinned kindly at me.

"I'm very lucky to have him in mine…Checkmate."

His jaw dropped in shock as he took a closer look at the board in front of him. I remained silent as he studied the pieces.

"Quite feisty," he muttered.

With a wry smile of defeat, he knocked his king over.

Two hours later, I helped Tom's mother prepare breakfast in the kitchen. Tom was still fast asleep and blissfully unaware of the fact I had been unleashed on his parents without a chaperone. Anne lived with a roommate in a flat about half an hour away, so her bubbly presence could not serve as a buffer.

"Are you sure you don't want more sleep, dear? Thomas stays out quite late when he spends time with his friends, and I don't want you to fall apart later on," she said with concern as I turned over the sausage in the frying pan.

"I'll be fine! I'm on my second cup of coffee so far, and I think I'll manage to keep it together. Maybe I'll try to grab a nap later this afternoon."

She studied my face carefully before replying. "Just don't let him drag you all over the city until you're half-dead. Sometimes he gets caught up in a moment, and someone has to bring him back down to earth."

"I really don't mind. I've spent most of my life grounded, so it's probably not a bad thing for me to learn how to fly."

She laughed in response. "Tom does fly, to be sure! That boy has always been a dreamer! I'm so glad he brought you to visit us. You're not what my husband was expecting, and I mean that in the kindest way possible. In fact, I was a bit surprised myself… not about the fact that you're wonderful; I never had any doubts about that. Tommy is far too particular to settle for anything less than wonderful. I was a bit surprised by how much he cares about you."

A flush crept up my neck, so I thought it was best to remain silent.

"I've never seen him look at any girl the way he looks at you, and I'm so happy for you both." She reached over to take my hand in hers as a lump formed in my throat.

"Thank you," I whispered.

"Of course. I hope you don't mind if I request a small favor: please don't break his heart; I'm becoming quite certain that he won't be able to get over it," she murmured tenderly.

I stared back into her earnest eyes, nodded, and cleared my throat to stifle the rising tide of emotion building in me. "Breakfast is almost ready. I'll make sure he's awake," I stammered.

I fled the kitchen before I cried on her shoulder and spilled my guts as if she were Oprah Winfrey and had just given me the keys to my first house. What a contrast Tom's mother was to his father! For every cold and calculating maneuver he made, she had one filled with warmth and openness to combat it.

I knocked softly on the door of Tom's bedroom. No response.

I pounded a bit more forcefully and heard a stilted groan that 153 reminded me of a grizzly bear being prodded out of hibernation. Trying the handle, I found it unlocked, so I pushed my way into his darkened bedroom. Just in case his parents held more conservative views on propriety, I left the door wide open.

"Tommy?"

Another groan.

"Thomas? Breakfast is ready. Wake up." I walked carefully over to his bed and leaned over his face.

"Get up...I made your father cry," I murmured in his ear.

His eyes shot open in surprise. "*What?*"

"I'm kidding. Get out of bed, lazy ass. I've been up for hours!"

"*I've been up for hours!*" he mimicked in a nasal voice. "God, you're annoying."

I sat on the edge of his bed and poked his ribs with my index finger. "Since I'm already annoying, I thought I might as well take it a step further."

Without warning, he sat up quickly and wrapped his long arms around my shoulders to restrict my movement. His hands grasped each of my wrists to prevent me from wiggling my way out.

"Game over." He grinned with half-lidded eyes.

"Fool, this game is far from over," I teased.

He laughed quietly and blinked the sleep away from his eyes. "Your face is a wonderful thing to wake up to, but your fingers between my ribcage are another story. Have you really been awake for hours?" He released me and ran his hands through his hair in an attempt to banish the bedhead.

"Yep. I couldn't sleep past six."

"What have you been doing since then?" He yawned absent-mindedly. His white T-shirt was wrinkled and askew on his chest, and that in combination with the unruly hair and bedroom eyes sent a flurry of tantalizingly inappropriate images through my head. Hah hah...if he only knew how dangerously sexy he was.

"I had coffee with your father, and we played chess."

He chuckled as he threw his legs over the side of his bed, stood, and stretched.

"How did that go?" he asked nonchalantly.

"Pretty well. I'm going to go out on a limb and say that your father thinks about things even more obsessively than I do."

"No kidding. It drives me insane." He grabbed some track pants from the floor and pulled them on in one fluid motion.

"By the way, you're having lunch with him today," I stated in a casual tone.

He froze mid-step. "What?" His voice was dangerously low.

"I told your father you would have lunch with him today."

He pursed his lips and cut his eyes at me. "I'm guessing that wasn't his idea."

"No, it was mine."

He took a deep breath to steady himself for a moment. "Cristina, why the hell would you do that?"

I was dismayed by the amount of anger I saw in his features, so I just sat there and stared at him in bewildered silence.

He took three long strides to his door and slammed it shut.

"Why?" he demanded furiously as he spun around to face me.

"I thought you should talk to him, so..."

"So, you just planned a sweet little father-son luncheon without even consulting me?"

"You want me to consult you?" I sputtered. "That's a joke! You never consult me about anything! Plus, we talked about this last night!"

"Talking about it and making me do something I'm not ready to do are two different things! I'm not going!" he said in a wrathful whisper.

I stood up from the bed and crossed my arms over my chest. "Yes, you are."

"No, I'm not!"

"You're acting like a spoiled brat! It's not going to fix itself, Thomas! Whether you talk to him now or next year, it will never get any easier. It will, however, get worse and worse if you keep acting like a brat about it, sitting there snorting at the dinner table and muttering under your breath. Grow up!" I spat.

"You think it's just that easy? You have absolutely no idea what you're talking about! Your father worshipped you and thought everything you did was worth its weight in gold. My father thinks everything about me is a fucking joke! You want me to sit across from him and pretend that I give a damn?"

"Yes, because you *do* give a damn! He needs to know that you give a damn! Maybe if he thought you cared, he would stop for a moment and look at things from your perspective!" I tried not to yell for fear that everyone in the house would hear every word we said.

"It's not that easy. Christ! It's a bit naïve of you to think you can fix this. This problem was here long before you were, and me forcing you to go to a party with people who don't matter is not the same 155 thing as you forcing me to have lunch with my father who hates me."

"He doesn't hate you! Don't say that!" I gasped.

"Just because you said so, it suddenly makes it true?" he shot back.

"No, but…you saying he hates you doesn't make it true either!"

"I'm not going," he stated flatly.

"Then don't go!" I said with exasperation. "But you have a choice: either deal with your father at lunch today, or deal with me for the rest of this trip. I don't have control over you or your father, but I promise to be the biggest pain in the ass you've ever seen!"

I marched over to the door and yanked it open with my heart rapidly beating in my chest.

Breakfast was interesting, to say the least. Tom sat in stony silence for most of the meal and attributed his lack of communication to the fact that he was still tired from the flight. Desperate to make up for his childishness, I overcompensated by talking entirely too much and laughing at things that weren't that funny. What I wouldn't give to have even a slight amount of skill when it involved acting. The irony. I was sure his parents knew something was wrong, but they didn't mention it. Midway through the meal, I started to feel guilty. I had raked Tom over the coals for taking me to the Vogue party without consulting me, and now I had definitely taken it upon myself to be a hero and "save" Tom's relationship with his father by planning their lunch of my own volition. He was right, I grudgingly admitted to myself. I had no business becoming an intermediary when it came to their issues. All I should have done was make suggestions and offer encouragement. I had gone too far. *Fuck.*

Tom walked upstairs after the meal, and I followed him to clear the air. I stopped in the doorway of his bedroom. "Um…Tommy?" I hesitated.

He glanced morosely over his shoulder at me and sighed. "Back for round two?"

I balked momentarily. "No. I'm—I'm really sorry."

He turned to face me.

"You're right—it's not my business how you choose to handle your father. I just…it hurts me to see you so frustrated about something, and I wanted to help. Please forgive me."

The tension on his face melted as I spoke. He wavered a bit and then smiled wryly. "I'm sorry I yelled at you like that. I know you were just trying to help."

"But still…I should have known better. It's your decision about whether or not you go to lunch. I won't say anything either way, and it was really shitty of me to issue an ultimatum like some crazy girlfriend with nothing better to do than make your life difficult."

He laughed softly to himself. "Self-aware to a fault. The ultimatum *was* a really shitty thing to do, by the way."

"I know. Truce?" I stuck out my hand.

"Truce." He took hold of my palm and pulled me into an embrace.

Without pausing to let me catch my breath, he pressed his lips to mine and lifted me off the ground. I wrapped my arms around his neck and kissed him back fervently, while my rationale tried to remind me I was in his parents' house. Thankfully, my ears detected the sound of falling footsteps on the stairs, and I struggled to push myself out of Tom's ironclad grip. He chuckled at my expression as I steadied my pounding heart and breath before anyone saw my flustered state.

"Stop laughing, Tommy!" I demanded under my breath.

"Incidentally, when did you start calling me 'Tommy'?"

"Um…I don't know. I think it's because Anne and your mother keep referring to you that way. If it bothers you, I won't do it anymore."

"No, no. It doesn't bother me. For some reason, I rather like it coming from you." He grinned.

"Cristina?" Tom's father called from the hallway.

"Yes sir?" I scrambled towards the door and into the hall where he stood waiting for me.

"I just wanted to thank you again for the book. I've already read some of it, and it was very thoughtful of you." He smiled earnestly at me, and I felt as though I had made a good deal of progress with the toughest member of Tom's family.

"It was my pleasure."

"I was also hoping…to have a chess rematch later on? A proper game, this time." The hopeful expression on his face made him look even more charmingly boyish.

"Absolutely."

He nodded in satisfaction, and then turned to walk back to his bedroom.

"Dad?"

Tom's father stopped in his tracks and twisted around awkwardly at the sound of his son's voice.

"Yes?"

157

Tom had come to stand behind me. He took a deep breath and placed his right hand on the small of my back before he spoke to his father.

"Where would you like to go for lunch? My treat."

I looked over my shoulder at his handsome face and beamed with uncontrollable pride.

# SEVENTEEN

Is what I'm wearing okay?" I asked Tom at the top of the stairs that evening.

"They're not the type of guys who care what you're wearing, so don't worry about it," he replied with amusement.

I tugged on the front of my fitted red shirt as I glanced down at my jeans and beige espadrilles one last time.

"I don't regularly hang out in pubs, and I don't want to stick out too badly."

"You're going to stick out no matter what you wear. It tends to happen to beautiful women," he noted.

I gave his arm a lighthearted shove before we made our way downstairs to leave.

"You don't need your 'disguise' here?" I asked after we bid his parents goodnight and strolled out the front door.

He shrugged. "I guess we'll find out. Honestly, I don't think many people know I'm in London at the moment. I haven't been back home for a while, so I guess I'll know soon enough if I made a bad decision about the disguise. Last time I was about, I didn't need anything."

He reached for my hand as he spoke. I noticed his stride seemed more at-ease here than the times we had gone out in public back home. He walked with unfailing confidence, and it was painfully obvious he felt a great deal more comfortable in this small section of London than at any fancy party or on any red carpet. His calm bearing was infectious, and soon I matched his relaxed gait and drank in the sights around me as though I knew exactly where we were and where we were headed.

"Your dad looked really happy when you came home from lunch," I commented casually.

He glanced at me with a wry smile. "It definitely went better than I would have thought. There's still a great deal that needs to be dealt with on both sides, but I was surprised by how willing he was to admit that he hasn't been very pleasant towards me."

I nodded silently.

"You're not going to say 'I told you so'?" he teased.

"There's no reason for me to be smug. Any progress you made is entirely your own. I'm not going to be a 'buttinski' anymore...but I'm really happy you spent time with him and that it went well," I replied in an even tone.

He responded by squeezing my hand affectionately. I noticed he navigated down many small side streets towards a destination I would never be able to find again, even on pain of death. The trail grew more and more narrow, and the asphalt became mottled with patches of cobblestone that grew in quantity with each passing step we made. Soon we came to a small alleyway that a car would never be able to traverse. The path before us consisted entirely of square grey stones that had eroded to smoothness by the passage of time and the soles of many feet treading upon their surface. The mortar between them was cracked and discolored. I had to slow down because my effing espadrilles kept turning precariously on the uneven surface. Several times Tom had to catch my arm before I pitched forward into a graceless pile that would undoubtedly leave the imprint of a two hundred year old brick on my forehead. Tom's step never faltered as he smilingly saved me from that fate time and time again. Damn him ...and the cobblestone.

When I nearly face-planted for the hundredth time, Tom decided he couldn't keep silent any longer. "I fancy those shoes were an ill-advised decision."

"The time to tell me these shoes were a bad choice was prior to leaving the house, smartass. I do recall specifically asking you about my outfit."

"Pardon me for not remembering that the last time I wore high heels in London, walking was a real bitch," he joked.

"You think you're *so* funny."

He laughed and came to an abrupt halt when he noticed a group of girls our age walking directly towards us while cackling and carrying on in a manner that suggested mild intoxication.

Trapped in the narrow alleyway, we stood still with baited breath and hoped they would pass by us without noticing anything.

And then...

A girlish screech pierced the night air.

"Holy shit! It's-it's...THOMAS ABRAMSON!" one girl cried. The others merely stood there and gaped at us for a lingering moment. Once the shock wore off, they rushed him without a second thought. One of the young women actually threw her arms around Tom's

160

neck for a hug! A flurry of comments flew around us, and it became difficult for me to process anything as their praise melded together to form a banshee wail of worship.

"Tom! Your last film was absolutely brilliant! Oscar-worthy!"

"God, my sister will never believe this!"

"What are you doing in London? Can I take a picture with you?"

"Where's my bloody camera when I need it?"

"Can I get your autograph?"

"This is unbelievable! I swear I'm not crazy, but I'm totally in love with you!"

"Does anyone have a fucking pen?"

Wordlessly, I reached into my purse and produced a black pen that was immediately snatched from my hand. Tom smiled and tried to field their questions with as much poise as he could manage while scribbling quickly on scraps of paper. Creases of strain marred his forehead when they pushed him for a picture.

"I'd really rather not," he said kindly as one girl flourished her camera.

"Oh, please! I promise not to sell it to a newspaper or anything!"

The look of sardonic dubiousness that graced his expression was completely lost on her as she tried to rally her friends for the photo. The hilarity continued when none of them would step forward to snap the shot, lest they risk being left out of the moment forever. Sense befell one of the girls as she spun around to look for help and unwittingly noticed me for the first time. Her face flushed crimson in realization.

"Blimey, is this your girlfriend?" she stated awkwardly.

"Yes," Tom responded. "Her name is Cristina."

"Oh! I saw a picture of her last week from a party in Hollywood. You looked so…. *different*!" remarked another girl.

Finally nearing the end of my patience, I forced myself to smile broadly at the brood before I stuck my hand out for the camera. "I can take the picture, if you like." Then please leave us alone.

I was treated to a chorus of "thank you" in exchange for my efforts.

After we managed to escape, Tom reverted back to his familiar stance of constant vigilance and slouched self-awareness.

"God, that was so awkward!" I remarked quietly as we continued to our destination. "Is that what usually happens?"

"More or less."

"Man, if people I didn't know ran at me for a hug, I would prob- 161 ably punch them before they could get close enough," I continued.

The lines on his face faded as he peered down at me and laughed. "Then it's a good thing they didn't try to hug you. Truly, I'm starting to get used to it."

"I don't think I could ever get used to complete strangers invading my personal space like that."

His expression was pensive as he paused for further consideration. "I wish I hadn't frozen in place like a moron when I saw them. I should have, I don't know… pushed us against the wall and starting snogging until they passed or something, but I couldn't think of anything to do at the moment… I just froze. Idiot."

"You've watched too many James Bond movies. Making out in a dark alleyway isn't the key to remaining nondescript. If I saw two people going at it, I would definitely stop to watch," I teased.

My cheesy attempt worked. He exhaled through his amusement and walked forward with a more lighthearted step. A few moments later, he stopped before an old wooden door with weather-beaten varnish and held it open for me. As I stepped into the dimly lit room, the scent of cigarettes and alcohol inundated me. Raucous laughter filled the air and a cloudy haze of smoke settled around us. The sparse lighting illustrated the unfurling wisps that twisted in response to the movements below in a macabre dance. The establishment was half-filled with patrons in varying degrees of inebriation.

Without pausing, Tom took my hand and led me to the back of the pub with purposeful strides. My eyes adjusted to the lighting as a booth directly ahead of us came into view where two men were seated.

"It's about bloody time! Did you leave your watch at home, mate?" one of them crowed in a mocking tone as we slid seamlessly into the booth.

"I actually left it at your mum's," Tom jeered back with a wide grin.

"Piss off!" He punched Tom roughly and clapped him on the back in a gesture of affectionate welcome.

"Thomas is buying the next round since he's a filthy millionaire. .. and the one after that, as well," the other guy said sarcastically.

Tom chuckled in acquiescence and turned to me. "Cris, this is Ben." He motioned to his friend who had mocked him about the watch. He had a curly mop of blond hair and an extremely friendly expression on his stout face. "And this ugly tosser is Philip." Tom smiled at the man directly across from us. Philip was a far cry from ugly with his thick, black hair and tanned skin. I was certain the brooding badass had broken the hearts of many women. He stared at me with striking green eyes filled with curiosity.

Ben leaned over Tom with his hand outstretched for mine. "Christ, Abramson! You did a shoddy job describing her to me. Cris, this pitiful sod here talks about you like you're his new religion, so it's really a pleasure to meet you."

I blushed furiously at his open gaze of admiration.

Philip smiled at me with a nod and said, "Really glad to meet you, as well."

"He talks about you guys and all the trouble you got him into all the time, so it's great to finally put names with faces," I said warmly.

"Us? He thinks we got him into trouble? Bollocks! This moron could act his way out of anything. Those big eyes worked miracles whenever we were caught doing something naughty. I always had to serve out harsher sentences than either of these two. Being cute has its perks," Ben commented.

"You idiot. You deserved to get caught. Every ill-advised thing I ever did was because I was daft enough to listen to you," Philip retorted at Ben.

"It's not my fault you're both so damn gullible!" Ben shot back.

"Gullible? More like conned! You'd sell crayons to the blind if you thought you could get away with it!" Tom jeered.

"Shut your face, you tosser!" He turned his twinkling eyes in my direction. "So tell me, what's it like dating a movie star?" Ben asked me in a teasing voice. His gaze shot over to Tom as though he knew he would emerge the victor in the Battle of Heckling.

Taken off guard, I blurted out the first thing that came to mind. "Dude, I have no idea how to answer that kind of question."

He laughed in surprise. "What do you mean?"

"Do you want a beauty pageant answer about how meaningful and eye-opening an experience it's been? Do you want me to tell you about being chased down the street by crazy fans? Do you want to know what it's like to have half the world's population hate me? What exactly do you want to know?"

Philip groaned. "Never ask Ben that kind of question."

Ben leaned forward in anticipation but was promptly cut off by Tom.

"No you don't! Don't even think about it!"

Ben ignored Tom with a wicked wagging of his eyebrows. "I think I'll settle for something . . . highly embarrassing and potentially 163 lucrative." He paused for effect. "Kiss and tell. What's it like to snog a movie star?"

"You bastard!" Tom moaned.

I couldn't help the laughter that bubbled from my lips at the sight of Tom flushing a deep red under Philip's watchful eyes and Ben's elated mockery.

"Nope." I shook my head through the mirth. "I'm not answering that one."

"I could make it worth your while. If we sell the tale to a trashy tabloid, I'm sure you could run away with me to a deserted island. It would make a brilliant story: 'Beautiful Idiot Dumps Handsome Movie Star for Chubby Best Friend,' " he pressed on, heartless in his attempt to make Tom squirm and get a good laugh in the process.

"See, I never know why these girls who hook up with a movie star go online or to these gossip magazines to blab about their story. They go on and on about 'what a great kisser he is' and whatnot. It just makes no sense to me," I stated carefully.

"Why not?" Philip asked, unable to conceal his interest.

"Personally, I wouldn't do it, and my reasons are far from being honorable," I hedged.

"Blast it, woman, just tell us!" Ben crowed with delight.

"Well, it stands to reason that if they 'kiss and tell,' they aren't likely to have any further encounters with their heartthrob. So, I won't kiss and tell because I definitely want more . . . much, *much* more." I winked at Ben suggestively, and Tom's countenance turned several different shades of mortified as they all digested the clear meaning behind my insinuation. Even Philip couldn't hold back his loud guffaw.

After Ben finished cackling at the look on Tom's face, he managed to bark out, "I'm marrying this woman. Seriously: smart, funny as hell, and completely gorgeous."

"You wish," Tom replied morosely.

"No, mate—you wish." Ben grinned at Tom.

The evening progressed as the level of comfort continued to increase between us all—aided by never-ending mugs of Guinness. Stories of the trio and their dastardly deeds throughout the years flew across the table, and the tales only made me even more enamored by Tom and his friends. Ben and Philip were witty and unfailingly loyal. They both tried to hide their pride in Tom's achievements, but it was so nakedly apparent in their affection that it was impossible to conceal it for long. Soon, Ben turned his torrent of mockery onto me with an ease that heartened my soul.

After three solid hours of conversation and more pitchers of beer than I cared to count, Ben made a suggestion that I initially thought was merely in jest.

"Gentlemen... and lady, of course! I suggest we return to my flat for a drunken round of Guitar Hero!" he proclaimed.

"What the fuck? Guitar Hero?" Tom replied dubiously.

I laughed; no one else did. "Are you serious?"

"I'm extremely serious about Guitar Hero," Ben asserted.

"He's not kidding. Every time he gets even slightly smashed, he wants to play that bloody game. I won't lie, it's great fun," Philip admitted.

"I don't know how to play!" I moaned.

"Neither do we. That's what makes it ridiculously fun. Of course, Tom is not allowed to play the guitar. That would be the grossest kind of cheating. I nominate Abramson to be our drummer," Ben announced.

"I thought the game was only for the guitar, hence the name Guitar Hero," Tom argued.

"No, no, no... that was then. This is now—the era of Guitar Hero World Tour. Watch and learn, you peon. Watch and learn."

"This should be interesting," Philip chuckled to himself.

"Final mike check... Testing, testing," Philip slurred as he clung to the microphone two hours later.

We all dripped sweat. Ben's flat was stifling with the combination of our body heat and the exertions of the last ninety minutes. The beer had followed us to our makeshift stage, and we stood in a semi-circle in front of the television. Tom had removed his soaked shirt and was seated behind a small ring of black "drums." Philip clutched the microphone as the bare-chested lead singer of our band. Ben played bass guitar.

"You can't fuck this up, Cris. We're all counting on you," Ben cheered with a huge grin of camaraderie on his face.

Yep, you guessed it. I, Cristina Pereira, had been conned into playing lead guitar by three drunken Englishmen. I will admit: it was a great deal harder than I ever would have thought. I will also admit I had a blast.

165

"Make sure you don't start the last riff until I finish singing the line, 'He doesn't look a thing like Jesus,' " Philip pressed.

"Piss off!" I replied drunkenly. "Ben, you worry about staying on beat because you weren't fooling me the second time we came to the chorus, and you'd better not forget the words again, Mr. I'm-So-Perfect Philip. This time, the one who ruins it has to put *two* shots of whiskey in their Guinness," I announced. My shirt was soaked through in an incredibly unbecoming fashion, and my hair was matted to my forehead as though I had spent the last hour swimming in a pool rather than playing a video game. I didn't care one bit.

"Agreed! God, I love this woman! Will you marry me?" Ben cried.

"For the thousandth time, no! You're too short for me!" I teased. The sound of my drunken giggling brought a huge smile to Tom's face.

"That's the tenth time you've been rejected, Benjamin. Just give it up." Tom spun his drumsticks clumsily around his index fingers and managed to release one too early. It vaulted through the air and nearly smacked Ben in the process.

"At least I have the balls to ask, you idiot," Ben mocked as he chucked the drumstick back at Tom.

"Enough! Focus! Final mike check!" Philip said forcefully.

Tom counted off the beat, and we all stood in readiness as Ben programmed our chosen song into his game console: *When You Were Young* by The Killers.

I directed my intoxicated brain to the TV in front of me and watched as the commands scrolled up the screen and into the flashing horizon on the game's prompter. As I had done many times before on this particular evening, I moved my left hand to the matching buttons at the end of the guitar and "strummed" along to the tune that I, thankfully, knew quite well at this point.

*"You sit there in your heartache, waiting on some beautiful boy to... to save you from your old ways,"* crooned Philip in the semi-chant of Brandon Flowers.

From the corner of my eye, I watched Tom pound away on the drum set and bob his head in time to the tune as he stared at the TV screen in deep concentration. I grinned like an idiot at him, and he winked back with a look that made my heart swell with pleasure.

"Right, Cris!" Ben shouted as I made it through the first verse and chorus without error. He mock head-banged with a look of boyish glee on his face that caused me to laugh like a little girl.

Philip jumped up and down as he continued to sing with a passion that suggested he fed his family through his efforts. It was adorable. We came to a lull after the second verse where Philip should have been the only one performing... and yet, all four of us proceeded to belt out the lyrics along with him. He even turned around to face us so that we could ham it up as one. I spun around to make sure Tom and I played exactly in time with one another as the drums and the lead guitar pounded out the melody in the song's biggest instrumental crescendo. We received sustained "Star Power" credits like crazy on the Guitar Hero system.

"Hell yeah!" Ben yelled energetically as Philip rejoined the chorus.

We all paused with our hands positioned on our "instruments" as the final notes rang from the speakers. Glancing at one another in awe at the fact we had managed to make it through the song perfectly, we reveled in the moment for a few seconds of silence... and then cheered raucously. I was yanked into numerous sweaty hugs and clapped on the back with a fervor that nearly caused me to keel over. Ben lifted me off the ground with the sheer exuberance of his embrace.

"Watch it there, mate," Tom chastised Ben affectionately as he removed me from Ben's arms to hold me in his.

"Fine, I'll let you borrow my wife for a few seconds but you have to give her back." Ben laughed with drunken abandon.

"Like hell," Tom murmured as he smiled and pressed his face into my neck.

"So, who has to drink the Boilermaker?" Philip asked jokingly.

"I say we all drink one!" Ben replied.

"I can't drink another one, you idiots! The wheels may still be turning, but the hamster upstairs is definitely dead! Plus, I'm like... half your size!" I protested.

Ben grabbed the beer and whiskey. "Half our size means half a drink! Bottoms up, love!"

Like an idiot, I drank.

Forty-five minutes later, I stumbled down the stairs leading to the street outside of Ben's flat. Philip was fast asleep on the sofa in the apartment, and Tom was trying to grasp onto a sliver of sobriety as he held me tightly in his arms to prevent me from killing us both.

"Oh God! I'm wasted!" I moaned as we made our way out the door and onto the *furshlugginer* cobblestone.

"Yes, you are," Tom agreed with a laugh.

"This is terrible! What are your parents going to think?" I cried as a hiccup escaped my lips. My ankle nearly twisted out from under me, and Tom's steady hands wrapped around my waist securely.

"Darling, it's past three. They've been asleep for hours," he said soothingly.

I hiccupped again and pitched forward as my shoe snagged on the edge of another ancient stone.

"Those damn shoes. This is not going to work." He bent over, wrapped his arms around my thighs, and hoisted me over his shoulder so I dangled unceremoniously upside down against his back. My arms hung a few feet above the ground, and my hair swung from side to side with each of his steps.

"Those effing Boilermakers!" I moaned.

"I don't know why you felt the need to keep up with three men. Three British men, at that," Tom teased.

"Anything you can do, I can do better!" I sang in a hideously nasal voice.

"Annie, get your gun...and shoot yourself. That was horrid."

"Psshh. You're just jealous," I slurred as my arms and hair continued to sway by my face.

He laughed as he walked towards a major thoroughfare where we could find a hack to take us home. All of a sudden, the motion of swaying while upside down affected me in the worst way possible.

"I think I'm going to be sick, Tommy," I lamented as I poked at his back, urging him to put me down.

He quickly removed me from his shoulder and placed me on the ground. I stumbled to the gutter for my penance.

"Don't come here!" I moaned. "This is so embarrassing!" I was sick again. He ignored my earlier request and collected my hair in his right hand so it wouldn't be in the way.

"Go away!" I cried. "I'm that stupid girl puking in the gutter... like some sad cliché of a tourist! Wooo, London!" I punched my fist weakly in the air, only to resume my position of prostration on Shakespeare's curb.

"Watch it now, that's my girlfriend you're talking about," he said soothingly as he rubbed my back with his free hand.

When I finished, he removed my shoes and lifted me once more. He cradled me against his chest and wrapped my legs around his waist. I rested my head on his shoulder and draped my arms behind his neck.

"You smell so good." I sighed against his collarbone.

"You smell like puke."

"I'm sorry. I'll understand if you never want to see me again," I slurred.

"I don't think there's much you could do that would ever make me feel that way."

"Hmmm." I barely managed to stay awake at that point.

"I'm addicted to you, Cris Pereira...and I don't want a cure," he whispered in my ear.

I smiled and clung even more tightly to his neck. That was the last thing I remembered from that night.

# EIGHTEEN

From: Lt. Ryan Sullivan <ryan.sullivan4@us.army.mil>
To: Cris Pereira <7crisp@gmail.com>
Date: Thurs, Sept 17, 2009 at 11:12 AM
Subject: ?

This is getting ridiculous. I guess the only way I know you'll hear what I have to say is through email. So be it.
I want you back. My life is shit without you. I'll do whatever it takes to make you believe me. At least give me the chance to say this in person.
Ryan

---

From: Cris Pereira <7crisp@gmail.com>
To: Lt. Ryan Sullivan <ryan.sullivan4@us.army.mil>
Date: Fri, Sept 18, 2009 at 4:41 PM
Subject: Re: ?

Too bad.

---

From: Lt. Ryan Sullivan <ryan.sullivan4@us.army.mil>
To: Cris Pereira <7crisp@gmail.com>
Date: Fri, Sept 18, 2009 at 5:09 PM
Subject: Re: Re: ?

Ouch. Do you want me to come to your house and beg? I can.
Ryan

From: Cris Pereira <7crisp@gmail.com>
To: Lt. Ryan Sullivan <ryan.sullivan4@us.army.mil>
Date: Fri, Sept 18, 2009 at 6:32 PM
Subject: Re: Re: Re: ?

No. I want you to leave me alone. Seriously, Ryan. I can't believe you think this is okay. I'm happy now. Stop trying to ruin it.
You don't deserve to set foot in my house, so don't show up here. I won't hold Mami back.
Cris

---

From: Lt. Ryan Sullivan <ryan.sullivan4@us.army.mil>
To: Cris Pereira <7crisp@gmail.com>
Date: Fri, Sept 18, 2009 at 6:51 PM
Subject: Re: Re: Re: Re: ?

You're not happy. You're dating a handsome man with a disposable income, so you think you have it made for the moment. But I know that's not you. Stop trying to trick yourself into thinking it is. I'm not trying to ruin anything. I'm trying to get you to see reason. Fairy tales are meant for children.
We can be happy again. I know it. It's all there, and I don't need a fairy tale to prove it.
Ryan

---

From: Cris Pereira <7crisp@gmail.com>
To: Lt. Ryan Sullivan <ryan.sullivan4@us.army.mil>
Date: Fri, Sept 18, 2009 at 8:01 PM
Subject: Piss Off

HOW DARE YOU? You have no fucking clue what 171

you're talking about! You think you can tear people apart and analyze them to death based on external factors alone because you're "smart." If you're so smart, why did you screw up a good thing? Oh, I know! Because you're pathetic. In case you haven't forgotten . . . we were happy. Until you ruined it by CHEATING ON ME. There are no second chances. You always knew that. STOP DELUDING YOURSELF. I'm happy because a good man loves me. If you think that's a fairy tale, then I feel sorry for you.
Cris

---

From: Lt. Ryan Sullivan <ryan.sullivan4@ us.army.mil>
To: Cris Pereira <7crisp@gmail.com>
Date: Wed, Oct 7, 2009 at 8:17 AM
Subject: Re: Piss Off

Just so you know: I didn't technically cheat on you. Thought it might be pertinent.
Ryan

---

From: Cris Pereira <7crisp@gmail.com>
To: Lt. Ryan Sullivan <ryan.sullivan4@us.army. mil>
Date: Fri, Oct 9, 2009 at 9:22 AM
Subject: Re: Re: Piss Off

I really have no idea what to say. I'm not interested in some Lewinsky story of how you didn't "technically" cheat on me.
For the last time . . . PISS OFF.

---

From: Lt. Ryan Sullivan <ryan.sullivan4@ us.army.mil>
To: Cris Pereira <7crisp@gmail.com>
Date: Mon, Jan 4, 2010 at 12:22 PM

Happy New Year, Cris. I'm really sorry if I upset you the last time I wrote.

I went to the grocery store yesterday and saw a picture of you at a New Year's Eve party in Hollywood with whatshisface.

You looked beautiful, mi corazon.

I'm so sorry I hurt you. I would do anything to take it back.

Ryan

---

I hauled my dry cleaning from the back of my Civic and walked into the family room to unload my burden on the first empty space I saw.

I loved Fridays. This weekend in particular was sure to be incredibly relaxing. I had absolutely nothing major planned. The list of "To-Dos" in my purse I wrote while at work included self-indulgent things like a mani/pedi session and the reorganization of my closet. After my crazy New Year's Eve in L.A. the weekend before, this would be a welcome respite.

The holidays had been a mixture of the mundane and the fantastical. Tom came to Raleigh for Thanksgiving, and we spent Christmas apart with our respective families. The time at home had been wonderful, but my mind was often preoccupied with missing Tom entirely too much. I had to confess that my heart felt noticeably lighter when the taxi dropped me off in front of his apartment before New Year's Eve. The raucous nightclub party we had attended left scattered remembrances of flashing camera lights, glittering jewels, and pounding music. Of course, all of those recollections paled in comparison to the best memory of all: the soul-jarring kiss we had shared to welcome in 2010.

I smiled to myself at the thought.

Mami came home as I prepared supper, and we passed the evening in each other's company with jokes and lighthearted conversation.

"You're so happy recently," she commented in Spanish during dinner.

I shrugged. "Life is good." Except for the intermittent emails of doom and gloom from my ex.

"It's more than that. I think it's because of Thomas. You know, I didn't want to say this, but I was worried for a long time you were too hurt by everything that happened last year. After your father died, I could see that you were only pretending to be happy, and it upset me a lot. I'm so grateful to see you smile easily again."

I grinned at her affectionately to further illustrate her point. "Don't worry about me, Mami. Everything's going to be okay."

My phone shrieked in my purse as I toweled off the last of the dishes. I checked the caller ID, and I couldn't stop myself from experiencing a small rush of contentment when I saw the words "Blocked ID" illuminated in the window.

"Hi," I said.

"What are you doing?"

"Drying dishes," I replied.

"That could be sexy."

"Only if you're a chauvinistic pig with a June Cleaver fetish," I chuckled. "How was filming today?"

"Hellish. It was impossible to manage the extras on set because they didn't have enough people organizing everything. Anyway, I think it came out well, and everyone was really nice. But it's kind of like forcing yourself to smile whilst listening to a broken drill right beside your head."

I laughed as I put the last dish in the cupboard.

"Still no plans for the weekend?" he queried.

"Nope. I'm totally free! I was invited to go dancing with some co-workers tomorrow, but I bowed out gracefully."

"Maybe you should do something more low-key," he mused.

"I'm sure I'll find something to fill the time with. It's impossible for me to sit still for long," I joked.

"I'm well aware of that fact. On that note, I think I've come up with something for you to do."

"Like what?" I teased suggestively.

"Well, for starters...you can open the door."

"Huh?" I gasped.

"Open the bloody door, love. I'm outside." He chuckled.

I dropped the dishtowel on the floor, raced to the front door, and yanked it open.

Sure enough, my tall drink of water stood in our front yard with a huge grin on his face and his cell phone in his hand. A taxicab idled in our driveway with its lights on.

"Wha- what?" I stammered as I clicked my phone shut.

"Do you want to go with me to a museum?" he asked without missing a beat.

I raced towards him and threw my arms around his neck.

"Are you crazy?" I demanded through my laughter.

"Yes. Do you want to go with me to a museum?" he pressed as he waved back at the house behind me. Mami had come to situate herself by the front door with a look of flabbergasted shock on her face.

"Um, what museum?"

"It's a surprise. You're just going to have to trust me. Yes or no?" His eyes sparkled with merriment as he gazed into mine.

"Yes, of course—but—"

He didn't let me finish. "Go upstairs and grab your passport."

"Are you nuts? Where are we going?" I insisted.

"I told you: to a museum. I know you'll like it."

"Thomas!" I cried.

"Cristina! Come on, you promised to live outside your head more. Trust me. Go get your passport." He placed a kiss on my forehead and strolled over to Mami and hugged her.

Confusion and excitement warred within me as I considered arguing further with my obstinate boyfriend but decided against it as I raced upstairs to retrieve my passport and brush my teeth. Upon further contemplation, I changed my clothes and threw some necessities into a small bag to take with me.

I came back downstairs. Tom and my mother were seated at the little table in our breakfast nook. She held both of his hands in each of hers and lavished words of thanks on him. He smiled kindly at her with such caring compassion that I could feel myself fall in love with him all over again. As I walked over to them, she released his hands, and he hastily rose to his feet.

"Mami, I guess I'll call you from…wherever it is we're going!" I shook my head at Tom and didn't even attempt to hide my bewilderment.

"Go, go!" she sniffed.

"Are you crying?" I demanded.

"No! *Esto*, I'm just surprised to see Tom. *Pero*, please call me when you get there!"

"Don't worry! I will!"

"I won't worry, *querida*. Not anymore," she said quietly as she hugged me. She turned towards Tom and positioned herself on her tiptoes to embrace him tightly. As she pulled away, she put her right 175 hand on his cheek in a gesture I always associated with deep affection. I guess my mother liked surprises more than I did.

In the cab, I wasn't too surprised when Tom directed the driver to take us to the airport since he specifically asked me to grab my passport.

"We're not really going to a museum, are we?" I intoned.

"Of course we are. I wouldn't ask you to go to a museum if I had no intention of taking you. Unfortunately, there are no museums open around here right now, so we have to go someplace else."

"Like?" I pushed.

"Like…a museum you need a passport for," he teased.

"Seriously, tell me! Anyway, I'll find out where we're going as soon as we get to the airport!" I said with exasperation. While glancing circumspectly at his disheveled good looks, I decided I needed a proper kiss, and he needed some "persuasion." I leaned over to him and pressed my lips lightly on his neck and across his jawbone. He sighed as his hands moved to my lower back to pull me closer against him.

"Tommy?"

"You're wicked." He groaned.

I grinned. "Tell me."

He smirked back at me. "I will. But first, let me tell you a story."

I shoved him away jokingly. He chuckled for a moment and proceeded with his tale.

"I promise it's relevant. Besides, you could use some patience.

"About a year ago, I was forced to attend these mall autograph signings all over the country. One particularly sad Sunday, I saw a petite girl with an angry face cutting her eyes at me from the queue. It intrigued me because she was clearly bored out of her mind. We definitely shared that sentiment. When she came closer, I saw that the angry girl was actually quite beautiful. Further intrigued, I attempted to engage her in dialogue with the help of some inane questions. She proceeded to accuse me of being a racist sod. I was hooked. So, I began stalking her through email and text messages. In a pathetic attempt to learn as much about her as possible, I asked random questions of her on almost a daily basis." He stopped to press a kiss to my forehead.

"Sounds like a really interesting story. Yet, I fail to see the relevance."

"It's relevant. You already know where we're going. You told me on Monday, January 12, 2009." He stared evenly at me with an intense look that suddenly made me feel lightheaded.

"What was the question?" My mind searched through tomes of emails.

He merely smiled back at me patiently.

Museums. Passports. Questions in January. No way. No *freaking* way.

"You're-you're…are we going to Paris?" I squeaked.

"Could you please pull around to the Air France terminal?" Tom said smoothly to the driver, faced me again, and wagged his eyebrows in a manner that clearly affirmed my rather inarticulate assessment.

Speechless, I threw my arms around his neck. He laughed softly as he returned the embrace.

"Happy Birthday."

"My birthday is not for another two weeks!" I croaked.

"I'll be in Madrid then. I changed your birthday this year. Temporarily."

I managed to find my voice again. "How omnipotent of you, oh mighty one!"

We breezed through airport check-in without any undue notice and were directed by the Air France staff into a private waiting area prior to boarding our flight. The plane sped down the runway at eleven that evening. I tried hard to fall asleep, and Tom continually pressured me to rest since we would arrive in Paris in the middle of the day. Honestly, it did not matter to me in the slightest if I spent the next forty-eight hours awake. I would gladly suffer the consequences.

We were going to Paris! The man I loved was taking me to the city I adored. It was wondrously cheesy, and yet it was also one of the most amazing things anyone had ever done for me.

Go to hell, Ryan Sullivan, and take with you every silly fairy tale you believed was meant only for children.

"Where do you want to go for lunch?" Tom asked as we waited for a chauffeured car upon arrival at Charles de Gaulle.

"I have no idea!" I laughed with exuberance as I absorbed the slightly overcast sky and the sound of the French language rolling off the tongues of those around me.

"That's not helpful," he replied merrily.

"Tell you what: you pick an arrondissement, and I'll pick a place to eat!"

After much debate back and forth, he selected the eighth arrondissement. I thought for a moment and asked the driver to take us to the area of Madeleine. A cup of piping hot coffee and a croque-monsieur from Fauchon suddenly sounded incredibly delicious.

One of the wonderful things about the stereotypical snobbery the world often accused the French of cultivating was the fact that they were rarely impressed by the things that drove the masses wild elsewhere. I was certain that people recognized Tom as we traversed Madeleine and spent a ridiculous amount of time browsing through the cases of pastries at Fauchon. Several times I saw a few individuals do a double take as their eyes glossed over us. Yet, not a single person approached Tom, nor did anyone give him any undue amount of attention. It was wonderful. The French were not easily overcome, and the British movie star traipsing through one of the loveliest sections of their city was not something that merited more than a cursory glance of appreciation. The bronze-skinned midget by his side was even more negligible. I can't think of a time where I appreciated being completely unimportant more.

As we strolled up and down the boulevards, and time passed with carefree swiftness, I noticed Tom glance at his watch more and more recurrently. He also grew increasingly quiet and introspective. For some reason, the faintest trace of anxiety marred his brow.

"Are you meeting your other girlfriend soon?" I joked as he noted the time once again.

"In a bit, yes. I was kind of hoping you would—"

I interrupted him before he could finish. "We may be in Paris, but you'd better not say anything that even remotely sounds like *ménage*!" I teased. I couldn't fathom what caused his unease, but levity was generally a good antidote.

"Shit. It was worth a shot. In all seriousness, we do have an… appointment in about half an hour."

"Why didn't you just say that? Let's get a cab." I started towards the street corner, but he grabbed my hand and stopped me.

"The car is coming to pick us up in five minutes."

I raised my eyebrows at him. "The car?" I jeered with a grin.

He did not release my hand. Instead, he focused his gaze on me with the same intensity I recalled during the cab ride to the airport in North Carolina. Behind his beautiful grey eyes, I saw a hint of something ineffable. Electricity sparked between us and radiated warmth in our shared glance. It wasn't confusion that I saw amidst the flecks of green and gold. It was…*fear*?

"Is something wrong?" I blurted.

He glanced down and chuckled. The odd moment faded as the current of charged energy broke free its hold on us.

"No, nothing's wrong. Everything's exactly right."

"You were just looking at me kind of funny," I mused.

"Sorry. I must be knackered."

"The car" rolled before us, and we stepped inside before I could think of anything else to say that would prod him to offer further explanation for his odd behavior.

"Where are we going now?" I asked cheerfully.

"You know that, as well. I was supposed to take you to a museum." He grinned as he inclined his head towards the driver, giving me leave to divulge the destination.

"*Au Musée d'Orsay, s'il vous plaît,*" I intoned.

"*Oui, Mademoiselle.*"

"Have you ever been before?" I asked Tom.

"No, but I spent some time learning about it prior to coming here. I'm actually a big fan of Impressionist art as well."

"I love Van Gogh. I don't know why exactly, but I've always loved his work," I commented.

"It's because you're a nutter. You understand him," he joked.

"There's a thin line between genius and insanity."

"And you've definitely crossed it," he continued. His left knee bounced up and down rapidly in a habit I knew indicated he was nervous about something.

"I'm not the one who showed up randomly at your door on a Friday night and decided to go across the Atlantic!"

He laughed and ran his fingers anxiously through his hair. What the hell was going on with him?

We rolled to a stop in front of the museum, and I was dismayed to see a mass exodus of art lovers leaving the premises. I checked my watch and came to a heart-sinking realization.

"I think the museum is closed already!" I moaned.

He took my hand and marched towards the entrance as though I hadn't said anything.

The guards nodded at Tom and removed the rope currently cordoning the entrance to let us pass through. Waiting beyond was a grey-haired man with a tag identifying him as "Head Docent."

"Hello, Monsieur Abramson. You're right on time," he said warmly in accented English.

"Hello, Henri," Tom replied as though he had known this man for years.

"And you must be Mademoiselle Cristina," Henri announced as he turned to me and smiled encouragingly.

*"Bonsoir, Henri."*

"Thanks again for being so accommodating. I promise we won't be long," Tom stated to Henri.

"Please, Monsieur. Take your time."

Henri led us towards the main Impressionist gallery and turned around to give us privacy as we strolled from painting to painting.

"Did you plan this with Henri?" I whispered to Tom.

"No, Henri and I go way back. I know he doesn't look it, but the man is a wicked poker player."

"Right. No, really…did you plan this?" I tried again.

"It's a lot easier to enjoy an art gallery when the tourists aren't paying more attention to my ugly mug, don't you think?"

I smiled indulgently as I considered all the trouble he went through to take me to my favorite place in the world for my birthday: the Impressionist gallery of the Musée d'Orsay in Paris.

Pausing before a Van Gogh painting, I leaned in to study the brushstrokes. They were almost violent in their quantity and texture. The tiny dashes of color crashed into one another with seeming simplicity, but the picture as a whole appeared anything but effortless. Each individual element of a painting always made me feel as though I received a tiny glimpse into the artist's mindset at the time. To me, Van Gogh's work was vibrant and a bit aggressive. I loved it.

Tom walked ahead to look at something by Gauguin. We shifted from painting to painting in companionable silence. Twice, I caught him staring at me when he thought I wasn't looking. Each time, he smiled with a trace amount of discomfort and pretended as though everything was fine. We continued to make our way down the gallery. As I neared the rear wall, I noticed Tom backtrack to a painting he had already observed.

His behavior really started to puzzle me, but I was too in my element to let it overcome the enjoyment of being here with him.

I paced the back wall and noticed a small glass case standing alone in the far right corner, nestled between a Pissarro and a Degas. Confused by the existence of a display case in the back of the Impressionist wing, I strolled over to it. From behind me, Tom exhaled slowly and audibly.

At first glance, I didn't see anything in the small case. Then, something sparkled from the center as I came closer to it. A small light shone on the art within, and it reflected back at me in flashing shimmers of incandescence.

I stopped a few feet in front of it as realization dawned on me.

It was a ring.

Not just any ring. This ring was truly breathtaking. It sat inside a red box with the moniker "Cartier" emblazoned on the inner lid in gleaming gold script. It was an emerald cut diamond, and the behemoth flashing in the center could be no less than three carats of pressurized carbon perfection. The ring was extremely modern in its setting and presentation. Tasteful, yet fabulous.

It was so Tom.

My heart pounded in my throat, and I gasped quietly for air.

Tom walked towards me and came to stand on the other side of the display case with the flashing stone situated between us. His eyes were wide and his breath was a bit shaky as he opened his mouth to address me.

To propose to me.

"I'm done," he began.

"Oh God," I croaked.

He laughed nervously. "Let me try that again." He paused to clear his throat.

"I'm done waking up and wishing you were with me.

"I'm done being apart from the only person in America who cares to hear what I'm really thinking.

"I'm done seeing something you would find ridiculously funny, and only being able to tell you about it.

"Mostly... I'm done being without you."

My heartbeat drowned out all sounds except his voice.

"I want you to be my wife."

I stared at his face. It was so full of earnest love that it consumed everything else around it in a fire of clarity. For a brief moment, I thought about the last time a man had proposed to me.

I had gone with Ryan to pick out my ring. Since he was certain that he would not be able to purchase the ideal one without my help, we had gone together. From many selections, I had chosen the ring that was perfect for me. It was everything I had ever wanted. I loved antique rings, and the center stone was round cut with tiny pave diamonds intricately woven around it and situated amidst delicate embellishments that were carved along the length of the band.

Exactly what I wanted.

The glittering rock in front of me was the last thing I would ever have selected if given the opportunity. It was so ... *big*. It almost looked like a piece of costume jewelry, flashing merrily at me as every ray of light was captured and refracted in its perfectly cut facets. 181

This ring was so Tom. So not me.

"What about…my mom?" I barely made out.

"I asked her last night. She said yes."

Bewildered as the image of Tom and my mother sitting at our breakfast table just the day before came to mind, I tried to change the subject. "It's huge!" I whispered.

He smiled crookedly back at me. "I work in Hollywood. I'd rather not have someone look at my wife's hand and think I'm a cheap bastard."

I couldn't say anything else as I stared down at what I believed to be the wrong ring. Utterly. Then I glanced back at the face…of the right man. He had to be the right man. Every fiber of my being wanted to throw my arms around his neck and shout "Yes!" to the world.

Why couldn't I do it?

I was so afraid. The last time I said "yes" to a man, he had left my heart in the gutter for me to find and resuscitate by myself. When I did unearth it, it was bitter and blemished. It had taken months of agony to make it function properly again. I couldn't go through that once more. I wouldn't make it.

"Stop thinking, Cris!" he whispered.

I snapped out of my fear-ridden reverie and stared back into his eyes. The eyes of the right man.

"Don't think, just do," he murmured with a careful smile.

I took a deep breath and raced over to him to press my lips to his. He lifted me from the ground as we kissed, and I tangled my fingers in his soft hair.

"Yes."

# NINETEEN

I left for work the next Monday morning twenty minutes earlier than usual. Even though I was sure to regret relinquishing those extra moments of sleep, I was more concerned with making it to my cubicle under the radar. Like a zombie, I shuffled to my desk and plopped into my seat with a yawn that rippled down my spine. Shuddering afterwards, I placed my hands on the keyboard of the computer to type in my login and password information.

There it was, resting innocuously on my ring finger for all the world to see. Yep, it definitely wasn't a dream. It sat there obnoxiously fat and painfully brilliant and was my reason for coming into the office before anyone else noticed me. If a gust of wind blew in my general direction, I knew which side a fall would favor.

This was completely ridiculous. A normal girl would be leading with her left hand everywhere she went, just as I did whenever I was first engaged to Ryan. That month, I began to point at everything, brush my hair over my shoulder, stroke my chin thoughtfully, and juggle bowling pins on fire with my left hand. I became the Ambidextrous Superwoman. It was impossible to miss my pride and pleasure at the shining rock of commitment glistening from my finger with every movement I made.

The man I loved wanted to cherish me. ~~For a lifetime.~~ For a little while. The simple truth of the matter: I was incredibly uncomfortable with the recent turn of events. Never before in my life had I made such an important decision so recklessly and impulsively. Usually, everything I did was done with careful consideration, weighing pros and cons until I felt at peace with my choice.

This decision was pure insanity. My heart had spoken instinctively, and my mind never even had a chance.

What had I gotten myself into!?

I should have spent the rest of the weekend talking at length with Tom about the intricacies that came with planning a life together. I should have asked questions about my mother, about how to deal with moving, about where I could work. Should have.

Instead, we had passed the time in a suite at the Plaza Athénée..

. laughing and reveling in one another's company with the shadow of the Eiffel Tower filling the floor to ceiling windows by the enormous bed. Completely carefree, as though the real world had been set on pause and nothing else mattered except enjoying the moment.

I blushed to myself as certain explicit memories rose to the surface of my sleep-deprived mind. Closing my eyes, I shook my head firmly in an attempt to focus on the work in front of me.

Today was sure to be... *interesting*.

Thus far, the only people who knew that we were... *engaged*... were members of our families. We called my mother first, and Tom had patiently smiled through her tears of happiness and almost incoherent pronouncements of joy. Anne had shrieked and carried on with abandon as soon as Tom said, "We have something to tell you." Of course, he had been unable to get a word in edgewise as soon as she gleaned the truth from him. She had ended the conversation by breathlessly saying to me, "I can't wait to call you my sister!"

The biggest shock of all was the reaction of Tom's father. Truth be told, I had chewed on my lower lip nervously whenever Tom pressed the buttons on his phone to call London. His father usually thought Tom was brash and impulsive, prone to making stupid decisions based on nothing more than a whim. I assumed he wouldn't take this news very well.

Upon hearing what had just transpired, his mother had been quietly ecstatic in the elegantly refined manner I had come to expect from her. After warmly wishing us well and conveying her delight via speakerphone, she had turned over the phone to her husband.

"Well, Thomas. I can't say that I'm surprised," he began.

Tom merely smiled at the phone resting in his hand.

"But... I'm proud of you, son."

Tom's eyebrows rose in reaction to his father's words. "Thank you."

"No, thank you. I thought long and hard about the things we discussed at lunch, and I need to take a step back and be proud of the man I raised, even if he is not how I pictured him being."

"I really appreciate that," Tom stated earnestly.

"You've chosen a magnificent young woman. She's strong and direct, with a great sense of humor and a good head on her shoulders. She's not likely to take any garbage you hand her way. There's little else I put more stock into than choosing one's partner in life. I guess you're not as daft as I thought you were. I'm happy to give credit where credit is due. Congratulations, Thomas and Cristina. I'm

184

very pleased for you both."

My jaw nearly hit the floor. Not a single admonishment. I could not even detect the slightest hint of judgment in his tone. *Hot damn.*

We had definitely used up all our luck on that one. Today, Tom would tell Melissa about the happy development that occurred over the weekend. *Yay.*

As I looked through my email, I saw that Hana had sent no less than four different messages to me over the span of the last three days. She wrote to tell me my phone was going straight to voicemail, and she wanted to make sure everything was okay. The last email was slightly more petulant and brought a wry smile to my face. *Crazy-ass stalker.* I needed to call both Hana and Gita on my lunch break.

My phone buzzed next to me with a text message.

> Blocked ID (8:49 am): fuck, it's early

I smiled to myself before responding.

> Me (8:49 am): Language! Tell me a/b it.
> Blocked ID (8:49 am): i'm entitled to foul language—it's six here
> Me (8:50 am): Blah, blah, blah. Poor u :-P
> Blocked ID (8:50 am): poor me is right, i didn't get much sleep this wkend ;-)
> Me (8:50 am): Whatever! I didn't hear any complaints while it was happening!
> Blocked ID (8:50 am): and u never will
> Me (8:50 am): That's good to know.
> Blocked ID (8:50 am): i wouldn't mind a distraction—seeing melissa in a few hrs
> Me (8:50 am): Keep a chew toy handy. Rub some catnip on it.
> Blocked ID (8:51 am): lol
> Me (8:51 am): Are u free later on?
> Blocked ID (8:51 am): no, i have a

185

```
date with a hot blonde
Me (8:51 am): Ha! No, srsly. We need
to talk a/b ... logistics.
Blocked ID (8:51 am): u would say
that-ur a total buzzkill
Me (8:51 am): I'm serious.
Blocked ID (8:51 am): i know-i'll
call u after ten tonight, ur time
Me (8:52 am): Thank you. J
Blocked ID (8:52 am): tell cletise
the security guard to "back up off my
shit" ;-)
Me (8:52 am): Your shit? You swine.
Tell Jenna to find another shoulder to
cry on.
Blocked ID (8:52 am): lol
Me (8:52 am): I love you.
Blocked ID (8:52 am): i love u
```

I put down my phone with a peaceful grin and turned to my mountain of work, temporarily separated from the storm of thoughts in my head. Perhaps it was weakness on my part, but Tom never failed to distract me from myself. Unfortunately, this proved to be quite problematic when I actually wanted to have a serious discussion with him about rather important things ... like getting married. His laissez-faire attitude was contagious, and I really needed to hash out some of the more pressing issues to appease my ranting mind—for a little while.

"Cristina?"

I jumped in my seat at the voice behind me. It was my boss, Marta.

"Hey!" I squeaked as I spun around and simultaneously shoved my left hand into the pocket of my slacks.

"I didn't mean to startle you. You're in early for a Monday."

"Uh ... yeah. Just wanted to get myself situated and organized," I stated lamely.

"Great. I'm glad you're here. I've been meaning to talk to you about that community outreach project you've been working on recently. 'Master Classes for Kids'?"

"Oh!" With inspiration from Tom and the support of my friends, I had contacted musicians from the North Carolina Symphony in Raleigh and put together four different master classes in public schools for members of the student orchestras. The principal violinist, cellist, flutist, and percussionist had volunteered their Saturdays for open forum lessons with gifted students that were meant to engage and inspire kids to continue pursuing music. It was amazing to witness the kids surrounded by the support of their fellow orchestra members and the positive encouragement from industry professionals. Many of these children had never had a private lesson and could not really afford to pay for them, so this sort of environment was perfect for cultivating their shared love of music. I know, I know … eat your heart out, Oprah.

"We've gotten terrific feedback from the community on it," Marta continued.

"Thanks. It was a lot of fun, and the kids really enjoyed it." There appeared to be no end to the lame sound bites on my part.

She nodded slowly. "So, I received a call on Friday from Mecklenburg County. They wanted to talk to you about helping them organize something similar there."

My eyes widened.

"Of course, we don't really have the budget to continue sponsoring these things, but Mecklenburg County recently received a donation from an anonymous patron of the arts. This individual indicated the desire to see something like 'Master Classes for Kids' develop into a recurring event in North Carolina," she continued.

"That's really wonderful. Seriously, Marta. It's definitely going to make such a difference. I know it was tough getting approval for any funding whatsoever on this, and I wanted to thank you again for all of your efforts."

"Thank yourself. You did all the work. So, are you interested in helping out Mecklenburg County? It should be a lot easier without the budgetary constraints we had here. Anyway, think about it. I'll email you the contact info. Of course, I don't want it to take away from your work here, but if you can manage the time commitment, I'm sure they would love your input," she finished.

I nodded. "Absolutely. Thanks so much for the vote of confidence."

She smiled back at me knowingly and turned to leave.

Puzzled by her strange expression, I sat still for a moment trying to figure out the source of her amusement. Whatever. It was probably just my paranoia rearing its ugly head.

I responded to Hana's emails by saying I would give her a call 187 at lunch—that way I could make sure I had the full functionality of both my eardrums for at least half of the day. Her reaction to Paris was sure to be heartfelt and deafening.

A few hours later, I made the trek to my car with the intention of sacrificing my hearing on the altar of undying friendship.

Shockingly, Hana failed to answer her phone.

Gita picked up on the third ring.

"Good, you're not dead," she bit sarcastically.

"Hah."

"I knew you weren't. Make sure to tell Crazy you're alive and well," she continued with a chuckle.

"I left her a message. Hopefully she'll call me back before my lunch hour is up."

"You should have heard her on the phone yesterday. She finally got in touch with your mother, and since Mami wouldn't throw her a bone as to your whereabouts, the speculations grew wildly out of hand," Gita continued.

I laughed nervously.

She paused for a moment, digesting the implications of my skittish giggle. "Oh lord. Please tell me you didn't run off to Vegas for an easily annullable wedding."

"No! I'm not quite *that* impulsive."

"That's a joke. You're not even slightly impulsive. Period. Why do I detect a note of hysteria in your voice?" she pressed.

I took a deep breath. Cut the shit. "I'm engaged."

Dead silence.

"Gita?"

"Dammit! I owe Hana fifty bucks!" she groaned.

Taken aback by her reaction, I merely said, "What?"

"I said it would take you at least two years. She said less."

"Wait... you're not... surprised?"

"I'm surprised at how soon it happened, but I'm not surprised by it happening. Come on, dude. You two are nuts for each other."

"Yeah, but... it happened so suddenly!" I lamented.

"Are you regretting your decision?"

I didn't hesitate to respond. "No. I feel like I made the right decision. I just don't... I'm not used to being so impetuous."

"Chica, I've held back for a while because I didn't want to proffer advice like an oldass crone chockfull of wisdom, but he's a lot better for you than that regimented fool you carted around for years. That decision was a far cry from reckless, and it didn't work out so

188

well."

I remained silent for a moment. Gita was the verbal equivalent of a Mack truck.

"Are you mad at me?" she demanded.

"No. I knew you weren't a huge fan of Ryan, but I guess I didn't realize until now how much of a non-fan you were."

"I wouldn't go that far. I was just never too impressed. You're like... this great breath of sunny, fresh air. He wasn't. Killjoy. In my mind, I always referred to him as Sergeant Killjoy. You don't want a spring day to come in contact with him," she stated flatly.

"Ryan wasn't... *that* bad," I retorted lamely.

"Whatever. He's a total moron trying to be wise beyond his years. Full of doom and gloom. Tom kind of reminds me of a kid sometimes, but he definitely suits you more. He's not laden with issues of self-loathing."

"How is he a kid?" I tried not to sound testy, but I was fairly certain I failed in my efforts.

"Come on, Cris. I meant it in a good way. Tom laughs more, jokes more, and stops to take in life without being forced to do so. I don't see him struggling with indecision. He knows what he wants and goes for it. A risk taker. Come to think of it, I wish I were more of a kid sometimes. They just want to have fun. If I functioned according to that premise, maybe I would stop myself from saying dumbass things to my newly-engaged best friend and upsetting her as a result."

I sighed with a half-smile. "I'm not upset."

"Liar. Let me try this again. Congratulations. Ryan sucked. Tom rules."

I laughed softly. "Thanks."

"Don't be uncomfortable. Even if I think it happened sooner than I would have guessed, I feel a heck of a lot better about you marrying a smiling risk taker than a grouchy douchebag."

We ended the conversation soon after that, but the unsettled feeling in the pit of my stomach had not dissipated. I expected Gita to share some of my more worrisome sentiments, and her open acceptance of the craziest decision I had ever made in my life unnerved me. She was my practical friend, and she had always been the one to see the forest through the trees. If she readily subscribed to Tom's school of life-changing spontaneity, I was more alone in my discomfort than I originally thought.

Was no one dismayed by the recent turn of events? How come

everyone saw this coming except for me? When were they planning to share their clairvoyance?

The last thing she said echoed in my mind: "You said it was the right decision. Why are you trying to kill it with worry? If it's the right decision for you, then everything else will fall into place. I'm not one for religion, but have some faith."

I sat in my car, staring at the steering wheel. Engrossed in my own thoughts, the sudden tapping on the window next to my head caused me to jump in my seat. If I thought the sound was startling, I was completely unprepared for the sight of its source.

Sergeant Killjoy stood at my door and peered down intently at me.

Ryan Sullivan: the man who broke my heart…my first love.

Shit. Double shit.

I scrambled to open the car door and scrambled up rather clumsily.

"What are you doing here?" I sputtered and shoved my palms in my pockets like a naughty child caught with her hand in Monsieur Cartier's cookie jar. Adrenaline made my motions jerky, and my pulse raced with the combination of shock and hyperawareness.

His hair was cropped short, and his beautiful blue eyes studied me with the same intensity that used to make my heart melt. Pain flew into my throat. The last memory of those eyes was one of devastation.

"I'm sorry. I thought I asked you a question. *What are you doing here?*" I bit out.

"Still a smartass." He chuckled.

"And you're still a dick," I kicked back.

"I always liked that about you."

"I don't have time for this," I retorted and made to return to the office building.

He caught my right arm as I tried to walk by. "Cristina. Please. Just give me five minutes."

"Let go of me." I gasped as the searing pain of his touch on my skin threatened to rip apart my tenuous hold on self-control.

"I'll just follow you inside if you try to leave."

I glared at him.

He glanced around. "I guess you're probably not going to get coffee with me."

"You think?" I shot back.

"Babe, stop pretending to be such a bitch. I know it's taking you a lot of effort. Just hear me out."

"I'm not your 'babe,' Ryan. Talk fast because I have very little patience for bullshit," I said begrudgingly.

His gaze softened at my apparent willingness to listen to him. "Look... I've been trying to talk to you for a while now, and I know you're probably not ready for me to jump back into your life like nothing happened, but there are a few things I need to say to you."

I closed my eyes and took a deep breath. "You suffer from the supreme misconception that I could *ever* feel as though nothing happened. You... *destroyed* me. There's no other way to say it. You left me to bury myself, and you didn't care one bit about what that meant. Luckily, I didn't crawl into a hole and waste away. Why are you trying to make me relive that agony?"

He grimaced at my flat tone of voice juxtaposed alongside the pain of my words. For the first time, I felt a pang of guilt for being so nasty to him. He was right... it wasn't easy being such a bitch.

"There aren't enough words in the English language to tell you how sorry I am for what I did to you. I know I owe you an explanation."

"You know what? I thought you owed me an explanation for a long time. Now, I don't really care," I responded matter-of-factly.

"You're lying. Look, I was... scared. There were so many things I wanted to do with my life, and I wasn't sure that getting married was the right decision for me."

"Then why the hell did you ask?" I grasped tightly onto the cell phone in my right pocket.

"Because I knew I'd never be able to find another woman like you."

"And yet, you tried," I stated quietly.

"About that... I meant what I said in the email. I didn't cheat on you. I did meet someone named Amber, and I was really attracted to her. I never did anything about it... but I knew you weren't going to just let me go without a fight. As terrible as it sounds, I knew the only way to get you to walk away and never look back was to tell you I cheated on you. I lied. I'm sorry." As he made his agonizing admission, he stared directly into my face to see if the weight of his statements would have any effect on my frosty demeanor.

I couldn't hide my painful dismay. "How could you do that? *Why?*" The last word sounded hideously similar to a sob.

He shrugged with a look of chagrin. "I made a mistake. You have to forgive me."

I looked about me in an attempt to bid some time and raised my left hand shakily to my face to press my thumb and forefinger into the bridge of my nose.

"What the fuck?" Ryan's voice was a tortured whisper. Even through my internal anguish, I realized my error.

His eyes froze on the giant cookie. I hastily shoved my hand back into my pocket.

"Are you insane?" he yelled.

I merely stared back in defiance.

"Please tell me that's merely a decorative deterrent. Please tell me you're not that stupid."

"How dare you?"

"Cristina, what are you thinking?" he demanded as he grabbed me by the shoulders and shook me gently.

"Let go of me."

"Are you actually planning to marry that moron? You're going to move to California? You want to be a real housewife of Orange County?" he jeered as he squeezed me even harder.

I shoved him away as the scent of painful remembrance washed over me. I was too close to the man responsible for a great deal of my suffering. Tears welled as my phone vibrated in my pocket.

"I don't have to listen to this. He's not a moron! You don't know anything about him, so shut up!"

"I know enough. The types of people who want that kind of life-style are crazy ones. They infect craziness onto those around them, and they're unfailingly selfish. Their marriages become statistics. I know why he wants you. You're selfless to a fault. When you love, you give everything," he stated with the rushed pace of desperation.

"Because that's what love is! This is the biggest problem with you, Ryan Sullivan! Love is not supposed to be convenient or easy all the time. Love is all-consuming and irrational."

"Only a fool believes that. I don't want to lose myself to love," he shot back.

"Why does it have to be that way? No one's asking you to lose yourself. This is what's fucked up about people who intellectualize love and try to repackage it as some new opiate of the masses."

"Look, I didn't come here to fight with you about the perils of co-dependence. In fact, I came to do the exact opposite. Maybe I think love is damaging just as much as it has its merits... but it doesn't matter. I love you. I want you back. Tell me it's not too late." He pulled me to him to stare down at my face openly. I tried to wriggle out of his grasp, but he held tightly onto my shoulders.

"Too late for what? I'm engaged. I love him even if you think he's crazy and selfish. Incidentally, you couldn't be more wrong. Before you point the finger at someone you don't even know, maybe you should take a good long look in the mirror." I twisted sideways and marched back towards the office building. He shouted after me.

"You're lost, Cristina! What are you going to do with your life? Are you going to take Mami with you? You know I'm not being harsh when I say that all those Beverly Hills snobs will think she's the hired help. Do you want to be responsible for that? I don't want you to change anything about yourself. Stay here. Be with your family. Be near your friends. Just be with me! I'll fix everything I broke if it takes me the rest of my life. We can be happy again!"

I stopped short as the tears cascaded down my face. Spinning around to glare at my first love, I froze at the sight of him rushing towards me to pull me into an embrace.

"Don't do this," he pleaded.

Even through the bittersweet sensation of hearing him say everything I had dreamed he would say each night I was forced to deal with my pain, I held tightly onto my pride.

"I didn't do this. You did." I shoved him aside and ran as fast as I could into the building.

My sobs were became audible, so I tore my way into the ladies room and slammed the stall door shut. Tears flowed down my face. All I wanted at that moment was to talk to Tom. I wanted to tell him everything. I wanted him to laugh at the things Ryan said. I wanted him to tell me I wouldn't be an Orange County housewife. I wanted him to say that my mother would be happy even though her only child lived three thousand miles away from her. Most of all, I wanted him to tell me *I* would be happy—away from my friends, away from my family . . . away from everything I knew.

But . . . I couldn't tell him. I couldn't bear to hear the pain in his voice when he realized Ryan was back in my life. He would feel betrayed. I pulled out my phone as a moment of weakness washed over me. A voicemail message blinked on the screen. I pressed the keys to listen.

"Cristina, this is Melissa Nash. I've just spoken to Thomas. I want to release a press statement at the end of the news cycle on Friday so we can control the flow of information. Thomas's publicist will be in touch. 'No comment' is about to become the most important phrase in your vocabulary. Against my better inclinations, 193

congratulations are in order. Do yourself a favor and either discon-
nect your home phone or get an unlisted number. Good luck. You're
going to need it. Hollywood is not for the fainthearted."

The phone clattered to the floor as a fresh stream of tears trailed
down my cheeks.

Cartier's cookie shimmered tauntingly on my hand.

I was so alone.

# TWENTY

Last weekend in Paris, British actor Thomas Abramson proposed to his girlfriend Cristina Pereira with a three-carat, emerald cut stone from Cartier. The two have been dating for approximately one year. London born Abramson is twenty-four years old and best known for his starring role in the film *Apparition*. Pereira is twenty-five years old and originally from Puerto Rico. She is employed by the state of North Carolina as a social worker. No wedding details have been solidified yet, but both the actor and his fiancée respectfully request that any inquiries be directed to Abramson's publicist, Alan Goefriller.

For the umpteenth time that evening, my phone screamed for attention from its location of exile under the coffee table. Groaning, I reached for it with wary apprehension, as if it were a clawing cat afflicted with rabies. Please, don't let it be another "Unknown" number. Sure enough, my caller ID failed to register any digits. I chucked Napoleon back to the Isle of Elba and prayed this anonymous individual gave up more easily than the others had.

No such luck. The Treo wailed again within mere moments.

"Hello?" I barked.

"May I please speak to Cristina...Pay-REE-rah?"

"Peh-ray-rah," I responded testily. Idiot.

"Yes, of course. That's what I meant."

"May I ask what this is in regards to?"

"My name is Candace Porter, and I work for the magazine Box Nine. I just wanted to speak to her for a moment regarding Thomas Abramson."

"Speaking," I sighed.

"Oh! Great! I don't mean to bother you."

"Right," I muttered sarcastically. Too late.

"Haha! First off, congratulations. I was just hoping to interview you for our 'Honorable Mentions' section of the next issue—just a quick blurb about where you want to get married or something about your wedding dress. Maybe a tidbit about the proposal? It's just for our readers."

"I'm sorry, but I think you meant to contact Mr. Goefriller. I have nothing to say at this time," I responded as patiently as possible.

"Can you just answer one question for us? Our subscribers love Tom, and they would be so excited to learn more about you."

"Again, I'm sorry, but…no comment." Give up, please!

The line disconnected. I pursed my lips together and slid Napoleon under a cushion from the couch.

"Just turn it off!" Mami exclaimed with frustration.

"Tom might call," I responded. "Hana or Gita might need something."

"Mira, they'll understand."

"Mami, I need to keep my life as normal as possible. We already had to get rid of our house phone! I don't know how these people found my cell number, but I swear I will find the individual responsible and glue a phone to their head while I sadistically hit redial for two days straight."

"Your life is not going to be normal, *mi amor*. Do what Thomas said and get another cell phone," she suggested.

I huffed through my nose with an expression of obstinacy. "Eventually they'll stop calling when they realize how boring I am."

She shook her head as she exhaled. "It's been three weeks since the announcement. They haven't stopped."

I didn't bother responding. She was right.

After disconnecting the home phone on Melissa's advice, I held my breath for the entire weekend following her Friday afternoon press release. Since no one bothered me for forty-eight hours straight, I assumed that meant we had successfully eluded the media spotlight. I wasn't that interesting after all, and I was incredibly grateful for that fact. Unfortunately, the subsequent Monday proved me horribly wrong on both accounts.

I was forced to leave my cell phone in the car for the afternoon portion of the workday after dealing with its insolence all morning long. When I retrieved it on my way home from the office, I had missed thirty-seven calls, and the voicemail box was full.

Tom was not happy about the leak of my personal cell phone

number. Honestly, it could have been any number of people, but I did have my suspicions. After the obsessive behavior I exhibited months ago when the grainy pictures of us in the hospital made the blog rounds, I wisely chose to use the internet strictly for email. I really didn't want to know if Amy in Boise, Idaho thought my hair was fugly at that movie premiere or if my ass was too big to be engaged to a movie star.

Unfortunately, I couldn't force my friends to do the same. Hana had placed several indignant phone calls to me when she came across articles depicting Tom Abramson's fiancée in an unfavorable light. Apparently, some anonymous individuals claiming to possess intimate knowledge were only more than happy to shed "light" onto the fortuitous turn of events that had led me into the arms of one of the most desirable males in the western world. Sure enough, the goldigging famewhore nonsense reared its ugly head ... again. I had to talk Hana down from her burning soapbox several times, and eventually Gita demanded that Hana stop informing me of all this blogsip crap immediately. Mind pollution at its best.

Why does anyone even care? I tried hard not to dwell too much on my internal lamentations, but this task had become increasingly more difficult with each passing day.

It grew late, and after I retrieved the wailing banshee, I went upstairs with the intention of packing for my trip to L.A. the following day. Inexplicably, a shade loomed over this sojourn, and I couldn't stop this foreboding from overshadowing my excitement. Some shit was about to go down, and I wasn't sure what caused me to feel this way. I hoped there wasn't too much truth to the phenomenon of self-fulfilling prophecies.

My phone rang again as I closed my overstuffed suitcase half an hour later.

"Hey!" I said with a tired smile.

"Hey! Are you all set for tomorrow?" Hana replied.

"More or less."

"Are you guys planning on doing anything wedding related this weekend?" she asked over-brightly.

"No. I don't think there's a pressing sense of urgency on either side, and the more I think about it, the more I'd like to do something small in a foreign country."

"Destination wedding! Awesome!" There was a note of false enthusiasm to her tone that definitely piqued my curiosity. She was hedging.

"Okay, what's going on?" I asked wearily.

"It's nothing..."

"Babe, I really don't have the time or the energy to pry it out of you. Just say it." I sighed.

"Well... look... Gita and I know that something is really bothering you, and I don't know why you haven't tried to talk about it with anyone. I keep waiting for you to mention it, and I don't have any more patience for this crap."

I paused thoughtfully. She wasn't my best friend by mere coincidence. "What are you talking about?"

"If I knew, I wouldn't be calling you. I can just tell that you're troubled, and it's gotten worse over the last week. Did something happen to you?" she demanded.

The burden of hiding my internal turmoil from the altercation with Ryan had taken its toll. Here was the proof.

"Cris, please talk to me. If something is bothering you, then let's deal with it. Don't dump it on Tom. You guys don't get to spend enough time with one another as it is. If I can tell you're hiding something, he will know as soon as he sees your face."

Her words were painfully true. Mendacity was incredibly unbecoming on me. "Please, don't be mad at me," I began tentatively.

"I can't promise that, but I will promise to hear you out."

I exhaled protractedly. "You're going to be pissed because... it's about Ryan."

"Fuck! I knew it!" She groaned. "Go on."

"He started... emailing me a couple of months ago."

"Please tell me you didn't respond!" she gasped.

"Well, not at first."

"Cristina Pereira! You idiot! Why did you respond to him?" she scolded.

"I couldn't help it! He was baiting me, and the shit he said just got under my skin!" I sniffed.

"If you knew he was baiting you, you should have controlled yourself better!"

"Are you going to keep yelling at me, or what?" I demanded.

"Sorry." She didn't sound sorry at all.

"Anyway, he kept begging me to talk to him. He said he had something important to tell me."

"I have something important to tell him too. It starts with an F and ends with a U."

198  "I refused to hear him out... and... he showed up at work a few

weeks ago," I mumbled with chagrin.

"WHAT? That interfering, backstabbing, mother—"

"Hana! Just let me finish." I waited for her to cease her ranting.

"He…told me he never cheated on me. He lied about it so that I would let him go."

She was momentarily shocked into silence, so I rushed onward in an attempt to tell her everything that had eaten away at me for the last few weeks.

"He…wants me back."

She cleared her throat. "No."

"Huh?"

"Never. Please, Cris. Please tell me you aren't even thinking about this." Her voice was deathly quiet.

"Of course not! I'm engaged!"

"But that's not the only reason, right?" she continued.

"What do you mean?"

"If you weren't engaged, you still wouldn't take him back, right?" she pressed.

"No. I don't…think so."

"No! Don't even think about it! Maybe you can forget what he did after he feeds you a couple of angst-ridden lines about fear and commitment, but I most certainly can not!" she shouted. "It doesn't matter if he didn't cheat! He's weak. He's not your equal!"

"He's not a bad person, Hana. He just made bad decisions."

"Fine! It doesn't matter if he's not a bad person. He doesn't deserve you. He lied to you, and he broke your heart!" she cried.

"Heartbreak happens every day…anyone can break your heart if you let them." Fear tinged my tone, and my perceptive best friend picked up on it immediately.

"I will never break your heart, Cris…and Tom won't break your heart either," she championed.

"I love you too, but…you don't know that. I never thought Ryan would break my heart, and you can't make promises on behalf of another person."

"Please, don't be like Ryan. Don't let your fear ruin something wonderful," she pleaded.

"I'm nothing like Ryan," I said angrily.

"I know. I just…I know you're afraid of trusting Tom, but he's earned your trust, chica. You always tell me—love fully or not at all. He deserves your love. Don't lose sight of that."

"I know you're right. I'm just so…scared of everything. All 199 of this change is really getting to me, and sometimes I feel overwhelmed," I admitted in a hushed tone.

"I completely understand, but don't punish the people who really love you for a man who wasn't sure."

When I didn't answer right away, she rushed through her next pearl of wisdom. "Tom's a good man, and you need to tell him about this. He deserves to know, and tell him to give me a call if he needs to hire some muscle for a much-deserved beat-down. I'm really cheap. In fact, for our purposes, I'm free," she joked tongue-in-cheek.

"He's going to be furious."

"Grow some nerve and deal with it. Ryan's ruined a good chunk of your life already; how about we place a moratorium on any further ruination?"

I smiled. "Thank you."

"Be a big girl. Don't screw this up. Even if your life isn't on a path you expected, it's the right one. I can feel it."

"Okay, Robert Frost. Goodnight," I teased.

"Love you. Call me later."

"Love you too. Will do."

Unfortunately, I didn't feel better.

I felt as though everyone thought my concerns were trivial and unfounded: fear-ridden angst that had no place in the world of a woman recently engaged to a wonderful man. Little did they know, a poison-laced virus had infiltrated its way into my mind, and the only person who could understand my anguish was the individual responsible for it.

A chauffeured Town Car waited for me by the curb at LAX when I arrived the next day. The driver stood by the passenger door holding a sign with the name "Chip" emblazoned on it.

With a half-smile, I ran to the automobile and slid into the backseat. Before I even had a chance to look around, I was yanked into a shameless embrace.

"You're mauling me!" I giggled as I playfully shoved Tom away.

"I can't help it. I'm starving, and you're delicious," he teased as he held tightly onto my body and pressed kisses against my neck.

"What's with the Town Car?" I asked.

He shrugged. "Melissa."

"Every so often, I start to hope that she hates me a bit less. This is one of those moments," I mused.

"She doesn't hate you. She's just a control freak, and she can't control you, so it rankles her a bit."

As he spoke, he studied my face carefully. My soul groaned as it braced for impact. *Damn the perceptiveness!* Wordlessly, he reached up with his right hand and rubbed my forehead with his thumb.

"These lines weren't here the last time I saw you," he began.

"I'm just tired. This week was tough. Managing work in Raleigh and helping with the master classes in Charlotte is a lot more demanding than I thought it was going to be," I replied lamely as I sped through my rehearsed explanation with a pace that clearly indicated nervousness.

He narrowed his eyes at me and ran his hand through my hair to brush it away. "We're getting you a new cell phone this weekend. End of discussion."

"It's really okay! I'm sure they'll stop!"

"And I'm sure I can't stand to see stress-induced wrinkles on your forehead. If you're not going to tell me the real reason behind them, then I'm just going to do what I want as well," he pronounced with a resolute tone.

"What makes you think it's not just because I'm overworked?"

"Cristina, I'm not that thickheaded. I want to be patient, but you're not making it easy," he said.

"Patient? I just got here."

"You know what I'm talking about. Ever since that conversation about the logistics of moving, you've been acting weird."

That was the day Ryan accosted me in the parking lot. I could feel my extremities start to shake as I considered telling him the reason behind my discomfort. I just couldn't. Not now. I wasn't ready.

"I do want to talk about it. Can you just give me a little more time?"

He looked at me with a grimace of displeasure, but didn't say anything to indicate he was unwilling to grant me this boon.

I laced my fingers through his and pulled his hand to my mouth to press a tender kiss near his wrist. "I promise. I've wanted to talk about it with you for some time, but at this moment, I just want to be with you. I'm also being a coward, but I'd really appreciate you being patient for a little while longer," I requested with a gentle smile.

He returned my grin with a slowly contrived one of his own. "I don't like cowards, but I do love you, so I'll play along." He cut his 201 eyes at me as a nonverbal indication that his good-natured acquiescence was merely temporary.

"Thank you. God, you're so cute," I joked as I rifled his hair and leaned into him. Our digression into difficult topics had happened much sooner than I would have liked.

"Flattery will get you everywhere."

"Especially with a movie star," I teased.

"I may be a narcissist, but you've just admitted to being a coward. We all have our flaws," he ribbed. The way his eyes became heavy-lidded with comfort combined with the gentle half curve of his smile never failed to kick my pulse into high gear.

"I'm willing to overlook your flaws... but I do have a request."

He chuckled. "Another one?"

"The best one. Kiss me."

We didn't surface for air until the car arrived at his apartment.

As we hauled my luggage through the front door, I noticed two large suitcases pushed up against the wall by the kitchen.

"Are those from Spain? Do you need some help unpacking?" I queried.

"I can't unpack. I have to go back on Tuesday," he responded.

"Yuck. I thought you had two weeks in L.A.!"

"I just found out before I left that they've moved up the timeline for filming my scenes," he stated.

"Why did you come all the way back to California if you only have five days off?" I cried.

"I should think that would be rather obvious." He grinned.

A flush rose into my cheeks as I stared back at him with a look of thanks.

"I missed the sunshine," he continued smarmily.

I punched his upper bicep with a quick jab. "There's definitely a shortage of that in Spain!"

"You know why I came back." He pulled me against him.

"Next time, just let me know. We can figure something out. I don't like you traveling unnecessarily."

"In that case, do you want to go to London with me in two weeks?" he asked.

"You're supposed to be spending time with your father."

"He's a lot nicer to me when you're there," he joked.

"I don't want to be a distraction."

"Just think about it. Anne would be ecstatic," he pressed.

202     "I'll think about it, but first, let's order some food. I haven't eaten

anything since breakfast."

"You know what? Let's go out," Tom announced.

I glanced at him with a dubious expression. "Are you sure?"

He nodded firmly. "I want to start acting normal when you're with me. There's a café a few blocks from here that I like, and I want to take you there for lunch."

Normal? Was it even possible? With a wry smile, I reached for his hand. He took it, and we made our way to the elevator and out the front door without any trouble from anyone.

After a leisurely lunch of sandwiches and soup in a charming delicatessen that was thankfully devoid of a crowd, we walked leisurely back towards his apartment. He moved to take hold of my left hand as he slid his aviator sunglasses onto his face.

"Bollocks!" he exclaimed after releasing my palm as though my touch burned him.

"What?" I said with alarm.

"That bloody diamond scratched my hand!"

I couldn't help the laughter that bubbled from my lips. "No one told you to get such a big one! It's the souls of modest people everywhere inflicting karmic irony on you!"

He lifted his hand to stare at the red scratch that swelled on the skin by his thumb. "This is bullshit. Shouldn't that thing have more respect?"

"You know, I've thought about it, and it's really a great weapon. Consider this: someone tries to mug me, and I reach over with my left hand... to slice their neck open, Mortal Kombat style."

He guffawed loudly. "It's a decidedly feminist take on blood sport. We could call your character Black Widow."

"Isn't there already a character with that name? Really, they shouldn't even let me travel with this thing on. I can't bring nail clippers onto a plane, but a monolithic rock with multiple sharpened edges, no problem!"

Punctuated by the sounds of laughter, the banter continued as we rounded the final curve before Tom's apartment. We were so busy joking with one another that we failed to notice the horde of people lying in wait by the entrance. Before we could process the situation and take pre-emptive action, cameras started to flashed like sparks from a newly tousled fire.

In the past, I had always been shielded from this insanity by some sort of barricade—a rope, a string of security guards, propriety, etc. This time, nothing prevented the paparazzi from shoving 203 their cameras right into our path, blocking our ability to move in any direction. They swarmed around us in a circle like vultures preparing to feast on the hapless dead before them. Tom grabbed me in a reflexive attempt to block their advances.

"Thomas! Look here!"

"Cristina! Let's see the ring!"

"Look up! Give us a smile!"

"Come on, you two! Show us the love!"

The directives were unceasing and grew increasingly more vehement as the shutters clicked around me. My heart rate increased and my breathing become haggard as a mild form of claustrophobia manifested itself. I looked around wildly for an outlet.

"Where's the ring? One picture!"

The paparazzo who made this demand took hold of Tom's arm in an attempt to pull me into view.

"Don't touch him!" I yelled angrily as Tom attempted to throw off his hand.

"She's a feisty one!" He reached over again, and my hand shot out in fury to shove his arm away.

Without warning, he grabbed hold of my wrist. Chaos ensued as the shutters clicked like bullets fired from a machine gun. The ring. Enraged by the fact this paparazzo had dared to manhandle me, Tom shoved him back with both hands. They responded by moving closer.

"Back off!" Tom shouted with fury. He again attempted to press them aside, but the pack mentality only increased the frenzy around us. They pushed him in an attempt to get their money shot. We were pulled apart, and I lost hold of my grip on his hand. Trying to rejoin him, I elbowed my way through the throng, and the combination of my movements along with the ebb and flow of the hands around me eventually produced disastrous results.

"I said back off!" Tom yelled warningly.

I fell to the ground as a wayward hand punched into my back with enough force to knock the wind out of me. Gasping for air, I struggled to regain my footing.

I heard the aftermath of this woeful predicament before I saw it.

"Get the fuck away from her!" Tom exploded at the top of his lungs. "Are you fucking mental? Back away! Get away from her! I swear to God, if you don't turn around and walk the fuck away, you'll be a hell of a lot sorrier than I will!"

I had never heard him this enraged before. He threw someone aside, grabbed my arm, and hoisted me up against him. The blood had rushed to his face and his eyebrows formed straight lines of fury over his darkly tinged pupils.

"Get the fuck away!" Tom bellowed. "Are you fucking satisfied? I don't give a fuck if you harass me, but I'll be damned if I stand by and let you trample her! Get out of the way!"

The group appeared just as shocked as I was. With huge eyes, they melted out of our path in a stupor of pseudo-remorse. It was then that I noticed the man with the video camera, quietly capturing every rage-filled expletive they baited Tom into spewing. Tom half carried me past the paparazzi with rapid steps towards the entrance of the building. We rode the elevator in silence as I surveyed the damage in the reflection of the sliding doors. My hair was a mess. As I reached up to fix it, I saw my hand shake in the image before me. I was too afraid to look at Tom.

He kicked open the door mercilessly and stomped into the living room. Spinning around to look at me, his anger had not abated to a manageable level.

"Are you all right?" he bit out.

"I'm fine."

He smashed his eyes shut forcefully, leaned against the wall, and slid to the floor. His palms pressed into his forehead with enough pressure to render their edges white. I slowly lowered myself next to him and placed my hand tentatively around his wrist so I could see his face.

"Tommy?" I whispered.

He exhaled and turned his gaze to me. The look in his eyes was so pained it hurt my soul. I curled up by his side and let my cheek rest on his shoulder. The adrenaline pounding in my veins started to subside, and I took in careful breaths to help in the endeavor.

"I'm sorry that happened," I said quietly.

He snorted with frustration. "Why are you apologizing? I should be the one to do that."

"Does that happen often?"

"Sometimes. They've never been this forceful, though," he admitted stonily.

"Is there anything we can do?"

Again, he pressed his palms into his eyes in aggravation. "Damn it all. I just wanted to take you to lunch."

My heart lurched with pity. This was reality. If I wanted to take a walk through the city with the man I loved, this was the risk I had to take. I couldn't just meet him at his office or grab a coffee with 205 him whenever I wanted. As long as people were crazy about Thomas Abramson, I had to hide my love behind security guards, velvet ropes, and locked doors. A quagmire of emotions swirled through my system, and my body chose the release of tears as a first response.

"Oh God, don't cry. You'll break me," Tom gasped out as he pulled me into his arms.

"I...can't..." I sniffed.

"You can't what?" He rubbed my back in an attempt to soothe me.

*I can't do this*, I wanted to say. Coward.

We sat there in silence until my tears subsided. The flurry of activity in my head had reached a level that was difficult to control. Fear was taking over. The tears would not be enough to keep it at bay.

Tom's phone buzzed in his pocket. I didn't even pay attention to his conversation because the demons carried on their feverish dialogue between my temples. When he was finished, he slid the phone away from us as though it were disease-laden filth. He laughed darkly and placed his hands on the floor to heave into a standing position.

"What's funny?" I asked.

"Nothing's funny. That f-bomb laden clip is already on Twitter. Melissa called. I'm apparently Christian Bale Lite. She's thrilled."

A small part of me wanted to smile at this news, but the situation was far from amusing. The demons would not shut up. This was such a bad time. I couldn't do this to him...not now. I stared down at the floor and willed myself to remain silent. I was so focused on this task that I didn't hear him continue to speak.

"Cris? Cris? Are you listening to me?"

I shook my head as though the gesture would mute the ranting within. "Huh?"

"That's it. What's wrong?"

"Nothing," I replied as the haze lifted infinitesimally.

"No." He sat back down on the floor in front of me. "I've had enough of this. I'm not in the mood to sit here and guess what's making the woman I love look as though someone murdered her best friend. I'm done with it. Let's have it out now."

My eyes widened with alarm at the same time my mind ached for this release. "Please. I'm just feeling...*overwhelmed.*"

"Then we need to talk about it," he replied. I could still see his handsome face marred by the anger festering on the surface and knew this was a really heinous idea.

"I don't think we should. Not now."

"I need to know. I'm feeling pretty shitty right now, so I doubt anything you could say would make it much worse," he intoned. "What's overwhelming you?"

I inhaled. "Fear."

He paused for a moment before continuing his merciless interrogation. "What are you afraid of?"

I stared into his eyes and made half of a decision. "Everything ... I'm afraid of moving, I'm afraid of what this will mean to my mother, I'm afraid of leaving behind everything I know and love, I'm afraid of trading in a life of predictability for a life of fantasy, and ... I'm just afraid of being a fool."

"A fool?"

"A fool who should have known better."

He lips formed a hard line as his eyebrows wrinkled into his forehead. "Where is this coming from?"

I looked at the floor. This was too painful. I pushed myself into a standing position and tried to walk away.

"Cristina. What happened that made you so afraid? For Christ's sake, just tell me!"

"I can't!" I replied.

"You can. You just don't want to." His tone was cold and hurt.

"I want to! I'm just a coward!"

He followed after me and blocked my ability to run away by pressing his hands against the wall on either side of my head.

"Stop being a coward," he demanded quietly.

I was trapped. The demons screamed even more loudly. With a pounding heart and an aching mind, I succumbed.

"Last month, I ... saw Ryan!" I gasped wretchedly.

The face of the man before me froze.

"He came to my office and demanded that I hear him out. Then he confessed to lying about cheating so I would let him go. He begged me to take him back."

The only movement I could register was the rise and fall of Tom's chest.

"I'm just completely ... mind-fucked. I have no idea what's going on, and I'm so afraid the world I built will come crashing down around me for the second time, and I can't stand it!" I shouted pathetically.

The arms dropped to his sides.

"Please! Say something!" I begged.

He cleared his throat. "Was ... was that the first time you spoke to him?" he asked hoarsely.

No lies. Only the truth. "No. We emailed a few times."

He turned his head to the side and closed his eyes. I gasped for air and watched the havoc my words rendered.

With his eyes still closed and his face averted, he asked the one question that would hurt the most. The question I couldn't answer.

"Do you want him back?"

My silence hung in the air like a twisted malediction. To my horror, I saw a strange trail of moisture on the cheek of the good man in front of me. The man I loved...the man I hurt.

The man who deserved better.

The sobs built in my chest, and I knew what I had to do.

Love fully, or not at all.

I stumbled to the kitchen counter and wrenched the ring off my finger. The sound of the diamond striking against the granite echoed through the room as the tears coursed down my face.

"I'm so sorry," I choked. "You deserve better than me. I can't do this to you anymore."

With this, the coward fled through the front door. As it slammed shut, the sound of a fist crunching through drywall echoed from within.

True to form, she left behind the devastation she wrought.

# TWENTY-ONE

First thing that Monday, I purchased a new cell phone with an unregistered number. I couldn't deal with any more calls from people I didn't know and didn't care about. Anyway, I didn't want to give them the slightest opportunity to sensationalize my pain for profit.

There was only one person's voice I wanted to hear in my phone, and I had made damn certain that would never happen again. Even so, it was with a regretful twinge that I discarded my old Treo, along with the last vestiges of my hope. If I could just disappear for a few weeks—I fantasized about fleeing to a third world country and getting lost on purpose in an attempt to "find myself." How cliché.

It took the passing of twenty-eight nights for me to smile in earnest again. The pain did not go away; it merely dulled in intensity …like the aftershocks of an earthquake. This time around, I did not have the luxury of righteous indignation to help temper my grief. This time around, it was entirely my own fault.

The worst decisions are the ones you regret with aching immediacy.

Coward.

From: Anne Abramson <anniea005@yahoo.co.uk>
To: Cris Pereira <7crisp@gmail.com>
Date: Thurs, February 25, 2010 at 4:09 PM
Subject: ?

Cris:

My brother would murder me if he knew I was emailing you, but I can't help it. He's trying so hard to act as though he's strong and able to handle everything. His eyes are destroying me. I just need to know that you're all right. I probably shouldn't give a rat's ass, but I'm not that fickle. One day, I'll probably hate you, but if Tommy's pain is anything like yours, I need you to know I still care. Dad is utterly devastated. He had a huge row with Tommy whenever he showed up from Spain a few days ago. Do you by any chance know why the knuckles on his right hand are mangled? Anyway, Dad completely blamed the poor boy for what happened with you. Some rot about Tommy failing to deal with matters before they got out of hand—and then some more about the fact that Tommy lives for the moment and never stops to think about the consequences. Mum screamed at Dad something awful for it. Part of me wants to beg you to call Tommy, but I don't think it would go well. Whenever I told him to call you, he yelled at me for a solid five minutes. He was furious.

I don't know what you did, but I'd bet meals for a month that he still loves you. So do I.

Yours, (until I start thinking straight)
Anne

---

From: Cris Pereira <7crisp@gmail.com>
To: Anne Abramson <anniea005@yahoo.co.uk>
Date: Thurs, February 25, 2010 at 11:47 PM
Subject: Re: ?

Anne,
I'm so very sorry. I hurt your brother irreparably, and I'm a coward.
He deserves everything wonderful that life gives him. I wish him the best with all my heart.

Love,
Cristina

---

*His eyes are destroying me.*

These words were seared on my vision as though Fate had devised a way to brand the evidence of my inadequacy onto everything I saw...making it impossible to forget, even for a moment. And man, did I try to forget. Those five words haunted my days.

And the memory of Tom's mother uttering this to me in her kitchen blistered my dreams: "Please don't break his heart...I'm becoming quite certain that he won't be able to get over it."

The recollection of this request became a rather strange precursor to my nightmare's ignominious return.

The first night it recurred was after a huge fight I had with Hana. For a week she pretended as though she understood why I walked out on my fiancé. Each time I called her, she listened with the ears of a friend who loved me unconditionally. I cried into the phone and blubbered through long-winded explanations and convoluted justifications. In turn, she murmured compassionate phrases meant to soothe my suffering and ease my nerves. But her heart wasn't in it.

On the seventh day, God meant to create patience. Instead, he went on vacation.

"I can't take it anymore!" she exploded that fateful night.

"Huh?" I sniffed.

"I've listened to this crap for a week now! I've lied to you for an entire week! Before this, I've never lied to you, and I can't deal with it anymore!"

"You lied to me?"

"I lied to you, I lied to Gita, and I lied to myself."

"What are you talking about?" I asked.

"YOU'RE AN IDIOT!"

"Huh?" The tears welled in my eyes again.

"YOU. ARE. AN. IDIOT. Just call him! You made a mistake. Tell him you're sorry, and then tell him how much you love him and want him back."

"Well, since you put it that way..." I spat.

"Table the sarcasm. Right now, you don't have the intellectual wherewithal to pull it off."

"Ouch. Tell me what you really think," I retorted. My melancholy overshadowed the beginning pangs of anger.

"You know what? I believe I will. So what if you were harassed by the paparazzi! So what if people kept calling your phone! So what if Tom is mad about Ryan! SO WHAT!"

The anger flared. "You have no idea what you're talking about! You think that all of this drama is fabulous and entertaining. You read your blogs and your People magazine, and you think this world is like the adult version of Disneyland! Newsflash: it isn't!" I shouted.

"This is exactly why you just fucked up your life, Cristina Pereira! You think that all of this has to do with Tom or Tom's profession. 211

Here's a newsflash FOR YOU: it has nothing to do with Tom! This is all you! You're terrified of trusting someone enough to believe in a future. Your mind needed to create some nonsensical reason for destroying a good thing before it progressed beyond your control!"

"Go to hell!" I cried.

"I'll take the seat right next to you! Only, my hell won't be one of my own making! Just call a spade a spade and admit that you dumped him before he could dump you, like some hormonal teenager with acne and insecurities!"

"HOW CAN YOU SAY THIS TO ME?" I screamed.

"Tell you what! I'll answer that question when you tell me why you bled internally for months after Ryan left, and then proceeded to inflict the same wound on someone else!"

"GOODBYE!" I yelled. I burst into tears and threw my phone on the bed.

I had never fought like that with Hana. We had our moments of mutual crankiness, but they were short-lived and laughed away. Most of the time, I loved her ability to see the root of a problem and figure out a solution that combined her acerbic wit and strong sense of compassion. She was usually so sympathetic ... such a wonderful shoulder to cry on.

She was never like this.

That night, right before going to bed, a fresh onslaught of tears snaked down my swollen cheeks at the gnawing playback of Hana's accusations combined with the memory of Grace Abramson's request.

Yet another failure. I broke his heart.

*His eyes are destroying me.*

I hiccupped my way into a restless sleep, and my chiaroscuro nightmare returned with a vengeance. Just like before, Ryan walked out on me through the front door. I was left in cold darkness and sank to the floor with a practiced motion full of antagonistic grace.

I froze in my heap to clasp the strands of itchy carpet and braced myself for the pain ... that didn't come. The long-familiar rush of anguish was strangely absent from this fourth-dimensional retelling.

My gaze shifted from the pilings before me towards the direction of the door. I was ... waiting. Waiting for the light and the warmth to radiate from the space Ryan had just vacated. I knew it was coming, and I waited for its hope and its promise.

And waited.

And waited.

It never came. The cold darkness was all that remained. Then the missing anguish slammed into me with startling ferocity.

I awoke with a gasp.

*Coward.*

"So, do you want to get dinner tonight?" Ryan asked me a week after my fight with Hana.

"I don't think that's a good idea," I said into the phone.

"How about tomorrow night? Aren't you tired of being cooped up at home in your self-imposed exile?"

I sighed quietly. Gita would be loath to hear it, but she had made the same point to me just that afternoon. Since I was not on speaking terms with Hana, she had been forced to deal with my misery a great deal more than usual this past week. Her only request was that I not force her to get involved in the spat. When contrasted with Hana, she had taken a decidedly different approach to my return to the world of Singledom.

"I have nothing to add. I told you everything on my mind whenever you first said you were engaged. My opinion remains the same. I'm here if you need me, but I won't lie and tell you what you want to hear," she intoned carefully. I knew what that meant: proceed at your own risk.

In short, we completely avoided speaking about Tom or Hana. I didn't want to lose the ear of another person dear to me by pressing the issue on either front. I was desperately thankful to have someone to talk to.

My mother tried hard not to burden me with her own disappointment, but I knew her well enough to be cognizant of it at all times. We were two silly women who lived together, cried ourselves to sleep, and pretended as though neither knew of that rather obvious fact. It was an excruciating farce to maintain.

Since one of my best friends was ignoring me, my other best friend desired painfully censored conversations, and my mother was trying her damnedest to win an Academy Award, I was forced to seriously consider having dinner with Ryan Sullivan. *Ugh.*

What a karmic twist of fate.

Anyway, there was something I had been meaning to give him for a while, and this seemed as good a time as any.

"I'll meet you for dinner tomorrow night, but there are several conditions. I want to go to Wendy's, and I'm paying for my own food. This is not a date, and the second that you even imply that it's anything more, I'm out the door in a heartbeat," I replied stiffly. How had it come to this?

The following evening, I met Ryan at Wendy's in sweatpants and a T-shirt. I would never admit it aloud, but it was nice to be eating with a person not peering intently at me over her glasses with a permafrown of concern. Poor Mami.

As I toyed with my chicken nuggets, I studied Ryan from across the table. He was oddly merry, as though he were satirizing himself.

"You don't have to try so hard. You suck at being cheerful," I said flatly and stabbed another fry into the pool of ketchup congealing on a napkin in front of me.

His nose flared and his eyes narrowed circumspectly. "Okay. You look like hell."

"Nice. Can you water it down a bit?" I demanded.

"You just asked me to be myself."

"No, I just asked you to stop being Mary Sunshine," I muttered.

"Fine. Are you sleeping at night? There are circles under your eyes."

"Now he cares about the circles under my eyes! Where the hell were you two years ago?" I sneered.

"Look, simmer down. I know you're going through a lot, but don't unload everything onto the first person willing to be honest with you."

"You're not the first person willing to be honest with me," I replied.

"And how well did you handle their honesty?"

The involuntary sadness that passed through my features was all the response he needed.

We exchanged mindless chatter about work as we made our way through the meal. After wiping the grease off my hands, I reached into my purse and pulled out a small velvet bag.

"I should have given this back to you two years ago. I don't want it anymore, and it really belongs to you," I said quietly as I placed it on the table between us.

He reached over with curiosity and pried apart the drawstrings on the small bag. After peering inside, he pulled the strings shut with a firm tug and put it back on the table.

"I gave that to you."

"It lost its meaning."

"No, it didn't. Not for me. Keep it. I'm going to try hard to make you believe the meaning behind it never left," he said with gentle eyes.

"I don't want the ring," I whispered. He had no idea how much that little piece of jewelry tormented me.

"You don't want it now, but you will one day. Keep it on you. There will be a moment when you believe in us again, and I want you to have it with you whenever you do."

"I don't think that's going to happen," I stated firmly.

"Nevertheless, give it at least six months. If you still don't want it in six months, I'll take it back. I promise."

"No. Please take it back now."

He shook his head with firm obstinacy, and I frowned with frustration.

It sat between us until we both rose to leave the restaurant. When he pulled on his jacket and walked quickly towards the door without retrieving it, I sighed and put it back into the zippered compartment of my purse. I didn't have the strength to argue about anything else.

He waited for me by the door.

"I had fun tonight," he said with a wry grin.

"Right."

He snorted with a sarcastic air that was sadly familiar to me. "I'm not lying. I love being with you...in fact, I belong with you."

"That's my cue to leave," I announced as I turned towards my car.

"Cris." He shifted into my path. "I'm not going to give up. Even when you look like hell, you're still beautiful to me. I know you're really confused right now, but when the dust settles I'll be here. We make sense, and deep down, you know it."

Wordlessly, I sidestepped him. "Thanks for grabbing dinner with me," I muttered as I rushed past him.

I cranked the engine of my car and leaned my forehead into the steering wheel to hide my tears from the world.

All you need to get the attention of a man...is another man. Hah, why didn't I think of that before?

Life most certainly goes on.

I went to work each day, and the predictable pattern of my existence slowly re-established itself, as though my time falling in love with a movie star had merely been an extended dream of epic proportions. I returned to the haze of before with penitent resignation.

I missed Tom so much it crushed down onto my chest with the weight of a million unspoken words. Weak and feeling alone in a hell of my own making (thanks again, Hana), I had lunch twice with Ryan the week following our dinner at Wendy's. After much prodding, I also went with him to see a documentary on evolutionary psychology at a nearby arthouse theatre. He tried hard to make me laugh, and I pretended that it worked so I wouldn't have to deal with worrying about his feelings on top of everything else.

That Friday, I went to the grocery store with the intention of buying frozen yogurt and renting a chick-flick from Redbox in the fashion of a normal girl who recently broke up with her boyfriend. In line with my yogurt, I saw a picture on the cover of Star magazine that made me drop my little carton and flee with deranged urgency.

Thomas Abramson had been caught exiting a bar in London. The magazine insinuated that he left with a beautiful blonde in tow.

I didn't even process the blurry picture of the accompanying woman.

*His eyes are destroying me.*

I went to bed early that night, curled in a ball of my own misery. The image of his haunted, grey green eyes...

My nightmare was harshly devoid of any warmth for the third time in a row. The next morning I decided something had to change. I couldn't continue living in this vacuum. As soon as I brushed my teeth, I pressed viciously onto the keys of my cell phone.

> Me (9:32 am): I miss u so much it hurts.

I waited with bated breath for a response.

> Hana (9:33 am): u woke me up

I exhaled with relief.

> Me (9:33 am): My bad. Can u ever forgive me?
> Hana (9:33 am): conditionally
> Me (9:33 am): ?
> Hana (9:33 am): only if u forgive me

**too**

For the first time in weeks, I smiled in earnest. Life most certainly goes on.

# TWENTY-TWO

I sat patiently outside of the hospital room holding a large covered dish in a towel on my lap. Next to me was a brown paper bag filled with drinks, fruit, and paper products. The smell of antiseptic filled my nostrils, and the glare of the fluorescent lighting triggered the beginning sensations of a headache. Nurses and orderlies blurred past me with their rubber-soled shoes squeaking against the white tile.

I hated hospitals. Come to think of it, I was certain this sentiment was one I shared with the vast majority of the population. The last time I had been in this hospital had been the morning my father died. I probably should have thought of that fact prior to volunteering for this task. Oh well. Good deeds are less powerful when they are driven by thoughts of convenience.

This afternoon, my co-worker Jennifer had mentioned a friend of hers who volunteered for Wake County Human Services every holiday season. Her name was Claire. Claire had been a student working on her Master's Degree in Elementary Education when she began to complain about frequent, fierce migraines and distorted vision. Soon afterward, she was diagnosed with brain cancer. Her family had struggled to come up with the funds to pay for Claire's treatment—she didn't have health insurance. Two weeks ago, the doctors announced the disease had metastasized, and now she floated in and out of consciousness. There was little hope that she would make it.

Jennifer brought up Claire's sad turn of events because it was her turn to bring dinner to Claire's family at the hospital. Unfortunately, Jennifer's son had been taken out of school that day with a bad stomach virus, and she was not certain she would have the time to prepare a meal to take to the hospital while nursing a sick child at home.

Moved by the situation, I had quickly volunteered to go in her stead. After leaving the office early at four o'clock, I put together some vegetable lasagna and drove over to the hospital to wait for Claire's parents to arrive from work. How sad that they couldn't sit by her side every second of every day... I felt fortunate that my father's illness had not burdened us with the insurmountable debt that it had Claire's family. We could afford at least one of us being there with him at all times.

Now, inundated by the sounds and smells that brought back the memory of a difficult time in my life, all I wanted was to give them the food and get the hell out of there. I closed my eyes and let the sadness wash through me in a moment of pithy self-indulgence. I could still conjure up the image of that morning with almost perfect attention to detail.

The opening of the door nearby startled me from my reverie.

"You know, you can go in there. Greg is waiting with her," the nurse said to me.

"Greg?"

"We call him 'The Barnacle' because he won't leave. He's Claire's fiancé. I'm sure he wouldn't mind your company."

"Uh, okay," I stammered as I collected my things.

"Have you never been here before?"

I shook my head. "No, I came because Jennifer's son is sick."

"Oh. Well, brace yourself. This one's a real tearjerker," she replied solemnly.

Isn't cancer usually a tearjerker? Puzzled by her statement, I merely smiled politely, pushed the door open, and walked into Claire's hospital room. The sight before me nearly made me drop the lasagna.

Strings that spanned from floor to ceiling swayed lazily in the breeze emitting from the air ducts and machinery in the room. Suspended on these strings were what appeared to be countless bits of colorful folded paper—some kind of origami. As I peered more closely at these strange decorations, I saw that they were cranes.

"There must be hundreds of them!" I gasped.

"There are six hundred and forty-seven," said a good-natured voice belonging to a dark-skinned man seated in the corner with a tiny table on his lap. He appeared to be around my age, and he looked tired, but happy. His hands held a half-completed crane on the flat surface before him, and a stack of origami paper waited for his deft ministrations.

"I'm so sorry to bother you," I sputtered as I peered around for a place to put the lasagna.

"Let me help you with that!" Greg stood and walked over to me. "You're definitely not bothering me! That smells wonderful." He took the lasagna navigated his way through the crane streamers, and set it on the counter by the small sink after.

219

"There's some fruit and utensils in this bag. I hope I brought enough," I explained.

"Thank you so much. I'm Greg." He put out his hand, and I shook it warmly.

"Cris. I'm Jennifer's friend. Her son is sick, so I said I would bring dinner. I didn't mean to interrupt... the nurse told me I could come in," I stated with chagrin.

"Please, don't worry about it. I'm sure Claire's parents will be here any moment. If you don't mind waiting, I'm sure they would love to meet you." He gestured towards the chair next to him, and I sat.

I watched as he sat back down to finish folding the crane he had discarded a moment ago. I couldn't help it. Curiosity was killing the cat. He glanced over at me and smiled in understanding at my inquisitive expression.

"You can ask me. It's okay," he stated kindly.

I blushed in embarrassment. "It's none of my business!"

"No, it's totally fine. Most people can't figure out what the hell I'm doing, so I've had to explain myself quite a few times. Once more won't hurt."

"Really, you don't have to explain yourself."

He chuckled. "I'm folding a thousand cranes."

I waited patiently for him to continue.

"Whenever Claire was first diagnosed, I didn't know what to do. I felt so... helpless. I couldn't make her pain go away, and it drove me crazy just sitting here doing nothing. I went online and tried to find a way to help. As silly as it sounds, I stumbled onto an article about a little boy with leukemia whose classmates folded a thousand cranes for him. The lore goes like this: if you fold a thousand cranes, your dearest wish will come true."

He shrugged. "So, I bought a book on origami... and started folding."

He grinned to himself as he put the finishing touches on the blue crane in his hands. When it was perfect, he looked over at the sleeping figure of the bald-headed girl lying on the bed with tubes and needles snaking from her skin. His brown eyes were so full of love, a rising tide of emotion gathered in me. There was no need for him to tell me what his one wish would be.

I cleared my throat so I could temporarily alleviate the pressure building in it. "Can I help you?" I whispered hoarsely.

220       He turned to me. "I want to do this myself, but thank you so

much for offering."

Not knowing what else to do, I took his hand and squeezed it tightly in mine. He peered more intently at me, squeezed back, and picked up another piece of paper to start the process for the six hundred and forty-ninth time.

"Do you mind if I ask you a personal question?" he queried.

"Not at all."

"Why do you look so sad?" His voice was incredibly gentle.

I stayed silent, momentarily taken aback by the fact that a man watching his love waste away before his eyes had the desire to care about others around him.

"I'm sorry," he said. "I couldn't help it."

"No. You don't have to apologize." I was normally an extremely private person, but since Greg had shared something intensely personal with me, I felt as though I needed to answer his question.

"I don't know what happened to me. I think I might have ruined my life."

His eyebrows furrowed, but he didn't look up from folding his crane. "I seriously doubt that. As long as you can find something that makes you happy, your life will never be ruined. You just need to fight for what makes you happy."

"How...how do you find the strength to fight for what makes you happy?" I asked in a tight voice.

At this, he put down his work and turned to me. "First, you have to know what it is. Then, you need to believe that you deserve it."

I stared back at him in tortured silence.

"What makes you happy?" he asked.

*Tom.* It was the first thing that popped into my head. He was the first thing my heart sought. His face, his laughter, his voice, his humor...his loyalty. His love.

He smiled again. "You look like you know what makes you happy."

When I didn't answer, he merely said, "Now believe you deserve it."

I stared down at my hands as my tears accumulated.

"I never thought I would be the type of guy to sit here folding little paper birds, but I can't tell you how happy I am when I'm here ...how happy I feel to know that I can do something for her. Every time she opens her eyes and sees the cranes, she smiles, and I can't remember feeling happier. She deserves to be happy. I deserve to be happy," he stated very quietly.

221

The tears slid down my nose, and I couldn't look up at him.

"You're a really good person, Cris. You brought dinner to a complete stranger's family just because you wanted to help. I know it when I look at you. You deserve to have whatever makes you happy. Just believe it."

Overcome with emotion, I grabbed my purse and stood up quickly. "I'm sorry...I...do you mind if I just go?"

He stared up at me with calm patience. "Of course. I'll tell them you had someplace to go."

"Thank you so much." I raced to the door awkwardly. As I touched the handle, I thought of something and spun to ask a final question. "Greg?"

He looked up. "Yes?"

"What happened to the boy with leukemia?"

He smiled serenely. "I have no idea." Then he picked up his crane and resumed folding.

Wasn't he curious? How did he know his efforts were going to work? Why was he so damn calm about everything?

The fact I didn't understand how he could be so happy in such a miserable situation tore at my heartstrings...

...and I envied him so much.

I ran all the way to my car and drove aimlessly as my mind replayed my conversation with Greg.

*What makes you happy?*

As I recalled my heart's deepest desire, the loss of it renewed the gnawing sense of grief I had managed to keep at bay for the last few weeks. Both my heart and mind came to the same conclusion without a moment's consideration, but my cowardice had ruthlessly precluded them.

At that moment, there was nothing I wanted more than to see Tom. I had to stop punishing myself. I had to move on. I had to find something that made me happy. Once upon a time, Ryan had made me happy. Could he make me happy again?

I turned my car in the direction of Ryan's home. Desperate for a measure of the happiness that brought Greg such peace and contentment, I raced to the door and rang the doorbell.

"What are you doing here?" he asked, clearly taken aback and pleased by my unannounced visit.

"I just wanted to talk," I replied breathlessly as I strode into his living room and plopped onto the sofa. I was surprised by the fact I didn't feel even the slightest ache at being in the home I had called my own for a few bliss-filled months. I had sworn never to set foot in this house again. Less than ten feet away from me was the place that inspired my recurring nightmare.

"What did you want to talk about?" he replied as he sat down in the armchair across from me.

I glanced about the room. Every piece of furniture in it I had helped to select, right down to the silly lamp with monkeys on its base—an inside joke with some long-forgotten significance. I glanced at the foyer near the front door and saw that the wall sconce had been removed and sat on the entry table with its screws nearby. A package of bulbs lay on the floor. The light had burned out.

"I just took dinner to a family at the hospital. Their daughter is dying of brain cancer," I stated matter-of-factly.

"That was nice of you," he replied.

"Her fiancé Greg was there."

"How's he holding up?" he asked.

"He's…great. He's…really happy."

"Sounds like an asshole," Ryan remarked with a puzzled expression.

He couldn't be further from the truth. "He's not. He was…folding cranes."

"Are you tripping on LSD?" Ryan teased.

"No. Can you refrain from being sarcastic for just a little while?"

"Okay, I'll play. Why was he folding cranes?" he asked with abrupt seriousness.

Suddenly, I didn't know why I had come here. Something strange had prompted me to drive my car in this direction and run to his front door. I knew I must have some kind of hidden purpose, even though I wasn't certain what it could be.

I sighed as the adrenaline began to pound with less intensity through my veins.

"Cris? The cranes?"

"She's probably not going to make it."

"Where was her family?" he asked.

"Working. She didn't have health insurance, and they're nearly bankrupt because of her medical bills."

"So why wasn't the fiancé out working as well?" he demanded.

My jaw snapped shut at this inquiry. I had not even thought about it. "I don't know. He was folding cranes by her bedside."

"You mentioned this. Why?" His eyes narrowed almost imperceptibly.

223

"Because…he…he read somewhere that if you fold a thousand cranes, your dearest wish will come true. He had already folded nearly seven hundred when I arrived. They were hanging like streamers all around her bed."

He pursed his lips together. "This guy sounds like a flake."

I was utterly confused by this reaction. I had found Greg's gesture to be so…inexplicably beautiful. "How do you figure?"

"His fiancée is lying on a hospital bed dying of cancer. Her family is working overtime to cover her medical bills. Instead of trying to organize a fundraiser or find a doctor who specializes in some sort of experimental treatment that might save her life, he's sitting there doing an arts and crafts project? Why doesn't he get a job and help in a constructive manner?"

My confusion only grew. "I hadn't thought of that."

"Apparently, neither has Greg," he pronounced with a trace amount of disgust.

"She loves the cranes. He told me they…they make her happy."

"He should work on saving her life first. Then he can worry about making her happy," Ryan stated bluntly.

My confusion was replaced with frustrated anger. "You're…you don't see anything beautiful about this?"

He shrugged dismissively. "There's nothing beautiful about waste. He's wasting his time, and he's wasting her chances."

"No! It-it's beautiful, Ryan. He sits with her all the time, and he makes her happy. When she's happy, he's happy. As long as they're with each other…doesn't that mean anything to you?"

"Maybe. All I'm saying is that he's going to feel less than happy when he folds his thousandth crane and his girl is still dying in front of him." Ryan was merciless in his appraisal.

And yet, I knew that he was…right. In a sad, twisted way, Ryan's dispassionate analysis had a ring of truth to it. There might be many more constructive things Greg could be doing with his time. Yet, everything Ryan suggested ignored the beauty of Greg's gesture. His undying devotion. His unwavering love. His quest for happiness.

What was I doing here? I stared at Ryan after he made his last coldhearted pronouncement…

…and I realized something.

"You don't get it, do you?"

"Get what?" he replied.

"You don't understand what he's trying to do, so you're ruining it by making it sound ridiculous."

"Now, *you're* being ridiculous," he scoffed as he leaned back into his chair.

"No, I'm not. I just figured it out. I get it. You don't. You can't stand that."

"Tell yourself that if it makes you feel better. I just feel bad for this girl," he remarked.

"I don't. I actually envy her," I said firmly.

"You sure you're not on drugs?"

"I envy her because she's happy. Even if it's just for one ridiculous moment a day when she sees hundreds of tiny cranes swaying around her, she's happy! He makes her happy!" I cried as I jumped off the sofa.

My rapid movement startled him from his posture of wizened judgment. Suddenly, he looked almost like a small boy afraid of the impending dark. As I stared down at him, I realized why I was supposed to be here. What I needed to do.

"They deserve to be happy. I deserve to be happy."

*Don't think. Just do.*

I reached into my purse and pulled out the little velvet bag with the ring. "I'm sorry, but I will never believe in us again, because there's nothing left to believe in."

"Cristina," he choked in shock as I put the bag on the coffee table. "I don't... don't do this. Why?"

"You're not the person I fell in love with. I will never be the person you want me to be," I whispered.

I could feel the invisible manacles drop from my arms. Free of their weight, I threw my shoulders back and lifted my chin.

"But I love you," he said in a tight voice.

"It's not enough. I'm so sorry."

I turned on my heel and walked towards the front door. As I passed by the light bulbs on the ground, I reached down and picked one up.

My heart pounded, and my hands trembled, but I refused to leave him in darkness as he did to me.

Standing on my tiptoes, I screwed the bulb into the wall sconce.

"Goodbye, Ryan," I breathed. I went to the door and flipped the light switch on behind me before pulling the handle shut.

The spring air smelled fresh, and the sun lying low on the horizon stretched its rays towards me with an embrace I had ignored far too long. Blissful ignorance always pales next to the electricity of awareness.

225

I yanked my phone out of my purse.

"Hello?"

"Hana? Can you help me find Tom?" I ran towards my car as I spoke.

My tires squealed as they hit the asphalt.

# TWENTY-THREE

I'm conferencing in Gita!" Hana shouted to me as I slammed the accelerator of my little Civic to the floor. It roared in protest, but I didn't care.

A few moments later, both of my best friends were positioned in front of their computers waiting for my directives.

"Where the hell do I even look?" Gita wailed.

"Try Twitter. Try fansites. Do a general Google search!" I replied.

"Can't you just call him?" Hana yelled with exasperation.

"I tried just now while you were calling Gita. The number I have doesn't work. It's out of service," I admitted.

"I *knew* it! I knew you were going to cave in!" Hana crowed.

"Focus! Okay, so I just did a Google search. Holy shit…there are fifteen million results!" Gita moaned.

"I'm looking at Twitter for links to fansites," Hana responded.

"Where are you?" Gita demanded.

"I'm on I-40 heading to the airport," I said.

"Do you even have your passport?" she demanded.

"I didn't get that far in my thought process. Hopefully, he's in the continental United States," I replied sheepishly.

"Hey! This site says he's attending a movie premiere in Chelsea tonight!" Hana cried.

"Can you guys try to verify that?" I pleaded.

"Shit, this one says he's in L.A.!" Gita stated with irritation.

"But I've already found two websites that say he's in New York!" Hana protested.

"Does he even have a Twitter thing? I ask because I've found no less than ten people claiming to be him, but they all have grammar skills Forrest Gump would openly mock," Gita said. "Two of them are clearly teenage girls."

"I don't think he has Twitter. At least, he didn't two months ago."

"Wait, wait, wait! This site says he's supposed to be at the Clearview Chelsea Cinemas on 23rd Street! The red carpet starts at nine thirty!" Gita yelled triumphantly.

"That's good enough for me!" I shouted back as I pushed the speedometer over eighty.

They both hollered in support, and I felt my heart soar with affection for them.

"Cristina, I'm so glad you're doing this," Gita said when the fervor died down.

"And I thought you were my sensible friend!" I teased. "Lately, your penchant for romanticism has shocked me to no end! I'm rather disappointed. I never thought you would be such a sucker for love."

"Piss off." She chuckled.

"There's a Delta flight leaving from RDU to LaGuardia in thirty-five minutes. How far are you from RDU?" Hana demanded.

"I'm ten minutes away," I replied.

"That's cutting it kind of close, Hana," Gita pointed out.

"Look, if she misses the six fifty flight, the next one leaves at eight thirty! She'll never make the premiere!" Hana exclaimed.

"I'll be on that plane," I vowed. Please, let me make it.

"I'm buying your ticket right now," Hana said with conviction.

I remained silent for a moment so I could reestablish control over my emotions. "Thank you so much. I love you both."

"Call us as soon as you get there! I'll book you a hotel room at the Marriott in Times Square! We have some points, and it's not too far from Chelsea!" Hana replied.

"Hopefully, she won't need a hotel room!" Gita teased.

"We love you too! Don't worry! It'll work out!" Hana called back.

"I'm not worried. Even if he doesn't want me, I have to do this. For me. I have to know that I fought for my happiness," I said firmly.

Even though it would cost me twenty dollars a day, I parked my car in the lot closest to the Delta terminal and ran pell-mell towards the electronic kiosk to print out my boarding pass.

Gasping for air, I raced down the corridor so I could get to the gate before the door closed and no one else was admitted onto the flight. I made it with moments to spare.

My mind whirred at a frenetic pace, and the short flight passed by in the blink of an eye. The only thing I could think about was getting close enough to Tom for him to see me. I squeezed my eyes shut and prayed my presence would be welcome, even if I did not deserve such a magnanimous gesture. I bounced my knee up and down as we sat on the tarmac for twenty grueling minutes before we were able to gain access to a gate and deplane.

228 Again, I flew through the airport and grabbed the first taxi I

reached. It was nearing nine o'clock.

"Clearview Chelsea Cinemas on 23rd!" I shouted to the cabbie. "Twenty bucks extra if you move it!"

Never tell a New York City cab driver to move it. The flashing lights of the city blurred by as he jerked through traffic and fit through spaces I was certain were way too small for an automobile. Each time, my fears were proven wrong.

Bless him.

"I can't get through," he complained in accented English as we neared the theater complex. "The traffic is terrible. Do you want me to go around?"

"No, it's okay. I'll walk." Correction: run. I shoved a handful of money towards him and murmured thanks as I lifted my sweaty, nerve-ridden self from the cab.

The cool April breeze blew around me, and the sticky strands of my hair curled in unbecoming whirls that framed my face like a Puerto Rican version of Shirley Temple. Nice. Oh well.

As I neared the theater, I faltered as I truly realized what I was up against. The large crowd milling by the entrance had obviously been there for quite a while, and the press contingency occupied the best location by the red carpet. This was a nightmare.

I gritted my teeth together and forced away my insecurities and hesitation. It didn't matter if I looked like shit. It didn't matter if it would take an act of God to put me in Tom's line of sight. It didn't matter if the fans tried to elbow me out of the way. The only thing that mattered was happiness. And I would fight for it, even if I had to claw my way through the crowd inch by inch.

"Excuse me," I began chanting as I tried to make it towards the front.

A collective scream rippled through the masses as the first of the celebrities proceeded onto the red carpet. The familiar bulbs flashed, and the questions flew through the air as people struggled to get the attention of their beloved stars. In the melee, I was able to press my way forward without drawing any ire from those around me. Another volley of shouts arose. I glanced towards the carpet and squinted. It was not Tom.

Each time the mob made an outcry, I looked up from my single-minded task to glance before me. A tall man who walked with a slightly awkward gait was the only thing my eyes sought. The process was excruciatingly slow. For every five steps I made forward, I was pushed back two.

And then…

"IT'S THOMAS!" screamed a girl less than fifteen feet in front of me.

I froze. The horde's uproar grew to reflect the magnitude of his arrival. My gaze zeroed in on the figure less than fifty feet to my left.

"Please," I begged under my breath as I moved forward with renewed zeal. I glanced towards him whenever the opportunity arose.

He was dressed in a charcoal grey suit, and his olive green button down was slightly wrinkled with the careless, devil-may-care style that was all his own. He wore polarized sunglasses, and when his right hand raked through his hair in an achingly familiar gesture, it took every ounce of my self-control not to scream for his attention at the top of my lungs.

He would never hear me anyway.

"Please!" I cried.

I pushed through the crowd and was jostled roughly by ever more fervent fans the closer I came to the front.

"Hey! I was here all afternoon!" a girl to my right yelled indignantly at me when I tried to elbow past her.

"I'm sorry! Please, I just need to see him," I stated with such desperation in my eyes that she decided to cut me a break.

"Jeez, and I thought I was nuts," she muttered.

He was less than fifteen feet away from me. My path would cross into his direct line of sight in mere seconds.

"Tom!" I reached out my hand towards him as though my palm would suddenly extend itself and grasp onto his. I knew I would never make it the last ten feet in time. There were countless bodies pressed tightly against one another, blocking my ability to move.

"Tom!" I yelled more loudly as I was buffeted against the people in my immediate vicinity.

"Thomas!" a girl nearby screeched.

A chorus of his name rose around me, and I knew it wasn't humanly possible for any person to pick out my voice from the rising din.

He was busy scribbling his name on every piece of paper shoved in his face. I tried again to move forward, but it was impossible to gain enough momentum to push through the crowd.

Nevertheless, I fought for every inch.

"Tom!" I screamed again.

He didn't even look up as a woman shoved a camera in his face and grabbed hold of his neck for a self-portrait. His security guard disentangled the lady's arms from around Tom and pulled him away from the line of people directly in front of me.

"Tommy!" I cried out again in desperation.

"Come back!" another voice begged. "Please! I want your autograph!"

He didn't even turn around as he was directed towards the press contingency.

It was too late.

The tears welled, but I refused to give up. I tried to move towards the flashing cameras, but my efforts were futile.

Before I had even made it ten feet in that direction, he turned to give the crowd a quick wave, and then followed Melissa Nash through the double doors and into the theater.

He was gone.

I stood in place and absorbed that fact as the crowd shifted its attention to the arrival of the newest celebrity.

Inhale. Exhale. Inhale. Exhale.

I squeezed my eyes shut and turned away. I began walking. I didn't know where I was going, but I knew that I needed to keep moving. I didn't even look around me as I willed my feet forward, step by step. The lights of New York twinkled in my periphery, and I could hear raucous laughter and the intermittent cry of colorful expletives, but these sounds and sights were slightly dulled by the sensation of recent events.

An hour later, the fog cleared... slowly but surely.

I continued to walk with my head down and my hands shoved into the pockets of my jacket.

Inhale. Exhale.

I tried.

I fought.

Until I was certain of the impossibility, I didn't give up.

I took a chance. I took a risk. I made a senseless decision.

And I didn't regret it at all. Not one bit.

With the healing power of this realization, I glanced up at the night sky and took my hands out of my pockets. In the distance, large trees loomed before me. Trees? In Manhattan? Central Park. Without hesitation, I shifted towards the beautiful cherry blossoms.

I slowed down and peered around. There were people everywhere. Some were taking their dogs for a walk, and others exercised on rollerblades or skateboards. Cheerful banter filled the air. I moved towards a bench situated between cherry trees and sat down. With every breeze, soft white petals cascaded to the ground and encircled me in their midst. They danced with abandon and fought to weave through each zephyr with graceful tenacity.

Straight ahead was a curve in the road. Strangely, I didn't feel the urge to see where it led. I smiled and looked up again. This was happiness, too. Maybe it wasn't the best kind of happiness I could imagine, but I knew beyond the shadow of a doubt that I felt a lasting sense of contentment sitting on this bench in Central Park. I had forgotten this kind of peace existed over the last few weeks. I tried. I didn't let fear motivate my decisions. I didn't let the threat of unpredictability overcome me. Tom would be proud . . . I lived outside of my head.

Gone was the shameful coward who only hoped her failures would never come back to haunt her. This time, I gained control by relinquishing it. Chuckling to myself, I thought about the fact I should have felt overwhelmed by all that happened to me today.

Instead, I was at peace. I was alone, and this time I was the only person I could hold responsible for that fact. This knowledge was incredibly liberating.

I sat on the bench and watched everything around me for a long time. As the spring air grew chillier, I pulled my jacket tighter and thought more about Tom.

One day, I hoped I would see him again so I could apologize in person for what I did. I wanted to explain everything to him because I had never been granted that level of honesty from Ryan. Tom deserved to have every question answered. I swore I would give that to him if he wanted it.

One day, I hoped I could tell him how much he meant to me . . . how much of an impact he had on my life. Most importantly, how much I loved him.

I retrieved my purse and left the park, full of peaceful gratitude.

"Times Square Marriott," I said to the cab driver after settling into my seat.

My phone buzzed.

> Hana (12:13 am): i'm dying here! what happened?
> Me (12:13 am): Nothing. I was too late.
> Hana (12:13 am): !! r u ok?
> Me (12:13 am): I'm perfectly fine.

```
Hana (12:13 am): where have u been?
Me (12:14 am): Central Park
Hana (12:14 am): r u sure ur ok?
Me (12:14 am): I'm positive. I'll
call u tomorrow. J
Hana (12:14 am): ok, i'm proud of u
Me (12:14 am): I'm proud of me too.
```

I smiled to myself.

I retrieved my room key at the front desk and made my way lethargically to the elevators. The reflection of the girl in the doors was an interesting one. Her hair was frazzled, her clothes were in complete disarray, and her makeup was smudged and useless. Her physical appearance contrasted sharply with the serene expression on her face. There were no more wrinkles on her forehead. I wiped away the ruined eyeliner and exhaled at the woman before me. She was strong and at peace.

Wearily, I shoved the card key into the door. I groaned whenever it didn't work immediately. All I wanted was to fall onto a pillow and sleep. I wasn't afraid of my dreams anymore. I mashed on the door handle and entered the hotel room. The lights were on already.

I exhaled slowly after pressing my back against the door. Gingerly, I slid my tired body to the ground and allowed myself a release of painless tears. They didn't burn, and they didn't ache. They were cathartic.

My phone buzzed again.

```
Gita (12:42 am): Hana called me. Just
wanted to tell you I love you.
Me (12:42 am): I love you too.
Gita (12:42 am): Sleep well.
```

I grinned in thanks and wiped away the last remaining tears before hauling myself into a standing position. With stumbling footsteps, I walked down the short hallway intent on my single-minded purpose of leaping into bed, fully clothed.

The room came into view…

…and I screamed involuntarily.

Standing between the two queen sized beds…was a movie star.

He was still dressed in his wrinkled grey suit, and the top buttons of his shirt were undone. There was a glimmer of a thin, silver chain 233 around his neck. His sunglasses hid his eyes from me, and he looked every inch of what he was: glamorous and unattainable.

"What... how... what?" I stammered. The fatigue I had been battling only moments before disappeared in a flash of panicked confusion. My entire body felt alive.

"Melissa... saw you at the premiere. I didn't know it at the time, but she spent the entire movie calling in favors. It turns out one of my security detail has a friend with the NYPD. He tracked you down."

The sound of his voice distracted me from any attempt at coherence.

"Oh," I breathed.

"What are you doing here?" he said quietly.

"I should think that would be rather obvious."

The right corner of his lip twitched minutely in remembrance. "It's not."

"I... I wanted to tell you something. Today, I lived outside of my head, and it was wonderful."

He waited patiently.

"I don't want to make sense anymore. I want to be happy. When I really stopped to think about it, I realized I'm happiest when I'm with you," I continued.

He looked down at the ground and took a deep breath.

"I know I have no right to do this to you, and I want you to know that no matter what, I promise to live life to its fullest. I'm an incredibly lucky woman, and I appreciate how rare it is to be given the gifts I've been given. I swear to you, regardless of what happens here tonight, I'll live my life to its fullest... I'll laugh loudly, curse emphatically, and cry with passion."

He sighed and reached up to remove his sunglasses. He tossed them onto the bed and pressed his palms to his face. An onerous moment later, his hands fell to his sides. When he glanced up, I saw the eyes of the man I loved for the first time in too long.

They were... torn, but I didn't see the colorless devastation I had feared for weeks.

"Why did you leave, Cristina?"

A fair question. I took a small step forward before I spoke. "I was ashamed of myself, and I didn't have the courage to face you."

"That's not an excuse."

"I know."

"You don't walk out on those you love." His expression hardened with this statement.

"Yes."

"I thought you of all people would know that," he said softly.

"Yes," I choked.

He paused before proceeding. "Why were you ashamed of yourself?"

I hesitated. "Because, I was afraid...of everything. I've found that where there's fear, there's also shame."

To my astonishment, I saw the trace of a smile on his face. "You've always been good with words."

"Here's hoping."

He studied me unabashedly. "So, you swore to live life to the fullest, right?"

"Yes."

"Well, I want you to swear something else...that you won't ever walk out on someone you love without a damn good explanation," he asked.

"I swear," I replied with unmistakable conviction. "But, I also have a request. Well, it's actually more like a confession."

"You don't need to confess to me. I'm not a priest, and I'm also at fault in this...as my father pointed out to me numerous times."

"No. I need to be honest with you about everything. I make lots of mistakes, and I have a tendency to want control and order in my life. Sometimes, I make terrible decisions, and then I struggle to figure out what to do in the aftermath. Yes, I will swear to *live* life, but...I'm also selfish. I want more. I want to *love* life in every way, and... *you* are what makes that possible for me."

I inhaled and closed my eyes to collect my courage. The moment of truth. "I love you, Thomas Abramson. You make my life whole. There are many things I could ask for of this world, but the only thing I *will* ask for...is to be with you."

My words hung in the air and echoed off every surface like the peeling tolls of a bell. I held my breath and stared up at the man in front of me. His face was impossible to read, and he appeared to be struggling with his unspoken thoughts.

He cleared his throat. "Well then...be with me."

Without thinking, I ran towards his outstretched arms and buried my face into his chest.

"Ow!" I cried as something sharp stabbed into my cheek. "What is that?"

He looked down at me without responding, and his eyes were 235 pools of light and warmth. I curled my fingers in his hair and stood on my tiptoes to kiss him.

"I'm so sorry," I murmured into his lips. "So very sorry!"

"Stop it," he chuckled. "I know you're sorry. Besides, it doesn't matter anymore." He embraced me tightly, pressed his face into my skin, his actions a perfect reflection of his assertion.

As we kissed, my fingers fell onto the silver chain at his neck. Curious by this new adornment, my hand traced down its length, and I lifted the trinket hidden under his shirt into view.

Hanging from the chain was my ring. My imperfect, perfect ring.

Words would have marred the significance of this gesture, so I let the ring fall back against his chest and rested my palm over his heart.

He pulled me to him and placed a gentle kiss on my forehead.

"I love you," he said clearly.

They were the three most beautiful words I had ever heard in my life.

They were my perfect happiness.

# EPILOGUE

A nd the Oscar goes to..."

Tom's hand squeezed mine tightly. Hollywood held its breath, and the silence was so deafening that I swore I heard Catherine Zeta-Jones's enormous diamond earrings tinkling in front of me. I still could not believe it was possible for me to reach out and touch Michael Douglas.

"Thomas Abramson, for *Copland!*"

The sound of the applause was overwhelming as I leapt to my feet. Tom's hands were grabbed from all sides, and the muscles in my face strained from the wide breadth of my smile. He yanked me against him for one heart-stopping moment, and then turned to walk awkwardly towards the stage.

The applause died down to a smattering as he clutched hold of the golden statuette and bent to speak into the microphone.

"Bravo, Thomas!" I heard the booming voice of Patrick Abramson from somewhere behind me.

Tom laughed. "Thanks, Dad." Anne whistled loudly in response.

"First, I... this is so surreal. I want to thank you all very much for believing in this film. It was an amazing experience for me, and I have to admit that I'm only as good as the material I'm given. This was such a collaborative effort, and I have to thank the director, the screenwriter, the producer, and everyone involved for putting together such a wonderful project. I'd also like to thank Aaron Copland's family for their insight and encouragement."

He ran his hand nervously through his hair, and my painful smile grew even more.

"Of course, I must thank my family. My parents, Anne... without you, I'd probably be a starving musician living on beans, coffee, and tobacco."

A ripple of laughter ran through the crowd.

In the past, I used to think *real* love was anti-capitalistic.

I believed love, as the modern world understood it, was an endless siege fueled by the impossibility of healthy co-dependence.

One person always gave. One person always took.

Selflessness and selfishness.

I was wrong.

Real love is unto itself. For every person, it's different, and no one can presume to explain its complexity using mere words.

For me, love comes down to the moments of pure, unadulterated happiness in your life.

"And finally . . . Cris." Tom paused to grin crookedly and then shifted his eyes to mine.

"*Tu eres la luz de mi vida.*"

Somewhere above me, I knew my father was smiling.

Let it wash over you . . .

. . . and believe you deserve it.


## THE END

# ACKNOWLEDGEMENTS

First, I want to thank my family for their love and support. My passion for the written word began at home with battered copies of the classics and tiny flashlights hidden under my pillow. Mom and Dad, thank you for passing your love of books onto me. To Victor, Erica, Ian, and Chris - we are parts of a whole. No story is complete without even one of you.

To my extended "family" - Ela, Gin, Sheila, Gautam, and Tabi - the nights of endless laughter and food are the fuel that fires my imagination and warms my soul. The words "thank you" are startlingly insufficient. I'm so lucky for each and every one of you.

Without the tireless advocacy of Laura Kreitzer and the gang at Revolution, *Fanfare* would still be a manuscript lost in the void. Laura, you have become much more than a colleague. You are a woman-extraordinaire, and I am in awe of your courage and conviction. Thank you, thank you, thank you.

Finally, to all the readers of my earliest attempts who pushed me to persevere . . . this book exists because of you.

# RENEE
# AHDIEH

Renee Ahdieh believes that life should be relished like a beloved book: one page at a time. When she's not writing, Renee enjoys traveling, cooking, and salsa dancing. Her award-winning blog on all things foodie can be found at www.thecandidcook.com.

She lives in North Carolina with her husband Victor and their dog Mushu.

*Fanfare* is her debut novel.

CPSIA information can be obtained at www.ICGtesting.com
Printed in the USA
BVOW08s2248210416

444905BV00001B/67/P